*By the same author*

Where the Fresh Grass Grows (1955)
A Path to the Bridge (1958)
The Van Langeren Girl (1960)
A Touch of Thunder (1961)
A Time to Retreat (1963)
Genesis 38 (1965)
A Mission for Betty Smith (1967)
Messiter's Dream (1990)
The Cross of San Vincente (1991)
The Singing Stones (1993)

*Non-fiction*
Transformation of a Valley (1983)

When the rector of the
body of Major Christop
staircase that led to the
no more than a tragic acc
Lubbock already knew sc

Tremellen had received
a biblical text, ending w
What did they mean? Di
deep in the Major's pas
young Detective Inspector
got to find out whether
whether he ever passed th
if he ever slept with a girl

It was a trail that wound
further six thousand miles
into Norfolk.

In this fascinating myste
ther the uneasy friendship
revealed in *The Cross of San*

# COVENANT WITH DEATH

## Brian Cooper

Constable · London

First published in Great Britain 1994
by Constable & Company Ltd
3 The Lanchesters, 162 Fulham Palace Road
London W6 9ER
Copyright © 1994 by Brian Cooper
The right of Brian Cooper to be
identified as the author of this work
has been asserted by him in accordance
with the Copyright, Designs and Patents Act 1988
ISBN 0 09 473590 5
Set in Palatino 10 pt by
CentraCet Limited, Cambridge
Printed and bound in Great Britain
by Hartnolls Ltd, Bodmin

A CIP catalogue record for this book
is available from the British Library

For
NEVILLE
in the hope that he may
one day find his way to Cawston
and after that to Salle

What fellowship shall the earthen pot have with the kettle?

Ecclesiastes: 13.2.

# PROLOGUE

## THE HIGH PLACE

Then I said unto them, What is the high place whereunto ye go?

Ezekiel: 20.29.

Promptly at seven o'clock on the morning of 29th June 1948, the Feast of St Peter and St Paul, the Reverend Eustace Blake, the rector of Salleston in the county of Norfolk, swung his legs out of bed.

He did so without hesitation: not that he was a creature of habit, but rather a man of firm resolution. Having, the night before, resolved to rise that morning on the stroke of seven, he thumped the palm of his hand on the clock alarm, flung back the bedclothes, stood up and stretched.

He then walked to the window, drew back the curtains, placed his hands on the sill, looked out at the dripping trees and the louring sky, and then switched his gaze to the tall grey shaft that was the tower of his church.

What he saw there was evidently not to his liking, for, washing and shaving in haste and dressing with speed, he called to his housekeeper to hold up the breakfast, pulled on a raincoat and plunged out of doors.

Striding up the slope of the long church path, he glanced once again at the top of the tower and frowned in some perplexity. The church was unlocked as he'd expected it to be, but the huge vault of the nave beneath its hammerbeam roof was silent and still.

He stood for a moment looking and listening, then turned and stepped across to the low wooden door that gave access to the bell tower. From there a stone spiral led up to the bells, with a wooden ladder and a trap to the top of the tower.

He lifted the latch and pushed. The door opened so far, and then refused to move. Forcing it back another couple of inches, he squeezed through the gap.

It was then that he saw the body . . .

# I

## THE HEWN STONE

He hath inclosed my ways with hewn stone, he hath
made my paths crooked

Lamentations: 3.9.

# 1

Tench sat at his desk in Norwich.

'Let's go through this again,' he said. 'What was the man's name?'

'Tremellen. Cornish. Christopher Tremellen.'

'An army major?'

'Had been. Invalided out, but clung to the rank.'

'Significant?'

'Could be.' Lubbock relit his pipe. 'Struck me as a bit brash. Not that I saw much of him. Had a good army record, so I was told. Won an MC in the battles around Caen.'

'Who told you?'

'Blake.'

'He's the rector?'

'That's right.'

'OK. Let's start at the beginning. You've been staying in Salleston. Why? Tracking down more windmills?'

Since his retirement some eighteen months before, the ex-Detective Chief Inspector had been travelling round the county in his Morgan three-wheeler making a study of all the surviving mills.

'Partly, laddie,' he said. 'There's a couple of interesting old survivals at Southgate, near Cawston: the Black and White Mills. I wanted a closer look at them, but that was by the way. I've been staying with a friend, name of Reg Denstone. Chief Super at Ipswich, but well before your time.'

'And you've been there how long?'

'A fortnight. Long enough to get to know one or two people.'

Tench pulled out his notebook. 'So tell me again what happened.'

'Well,' – Lubbock drew hard on his pipe – 'seems that when

Tremellen was discharged from the army – got a head wound during the Normandy advance – he bought a cottage at Salleston. Been there three years. Set up an advertising business here in Norwich. Self-assertive sort of chap. Made himself very much a part of the community. Organized local functions, helped with church work, though I wouldn't have said he was deep in religion. Far from it, in fact. Probably did it just to give himself some standing. No doubt the publicity helped in his business.'

'You weren't too impressed with him.'

'Not overmuch. He was hardly my type.'

Tench nodded. His former Chief had never shown much patience with those who held good opinions of themselves. His method had invariably been to cut them down to size with a few well-chosen words.

'You said it was his job to raise the flag on the church?'

'Volunteered to do it, from what I could gather. Helped the community and Major Tremellen. Apparently it's flown on certain days of the year, and yesterday was one of them: the Feast of St Peter. According to Blake, he was meticulous about it. Always got up at the crack of dawn and had the flag flying as soon as it was daylight.'

'But not yesterday.'

'No. The rector climbed out of bed, couldn't see the flag and wondered what the hell had happened. Couldn't understand it. The Major had never once failed him before, so he had a quick lather and skipped across to take a look.'

'And found Tremellen dead.'

'That's what he says. Found him at the bottom of the spiral stair that leads up to the tower. Looked like he'd fallen and broken his neck.'

'So what did he do?'

'Well, he's not the sort of chap to do things by halves or to waste any time. He hared it back to the rectory, phoned the village doctor, called for an ambulance and rang the local constable.'

'What's his name?'

'Grenville. Young, but reliable. A bit inexperienced, but that's to be expected.'

Tench made a note, and then laid down his pen. 'I take it this Tremellen was dead right enough.'

'Dead as a coffin-nail, and the rector was right. Seems he had a broken neck among other things.'

'And what were the other things?'

'Injuries to the head and general contusions.'

'Consistent with the fall?'

'Yes, laddie, I'd say so. The sort of things you'd expect if a man took a header down a flight of stone steps.'

Tench frowned at his notebook. 'How old was Tremellen?'

'Mid-thirties, thereabouts.'

'But he had been discharged from the army with a head wound.'

'And fully recovered, according to the doctor.'

'Even so, he could very well have lost his balance. Those spiral stairs in churches are enough to make anyone feel a bit dizzy.'

'He could, that's true, but I don't think he did.'

Tench drew a deep breath.

'Go on then, sir,' he said. 'Tell me why not.'

'He was being threatened,' said Lubbock. 'He told me so. Someone, somewhere had it in for the lad.'

## 2

Tench stared at him. 'He told you? When was this?'

'The evening before he died.' Lubbock took out a match, poked fretfully into the bowl of his pipe, and then knocked it out on a sheet of paper. 'There's a village society, the Salleston Circle. You know the sort of thing. They invite speakers to give talks and then answer questions. Coffee and biscuits. Not my kind of caper, but Reg had offered to give them the fruits of his experience: "My Time in the Police" or some such nonsense. I went along to lend him some moral support. Oh, it all went pretty smoothly, plenty of questions, and one or two of them he pushed across to me. Well, Tremellen was there, and when we reached the coffee-and-biscuits stage, he tacked himself on to me and started to talk. I'd met him before – Blake had introduced us – and he wasn't the sort of bloke I was inclined to encourage, but then he got on about these letters he'd had.'

'Threatening letters?'

'He seemed to think they were. Said he'd had more than one, and he'd a pretty good idea who it was that was sending them. I asked him had he saved them, expecting him to say no, he'd simply torn them up and thrown them away; but he said, oh, yes, they were all in his desk, he didn't believe in destroying evidence, but he needed some advice about what steps to take.'

'He was worried about them?'

'Well, let's put it this way, laddie. If he hadn't been, he wouldn't have mentioned them to me.'

'So what did you tell him?'

'Said he ought to take them across to young Grenville, but he didn't seem to have much faith in the locals. Asked me would I take a look at them, so I told him I'd drop round and see them next morning, but by that time he was dead.'

Tench pushed aside his notebook. 'So you think someone from here ought to go and investigate.'

'Not exactly,' said Lubbock. 'I think you and I should. No point in stirring things up unless we need to. There may be nothing in it. On the other hand, who knows? Maybe it's just my suspicious mind, but someone could have given him a shove down those steps, and unless he lost his footing some-where near the bottom, then I reckon they did. Look, Mike, this is a spiral stair. The tower's a tall one. There must be close on a couple of hundred steps. Now I look at it like this. If a man's at the top and you give him a push, he's not going to tumble all the way to the bottom: not with the staircase curving as it does. The body's going to land up part-way down, lodged against a wall. To get it right to the bottom, someone's going to need to give it an extra nudge, possibly two or three. Blake found Tremellen right at the foot, slammed against the door.'

'Is there a handrail?'

'Not that I know of. Just the bare walls.'

'Then he could quite well have done as you said: lost his footing near the bottom.'

'It's possible, yes, but it's equally possible that someone was waiting for him up at the top.'

Tench pondered the point. 'Have you mentioned any of this to Grenville?'

'No, not a word.'

'So you don't know what he thinks.'

16

'From what I've gathered, he just accepts it was an accident. Hasn't any reason to think otherwise, has he? But to me it's a case of suspicious death, and someone ought to make a few inquiries about it.'

'Meaning a certain detective inspector personally known to an ex-DCI?'

'Yes, you could put it that way.'

'With the able assistance of a former member of the force?'

Lubbock screwed up the paper and dropped it in a waste bin. 'Well, I might be persuaded to offer a few suggestions. Based on local knowledge.'

Tench seemed amused. 'Persuaded, sir?'

'Of course. I wouldn't want to offer gratuitous advice.'

'You wouldn't?'

'No, laddie. Certainly not . . . Unless I thought it might be useful.'

They looked at one another, then both of them laughed. Tench pushed back his chair. He was suddenly serious.

'I think you're right,' he said. 'It does need looking into. This cottage of Tremellen's. You know where it is?'

'Yes. Top of the village, on the Cawston road.'

'Who's got the keys?'

'They're with Grenville at the moment. Till the sister arrives.'

'He wasn't married then, Tremellen?'

'No. Both parents dead. Only relative's his sister. Lives somewhere near Truro, but she's sunning herself in Switzerland.'

Tench swept up his notebook.

'Right,' he said. 'Let's go. I'll leave a message for Maitland. You lead the way and I'll tag along behind.'


# 3


Tench spread out the letters and their envelopes on Tremellen's oak table.

They'd been posted on successive days between 21st and 27th June from a variety of places in Norfolk, Suffolk and Cambridgeshire.

The first had come from Newmarket.

'Revelation 22.12,' it read. 'Behold, I come quickly; and my reward is with me, to render to each man according as his work is.' It was signed 'Remember B'.

The next was from Ely.

'I Peter 3.12. For the eyes of the Lord are upon the righteous, and His ears unto their supplication: but the face of the Lord is upon them that do evil. Remember Ba'.

The third was from Diss.

'I Peter 4.17. For the time is come for judgement to begin at the House of God: and if it begin first at us, what shall be the end of them that obey not the gospel of God? Remember Bar'.

They followed in similar vein day after day.

On the 24th from Thetford.

'II Peter 1.9. For he that lacketh these things is blind, seeing only what is near, having forgotten the cleansing from his old sins. Remember Bara'.

The postmark on the fifth one was smudged, but, peering at it closely, Grenville said he was ready to swear it was Beccles.

It contained what appeared to be more detailed accusations.

'I Peter 4.3. For the time past may suffice to have wrought the desire of the Gentiles, and to have walked in lasciviousness, lusts, winebibbings, revellings, carousings, and abominable idolatries. Remember Barad'.

The next came from Wymondham and carried the first direct threat.

'II Peter 1.13. And I think it right, as long as I am in this tabernacle, to stir you up by putting you in remembrance.' It was signed 'Remember Barada'.

The last was more specific. Half the postmark had missed the envelope, but it was clearly Norwich.

'II Peter 3.17. Ye, therefore, beloved, knowing these things beforehand, beware lest, being carried away with the error of the wicked, ye fall from your own stedfastness.'

The signature on this one was further extended: 'Remember Baradar'.

'Sounds like some religious nutter, sir,' said Grenville. 'Could be someone from the church.'

Tench leaned forward, his hands on the table. 'Anyone in mind?'

'Not offhand, sir, no. But one of them does say "as long as I am in this tabernacle".'

'Whoever it is,' said Lubbock, 'he's time enough to spare. If he posted them himself, he's ranged around quite a bit in the last seven days.'

'The writing,' said Tench. 'D'you think it's disguised?'

'Well, it's copper-plate.' Lubbock frowned. 'Looks as if it's been done with an ordinary nib-pen.'

'Someone used to writing out marriage certificates, baptisms? What about the paper?'

'Notepaper. Blue. Torn off a pad, and the envelopes match. I'd say it was common enough. Sold by the ton in stationers' shops. Forensics'll tell you . . . It's the signatures, laddie. They're what intrigue me. They grow by the day.'

'Who the hell's Baradar?'

'God knows,' said Lubbock, 'but it may not be anyone. You're running ahead too fast, Mike. It could be just a warning. It doesn't say "Remember full stop Baradar". It says "Remember Baradar".'

'Then what the devil's Baradar?'

'Your guess is as good as mine.' Lubbock bent over the letters. 'Notice something?' he said. 'There isn't a full stop after any of the signatures, not even the last one, and on each occasion he's added a letter. Now what does that mean?'

'That the word's not complete?'

'When was the last one posted?'

Tench picked up the envelope. '27th June.'

'Last Sunday. And Tremellen died when?'

'Early on the 29th, sir. Tuesday,' said Grenville.

'There's a letter-box behind the door. Has it been checked?'

'Not by me, sir, no.'

'Check it now, Constable, will you?' said Tench. He turned towards Lubbock. 'You say Tremellen told you he knew who was sending them?'

'Said he had a fair idea.'

'Pity then he didn't say who it was.'

Lubbock pulled out his pouch and began to fill his pipe. 'That's the way things fall in murder cases, laddie. If there weren't pieces missing, then you and I wouldn't be needed at all.'

19

Grenville was in the doorway, holding two envelopes.

'A couple more,' he said.

Tench took them from him and studied the postmarks. 'One sent on the 28th from East Dereham.'

Lubbock tapped it with his pipe stem. 'That'd be delivered on the morning he died.'

'And one on the 29th.' Tench turned the envelope round several times. 'Looks to be from Aylsham . . . But why would he send a letter if he knew that Tremellen was already dead?'

'Open them,' said Lubbock.

Tench slit them with a penknife.

'That's the first one,' he said, and smoothed it out on the table. 'First Epistle of Peter, chapter 2, verses 7 and 8 . . . Seems fond of Peter, this Bible-reader, doesn't he?'

'Well, it is St Peter's church.'

'What is?'

'Here at Salleston.'

'Oh, is it? Well, at least that seems to add a piece to the puzzle. Looks like the constable could well be right. It's somebody local.'

'Could be.' Lubbock shrugged. 'Or it could just be a trick to throw us off the scent. What gems in this one?'

Tench read it out. '"For such as disbelieve, the stone which the builders rejected, the same was made the head of the corner; and a stone of stumbling and a rock of offence; for they stumble at the word" . . . Then "Remember" again, and it's signed "Baradari".'

'With a full stop?

'Yes.'

'Then what about the last one?'

Tench pulled it from the envelope. 'This isn't Peter. It's Acts 1.18.'

'Doesn't mean a thing to me,' Lubbock said frankly.

'It may do when you've seen it.' Tench sounded grim. He passed it to Lubbock, but it was Grenville who read it, slowly, deliberately, looking across his shoulder.

'"Now this man obtained a field with the reward of his iniquity; and falling headlong, he burst asunder in the midst" . . . And it's signed "Baradari", with another full stop.'

'And this time, no "Remember".' Lubbock lit his pipe. 'Well,

20

if Tremellen was dead, he could hardly remember. So there's one thing about our biblical prophet. He was sure of his facts.'

# 4

Back in Norwich, Tench received the summons he'd expected. Detective Chief Inspector Maitland wanted to see him as soon as he returned.

Maitland was the man who'd taken over from Lubbock. He'd been transferred from Ipswich, where he'd served for some years as a detective inspector. Rumour had it that he hadn't been the Chief Super's choice, nor would he have been Lubbock's, though the old man had never once ventured his opinion. He was certainly a very different type from his predecessor. A burly, abrasive character, who prided himself on speaking his mind, he'd already put one or two noses out of joint, and Tench still approached him with the wariness of a bomb-disposal man approaching an unfamiliar, unexploded device.

It was clear that afternoon that the Chief Inspector wasn't in the best of tempers. He scowled across the desk at his young assistant.

'What's all this about Salleston?'

Tench, for all his caution, had long ago concluded that Maitland's harsh words weren't likely to break even his slender bones. Persistent and determined, he could also be diplomatically bland, and this was clearly an occasion that demanded smooth words.

'Case of suspicious death, sir. Had to investigate.'

'Well, go on,' said Maitland. 'Don't leave it at that. It's your job to inform me. Was the victim male or female?'

'Male, sir. Ex-army major.'

'Shot, was he?'

'No, sir. Fell down some stairs.'

'Anyone can fall down the stairs, Inspector. You mean he was pushed?'

'Could have been, yes, sir.'

21

'What makes you think so?'

'Letters, sir.'

'Letters?'

'These, sir,' said Tench. He handed them over: nine transparent plastic envelopes each with a sheet inside.

Maitland took his time. He read through each one twice, then he shuffled them together.

'This Bara-bloody-darri. Who is he? Some crackpot?'

'Don't know for sure, sir. Might be someone connected with the church. The body was found there.'

The Chief Inspector looked down his nose. 'Are there stairs in a church?'

'Up to the tower, sir. Deceased was supposed to be raising the flag. The rector found him at the bottom.'

'And suspected foul play?'

'The rector, sir? No.'

'Then who did? For God's sake get on with it, Tench. I haven't got all day. Who put you on to this?'

'One of the residents, sir. The Major had mentioned the letters in conversation.'

'And?'

'The village constable and I searched his cottage, sir, and found them.'

Maitland eyed him doubtfully. 'Well, it looks like you'll be setting things up on your own. I'm away off to Ipswich in a couple of hours.'

'I had heard, sir, yes.'

'Remnants of that robbery at Nettlefield Hall. The Dutch connection. I'll probably be hanging around all tomorrow waiting to give evidence, so you'll have to do without me for twenty-four hours . . . Think you can cope?'

Tench was well aware that Maitland regarded him as wet behind the ears, if not just out of nappies.

'Do my best, sir, yes.'

'Not my sort of case anyway. Never had much time for these God-sent-me-down-to-clean-up-the-world maniacs . . . Wasn't your father a rector?'

'Canon, sir. In Manchester.'

'Pity it's not a shooting affair then, eh?'

Tench forced out the faintest of dutiful smiles. 'Very true, sir, yes.'

'Right.' Maitland was on his feet. 'What have you done so far?'

'Locked up the cottage and told Constable Grenville no one's to be admitted . . .'

'He's the local plod.'

'Yes, sir, that's right.'

'Anything else?'

'No, sir. Thought I'd better check with you first.'

The Chief Inspector nodded approvingly. 'Correct. So you should . . . So what are you going to do?'

'Get those letters copied and then sent to the lab. We need to know about the paper, the ink and any fingerprints. After that maybe a handwriting expert . . .'

'Dicey devils they are. I've never found two reach the same conclusion.'

'We need to know all we can.'

'What about the post-mortem?'

'It's a suspicious death, sir. It'll have to be Ledward.'

Reg Ledward was the Home Office pathologist for Norfolk. He'd worked with Lubbock for years.

'You'll arrange that with the coroner?'

'And Ledward himself, sir. Get things done quicker.'

'And what else? Come on, lad. There's a train I've got to catch.'

Tench had prepared himself against the inquisition. 'I want the scene-of-crime squad to examine the staircase . . .'

'How big's this place Salleston?'

'Small village, sir. Five hundred people. Round about that.'

'Out in the Norfolk backwoods?'

'Yes, sir. A fair description.'

'Then set up a house-to-house. In places like that everyone knows everybody else's business . . . And you'll need accommodation for an incident room.'

'Right, sir.'

'And keep the press out as long as you can. I don't want a horde of newshounds baying at the door. Anything else?'

Tench didn't feel inclined to prolong the proceedings. 'I don't think so, sir, no.'

'Good.' Maitland nodded briefly. 'I'll speak to the Chief Super and get it all cleared. It's your job to see that everything's lined up today. Don't leave until it is. I'll be down there just as soon as I possibly can . . . Where is it, by the way?'

23

'Salleston, sir? It's a dozen miles out, just off the road to Holt.'

'Never heard of the dump. Is there a good pub?'

'Reasonable, sir.'

'What's it called?'

'The Cow and Heifer.'

Maitland gave a hollow laugh. 'I should bloody well have known without asking,' he said.

# 5

'Perhaps he'll break a leg.'

'No such luck,' said Tench. 'If he tripped on a steel rail, he'd just split it in two.'

McKenzie gave a grin, and ground his cigarette stub into the car ashtray. 'Say a prayer in the church, then.'

'Not much use, Mac. He's immune to any divine intercession . . . Talking about the church, have you ever been inside it?'

The sergeant, heavily moustached and broader round the waist than he cared to admit, shook his head forcefully.

'Never,' he said. 'When I get a day off, churches aren't the spots that first spring to mind. I save 'em up for events like weddings and funerals . . . Why? Is there something about it we ought to be knowing?'

'Looks a pretty big place for such a small village.'

'Oh, well,' – McKenzie yawned – 'that's par for the course in Norfolk. All those wealthy wool merchants trying to save their souls. It's the same down in Suffolk. Camels and needles' eyes. Build yourself a church to the glory of the Lord, and Peter'll hand you the keys of the kingdom. From what I can see, there's almost as many churches in Norfolk as rabbits. Even with the witch-finders prowling around and pointing the finger, they never half filled 'em.'

Salleston, like many villages in Norfolk, was a single street of brick and flint-cobble cottages, and Tench slowed down as he threaded his way between them; then, turning up a side lane, he parked by the church, and he and McKenzie climbed out of the car.

'OK, Mac,' he said. 'You go and see Grenville, and put him in the picture. Warn him about the house-to-house, and see what you can find in that place of Tremellen's. I'm going to have a little chat with the rector. Let's say we meet back here in an hour. That should give us enough time.'

He stared at the church. 'Strange place for a murder.'

McKenzie shrugged his shoulders. 'Happens to the best of 'em. Wasn't there one at Canterbury?'

Tench didn't answer. He was gazing up at the tower.

'Well,' he said, 'there's at least one piece of evidence we can file right away. Major Tremellen wasn't afraid of heights. Look up there, Mac. That tower's got no parapet. Can't say I'd feel very safe myself, if I had to stand on the top and raise any sort of flag.'

He was still casting a doubtful eye at the tower as he knocked on the weatherboarded door of the rectory, but the sound of a bolt being drawn back inside gave him no time for a longer inspection. The weatherboard clattered, the door was wrenched open, and he found himself facing a broad, heavily built man in a waistcoat, grey shirt and clerical collar.

He looked down at his visitor, which, according to Tench, who was six foot himself, made him at least five or six inches taller.

'Inspector Tench?'

'That's correct, sir.'

'Please step inside. You'll find my study through the door on the left.'

The voice was a deep and resonant bass. It followed Tench all the way down the dingy hall and into the study: the voice of a man who knew his own mind and, more often than not, disdained others' opinions.

'I was frankly puzzled by your telephone call, Inspector. You said it was connected with the Major's death . . . Please sit yourself down.'

He gestured to an ancient horsehair sofa, and Tench, who remembered one all too similar in his father's study, perched himself on the edge.

'Yes sir, it is about Major Tremellen's death.'

'The inquest, you mean. Of course, there'll have to be one. Most regrettable really . . .'

'That among other things.'

'Other things?' The rector narrowed his eyes. 'And what would they be?'

'We've reason to believe, sir, that the Major's death may not have been an accident.'

The Reverend Mr Blake was clearly taken aback. 'But that has to be preposterous. He fell down the steps. I found him at the bottom. Are you telling me he didn't?'

'Oh, he fell, sir. There seems little doubt about that. The question that concerns us is how did he come to fall.'

'But surely he must have tripped. Lost his footing in some way. People do it at home, let alone on a spiral stair without a handrail. The steps down from the tower need care to negotiate. That's why we never allow visitors to use them . . .'

'I think I should explain, sir.' Tench intervened. 'We searched the Major's cottage and found some letters. These are copies.' He handed them over. 'The originals, of course, are being photographed and analysed.'

The rector stared at him for a moment. Then he laid the sheaf of papers on a table at his side, removed his spectacles from a leather wallet, put them on and began to read.

Tench waited. Blake read slowly, deliberately, making no comment; then he turned the last letter face down on the others.

'I can hardly believe this, Inspector,' he said. 'You say you found these in Major Tremellen's house?'

'In his desk, sir,' said Tench.

'And the envelopes were addressed to him?'

'Yes, all of them, quite clearly. And all posted from places within fifty miles.'

'But who on earth would choose to do such a thing? And use the scriptures for such an abominable purpose? Have you any idea who this,' – he picked up the top letter and peered at it closely – 'this Baradari is?'

'No, sir. We thought perhaps you might be able to help us.'

Blake shook his head. 'I'm afraid I've no such knowledge.'

'We believe that the Major may have known who he was.'

'He said nothing to me. Never even told me he'd received any letters. What is it leads you to think that he knew?'

'He said so. He was speaking to one of your visitors. A Mr Lubbock.'

'Chief Inspector Lubbock?'

'He was until recently, yes, sir,' said Tench. 'The Major mentioned the letters to him and asked for advice.'

'And said he knew who'd sent them?'

'Said he had a good idea.'

'But he didn't name anyone.'

'Not at the time, sir, no. They made an arrangement to meet the next day, but unfortunately . . .' Tench spread out his hands.

'Yes. Yes, I see.' The rector picked up the letters and studied them again, then he raised his eyes and looked directly at Tench. 'You must understand, Inspector, that all this has come as a considerable shock.'

'Naturally, sir.'

'And I'm afraid I can offer little in the way of assistance . . . But one thing does strike me . . . The scriptural extracts are accurate, at least as I recall them, and most of them are taken from Peter's Epistles.'

'You think that's significant?'

'Possibly not, though this is St Peter's church . . . But I'm reminded, Inspector, of his ultimate fate. He died a martyr, as you know. It's said that his body lies somewhere below the high altar in Rome, though that, of course, is yet to be confirmed. But what strikes me is this. According to tradition, he always maintained he wasn't worthy to die as Christ had died. So, at his own request, he was crucified head downwards . . .'

The rector seemed uneasy. He hesitated as if wondering whether to continue.

'And?' said Tench gently.

'I don't really know.' Blake stared at the letters. 'When I found the Major, I was, understandably, somewhat distraught. It never occurred to me then that what had happened that morning was anything but an accident. And yet . . . he was lying on the stairs in a very peculiar position, Inspector. Head downwards to the door, and his arms were spread wide. I remember thinking for a second that he looked for all the world like a cross.'

27

# 6

Tench frowned. 'You're saying that the body might have been placed deliberately in such a position?'

The rector was unwilling to commit himself.

'No, I'm not saying that. I've no means of knowing one way or the other. But the way he was lying seemed to be unnatural.'

'How unnatural?'

'In a word, Inspector, it was far too neat. The arms and legs were stretched out. Perfectly straight.'

'Was he lying on his back, sir, or facing down?'

'He was facing the ground.'

'So he could have fallen forwards, and reached out with his hands to break his fall against the door.'

Blake took his time, trying to recall precisely just what he'd seen.

'He could have done, yes . . . but the position of the body seemed somehow . . . contrived.'

Tench switched the subject.

'What sort of a man was Major Tremellen?'

'He was a forceful personality.'

'Brash?'

'Not exactly. Self-confident, I'd say, rather than brash.'

'A self-publicist?'

'Perhaps, but he did a great deal of work for the village. He had energy and drive.'

'He imposed himself on others.'

'There may have been people who thought so.'

'He wasn't, then, universally popular.'

The rector was cautious. 'I think that might perhaps be a fair assessment.'

Tench paused. 'You must have a certain number of helpers. Church members who assist in the running of affairs.'

'Quite a number, yes.'

'Are there any among them who – let's say – actively disliked the Major?'

The rector's lips tightened.

'You can hardly expect me to answer that, Inspector. It isn't my place as a Christian pastor to point the finger at any of my flock.'

Tench back-tracked a fraction.

'No, sir, of course not, but we are treating this as a case of murder and we need all the help we can possibly get.'

'And I'm willing to help' – the rector's attitude had visibly stiffened – 'within the bounds of my province.'

'Then you'll be willing to supply me with a list of your helpers.'

'Naturally.'

'Thank you. And lay the church records open to inspection?'

'Records?'

'A matter of elimination, sir, nothing more than that. We shall need to compare samples of handwriting. For instance, your marriage and baptismal registers. Can you tell me who keeps them?'

'I do. They're held in the vestry under lock and key.'

'You actually make the entries?'

'Not myself, no. They're written in by the parish clerk.'

'And his name, sir?'

'The clerk is Mr Bebbington. Henry Bebbington.'

'He lives locally, does he?'

'Yes, at Maple Cottage, two doors beyond the church.'

'A respected member of the congregation?'

Blake looked at him sharply. 'Very much so. He assists the church in a great many ways.'

'Such as, sir?'

'Oh, choirmaster, sidesman. He also runs the Sunday school.'

'A useful man to have around. Has he lived here all his life?'

'I believe so, yes.'

'And he's been holding these offices for a number of years?'

'Since long before my time.' The rector peered at Tench, and furrowed his brow. 'I fail to see the purpose of these questions, Inspector. Mr Bebbington has no connection with this business. None whatsoever.'

Tench showed no surprise. 'Then perhaps we might turn to more pertinent matters. You said that visitors weren't allowed up the tower.'

'That's perfectly correct.'

'Then the door at the bottom. Is it kept locked?'

29

'Yes, invariably.'

'Who has the key?'

'There are two, Inspector. I have one, and the Major had the other.'

'When you found him, was his key in the door?'

'No.'

'You're sure of that, sir?'

'Absolutely certain. I remember thinking at the time that perhaps he'd overslept, though that would have been most unusual. So I lifted the latch and pushed. The door was unlocked. I can only assume that, having unlocked it, he put the key in his pocket.'

Tench nodded briefly. 'Since then, has anyone been up the tower?'

'Not to my knowledge. Once the Major's body had been taken away, I locked the door myself.'

'And you keep the key where, sir?'

'Here, in my desk.' The rector pointed to a roll-top desk, away to Tench's left.

'Can I see it, sir?'

Blake felt in his waistcoat pocket, took out a small key, unlocked the desk, opened one of a small clutch of drawers inside, and handed a somewhat larger key to Tench.

The inspector examined it.

'I shall have to keep this for the moment, sir,' he said. 'Before anyone else goes in, the forensic team needs to examine the stairs.'

'Yes, I understand that. And the other key?'

'One similar to this, sir, was found in the pocket of the Major's trousers, so I think we can be certain the place is secure. What about the church itself? Is it normally left unlocked?'

'During daylight hours, yes. I lock it at dusk.'

'And you locked it as usual last Monday night?'

The rector nodded. 'I did.'

'Right, sir.' Tench dropped the key in his pocket. 'Now tell me about the tower steps. How many are there?'

'A hundred and forty. At least, so I'm told. I've never counted them myself. The tower is a hundred and twenty feet high, and that includes the belfry. There are short landings after every thirty-five steps, and a ladder leads up from the bells to the top.'

'Are there any lights?'

'Only in the belfry. No one uses the stairs except in daylight.'

'Not even the Major?'

'No. He always waited till the light was good enough to see.'

'Tuesday morning was very dull.'

'Yes, it was.' The rector admitted as much. 'But there are slit windows that illumine the stairs, and he'd been up and down many times before.'

'I was told he volunteered to put up the flag.'

'Yes, he did. Soon after he came to Salleston. I accepted his offer at once. I felt that George Starling, who'd done the job for years, was getting a bit beyond it, and I'm afraid, Inspector, I've no head for heights.'

Tench looked down his nose. 'A bit risky though, wasn't it?'

Mr Blake seemed surprised. 'Good gracious, no. Why should it have been?'

'A man who'd suffered a head wound in the war . . .'

'Ah.' The rector relaxed. 'I see what you mean. But it wasn't a head wound in the sense that he was likely to suffer dizzy spells.'

'It wasn't?'

'No, indeed. The Major had a part of his jaw shot away. The surgeon, I believe, inserted a metal plate, but there was never any danger of him losing his balance. The man was very fit. A good deal fitter than I am.'

'I see. Yes, of course.'

Tench eased himself up, reached across to the table and picked up the letters.

'Thank you for answering my questions,' he said, 'and now, sir, would you care to show me round the church?'

## 7

'A hammerbeam roof.'

'Double hammerbeam. With angels.'

Tench saw them, spreading their wings below the rafters.

'Fifteenth century?'

'Mainly fifteenth, though building started much earlier.' The rector was in his element, proud of his church. 'In the early days, of course, the whole effect must have been much more impressive. No pews at that time. People simply stood or knelt for the services. The windows were a rich stained glass in those days, not the clear diamond panes you see round you now. The guilds had private chapels, their altars hung with cloth of gold and brocade. The place was lit by candles, and the colours on the rood screen must have been truly splendid . . .'

Tench listened, mentally docketing what was said. His training under Lubbock served him well in that respect. To listen was to learn, though exactly what it was that he learned by listening often took time to make itself apparent. His years as a history student at Cambridge, before he'd been drafted into the army, had taught him the value of accumulating facts and sifting what was important from what was merely dross. Since then he'd acquired patience and the growing conviction that, especially when it came to dealing with murder, there was much to be gained from letting people talk. Much of what they said was, in the end, irrelevant, but Lubbock had always maintained that it paid to absorb every scrap of information. Somewhere along the line something would be said which, immediately, meant nothing, but which sooner or later would click into place, tally with something that someone else had said, and open up a fruitful line of inquiry. Because of that, he was prepared to let the rector rumble on in the echoing, empty vastness of his church, in the solid conviction that, somewhere among the words that he flung to the angels, there was bound to be some idle snippet of information that would prove in the end to be of more than merely passing significance.

The Reverend Mr Blake was now in full flow.

'When they were first painted,' – he raised a hand towards the roof – 'the feathers on the angels were white, green and red, and the colours on the screen must have glowed in the candlelight with a richness that now we can only dream of. They should really be restored, and we did start a fund for the restoration. That was some years ago, but the village and the church both needed a communal meeting place, so the money was used to build the village hall . . .'

'That's the new building?' Tench said. 'The one that stands back, half-way up the main street?'

'Yes. Brick and flint, to tone with the rest. It's used for parish

32

meetings, dances, whist drives, you know the kind of thing. The Salleston Circle meets there, as well.'

Tench turned and began to walk back down the nave. 'This Circle . . . Who runs it?'

'It's run by Mrs Reynolds.' The rector's voice betrayed nothing at all.

'She's one of the residents?'

'Yes. She lives at Number 69. Opposite the hall.'

'How long has it been functioning?'

'The Circle? Oh, some four or five years. It was started during the war when it was difficult for the people here to get into Norwich.'

'And still flourishes?'

'Oh, yes. The meetings are well attended.'

'How often are they held?'

'The last Monday of every month. We had one the evening before the Major died.'

'He was there?'

'Yes, indeed. He very rarely missed.'

'I believe Mr Denstone gave the talk that night.'

The rector nodded in reminiscence. ' "My Time in the Police". He provided us with some fascinating insights.'

'You get a wide variety of speakers?'

'We try to. On all kinds of subjects: agriculture, industry, travel, the arts. And different nationalities. In the last couple of years we've had a US Army colonel, a German Jewish historian and an Indian research scholar from Cambridge. He contrasted his life in England with the one he'd known in India. We had him back again recently, and he was equally good on a very different subject.'

Tench came to a halt. 'Is this the door to the tower?'

It adjoined the south porch, low and heavily studded.

'That's the one, yes.'

Tench noted both the latch and the lock, took the key from his pocket, inserted it, turned it, lifted the latch and pushed the door open. It was solid, weighty, and needed some effort. By the light from a slit window set in the wall, he could see the steps twisting upwards. The turn was quite acute. The turret must be narrow.

'Not an easy climb,' he said.

'Spirals never are.' The rector was bland.

'And a very tall tower for a Norfolk parish church.'

'The second highest in the county, though Cromer tops it by a clear forty feet.'

'Yet it seems to have no parapet.'

Blake's face, for the first time, showed a trace of a smile. 'That's perfectly true. No parapet and no pinnacles. Legend has it they were stolen by the people of Clunch and used for their church.'

'Clunch?'

'The next village. Mine is a dual benefice. The parish is known as Clunch-with-Salleston. There was a time, you see, Inspector, when Clunch was bigger and more important than Salleston. Now it's no more than a cluster of cottages. The church is only opened one Sunday in the month . . . I'm afraid I find the legend a little far-fetched. The explanation is almost certainly far more mundane. You'll notice how the buttresses – double buttresses – reach to the very top of the tower. I think the builders were planning to add a spire to the church, but the money ran out.'

Tench stood back from the door, and looked up the tower to the hanging bell ropes.

'Doesn't that make the raising of a flag pretty dangerous?'

The rector gave a shrug. 'In frosty weather, yes, very danger-ous indeed. Or in a high wind. Not that anyone's ever fallen. At least, there's no record of any such incident. But I did forbid the Major to try and raise the flag on a number of occasions when the weather was inclement.'

'Did he need you to tell him?'

'Unfortunately, yes. He regarded the operation as something of a challenge.'

'Did you give him any instructions on the Monday evening?'

'No, Inspector. I didn't speak to him at all.'

'There were thunderstorms round Norwich early on Tuesday morning.'

'So I'm led to understand.'

'And presumably here, too.'

'I believe there were, yes, though I must have slept through them.'

Tench was still determined to probe the chance of an accident.

'Would the Major have gone up the tower to raise the flag if there'd been lightning about?'

'Who can possibly answer that?' The rector gave a somewhat impatient sigh. 'He might well have done. The point is, Inspector, we'll never know, will we?'

'Oh, I wouldn't be sure about that, sir,' said Tench. 'It's surprising what people see when they happen to look out of their bedroom windows.'

# 8

He walked slowly back to the car.

McKenzie was there already, lolling against the bonnet, hands in his pockets.

'Anything worth reporting?'

The sergeant uncoiled himself. 'Incident room's fixed. Grenville's arranged it.'

'Where?'

'There's a wooden annexe tacked on to the village hall. It's big enough for us. The lads can move all the stuff in tonight. Key's at the police house.'

'Good.' Tench slid behind the wheel. McKenzie slumped down beside him and slammed the car door.

'You warned him about the house-to-house?'

'Yes. It's all set up.'

'What about Tremellen's place? Anything there?'

'Documents, no. Nothing significant. Doesn't seem to have been a letter-writer. Odd business papers connected with this advertising firm of his in Norwich. Bank book and cheque book, both in good order. Oh, and an invitation to some regimental reunion. They're all in that envelope on the back seat. Apart from that, nothing.'

'What about impressions?'

'Yes, one or two.'

'Tell me.'

McKenzie shifted in his seat.

'First impression,' he said. 'The bloke who lived there was neat. Incredibly neat. Even made his bed the morning he went out to run up that flag. Now what kind of man, for God's sake, makes his own bed at five o'clock in the morning?'

35

'One who's spent a good bit of time in the army?'

'No, Mike, not a chance. This one was a major. He must have had a batman to do that sort of thing.'

'Well, perhaps he was organized. Schooled in discipline. Carried it into civilian life.'

'Or again, perhaps he wasn't.'

Tench frowned. 'Why not?'

McKenzie lit a cigarette.

'Impression number two,' he said. 'Maybe the Major didn't sleep there Monday night.'

'Any evidence for that?'

'At the time, you mean? None. It was just a passing thought . . . But then I was accosted.'

'In daylight?'

'In sunshine. Right here in Salleston.'

'Who by?'

'His next-door neighbour. She's a Mrs Bedwell.'

Tench raised his eyebrows. 'Young and attractive?'

'As it happens, no. Middle-aged and blessed with a face like a walnut . . . Was I police, she said?'

'You confessed?'

'Thought I'd better. She wanted to talk, and you never know just what's waiting on somebody's tongue.'

'So what did she tell you?'

'Quite a lot,' McKenzie said. 'Seems her husband has to be up and moving at the crack of dawn – his job's to milk the cows at some God-forsaken farm – so she gets up as well to cook him a breakfast. And last Tuesday morning she looked through the curtains – just by chance, of course – and there was Major Tremellen toddling back home.'

'What time was this?'

'Just after four o'clock. "And," she said darkly, "it's not the first time." Then she edged a bit closer, looked around twice, and said, "Where'd he been? That's what I'd like to know."'

'Did she give you a hint?'

'Oh, yes. More than that. She told me just where he'd been and what he'd been up to. In explicit detail.'

'Gossip?' said Tench. 'A woman with a grudge?'

'Could be.' McKenzie shrugged. 'I'll admit the idea did flick through my mind. So, when I saw Grenville, I mentioned what I'd heard.'

'And what did he have to say?'

'Well, he wasn't exactly shocked. Said yes, it was a well-known fact in the village. Apparently our friend the Major's been dipping his paddle in someone else's pond.'

'Has he, by God? And who's at the sticky end?'

'Some post office sorter at the GPO in Norwich. Works on night shift.'

'Does he know what's going on?'

McKenzie tapped the ash from the end of his cigarette.

'In a small place like this? Odds on that he does. But there's an old adage, Mike . . .'

'The husband's always the last to know?'

'That's the one. Right on the nail. So the answer to the question's maybe yes, maybe no.'

'Who is she, this woman?'

'According to Grenville she's a ravishing redhead, smart, with a figure like Rita Hayworth, something of a social climber and fancies herself as a cut above her husband.'

'And what's her name?' said Tench.

'Reynolds.' McKenzie leaned back in his seat and blew himself a smoke ring. 'Velda Reynolds. Very fond of getting together is Mrs Reynolds. I'm told she runs this thing called the Salleston Circle.'

# II

## THE WISDOM OF SOLOMON

My son, attend unto my wisdom, and bow thine ear
to my understanding

Proverbs: 5.1.

# 1

Late the following morning, Tench sat at his trestle-table in the village hall annexe and stared out across the fields. He was feeling more than a little perplexed. He kept telling himself that there was another old adage: still waters run deep; but the plain fact was that he hadn't been prepared for the murky depths that lay below the placid surface of Salleston. To a stranger like himself it had seemed at first sight a typical Norfolk backwater: one of the innumerable villages in the county, off the beaten track, which pursued its own life in a peaceful seclusion; a summer-still place where nothing much happened save that people came and went, the blackbirds sang and the haycocks stood dun and dry in the fields. Almost another Adlestrop.

But that wasn't a true image. The morning's encounters had soon disabused him. Salleston was no spotless, halcyon heaven untouched by the world. It had more than its share of the seven deadly sins. It had Pride and Wrath, Envy and Lust, and one or two others that even Solomon had never mentioned. It's residents, such of them as he'd met, had already made that abundantly clear.

The first was Henry Bebbington, parish clerk, choirmaster and superintendent of the local Sunday school: a tall, thin-lipped man with a snow-white beard and a harsh, rasping voice. Summoned from Maple Cottage, he was not in the best of moods. A zealot, girt around with the armour of God, he was convinced beyond doubt that no mortal hand, even that of the law, could possibly touch him.

'I wish to see Inspector Tench,' he said. 'Bebbington. Henry Bebbington.'

Tench had made himself known, and Bebbington had eyed him with evident mistrust.

'Remarkably young,' he said. 'However, let it pass. I was asked by the rector to deliver the registers.'

He set down on the table two leather-bound volumes, the one labelled Marriages and the other one Baptisms.

'Thank you, sir,' said Tench.

'You realize that these are the property of the parish and constitute an irreplaceable record?'

'Naturally, sir. We'll return them safely once they've been examined.'

'I hope so, indeed.'

'You can be certain of it, sir. They'll be well looked after . . . Please take a seat.'

Bebbington pulled a fob-watch from his waistcoat. Then, with seeming reluctance, he perched himself on the edge of a chair.

'I can give you ten minutes,' he said, 'and no more. I have shopping to do in Aylsham.'

Tench held himself in. 'Then we'd better not waste any time, sir, had we? I believe you're the parish clerk, and you hold a number of offices connected with the church. You run the choir and the Sunday school.'

Bebbington nodded stiffly. 'That's perfectly correct.'

'How long have you been the clerk?'

'Eighteen years come Michaelmas.'

'And you've run the choir and the Sunday school for much the same time?'

'Longer.'

'How much longer?'

'Nigh on twenty-two.'

'And you've lived in Salleston for how long?'

'Sixty-two years, winter and summer.'

'You were born here?'

'I was.'

'Where exactly?'

Bebbington glowered beneath his heavy grey eyebrows.

'I can see no purpose in these questions,' he said, 'and my time is running short. What value can it be to you to know where I was born?'

'Please just answer the question, Mr Bebbington.'

'Very well. I was born in Maple Cottage, I have lived there all my life and, failing some unpredictable natural disaster, I intend to go on living there until the Lord calls me.'

42

'Have you ever been abroad?'

'No, sir. Never. I have always believed that the lure of travel is a false abomination that contaminates the mind.'

'You didn't serve overseas in the First World War?'

'No, I did not.'

'Did you serve at all?'

'I repeat to you now what I said at the time, Inspector. Thou shalt not kill.'

'You invoked the conscience clause?'

'Let us simply say that I was martyred for my faith.'

Tench wondered to himself what the little martyrs of present-day Salleston made of this man. Perhaps parents used the Sunday school as a penance.

The time had come to change tack.

'You knew Major Tremellen?'

'Yes.' The answer came in a single grim syllable.

'You worked with him on church affairs?'

'Only when I had to.' Bebbington gave no ground. He was clearly determined not to compromise the truth.

'You didn't get on with him then?'

'Far from it.'

'Why not?'

'He was a foreigner.'

'A foreigner?'

'Not a Norfolk man.'

'You looked on him as an interloper?'

'Yes, if you like.'

Tench at last showed a flash of irritation.

'It's not if I like, Mr Bebbington,' he said. 'I'd remind you that we're treating Major Tremellen's death as a case of murder. There are questions I need to ask . . . Now, did you have occasion to go into the church at any time last Monday?'

'Not last Monday. No.'

'Not even in passing?'

'I did no passing. I was working in my garden all through the day.'

'And what about the evening?'

'I listened to the wireless and then went to bed.'

'You slept soundly?'

'Yes, I always sleep soundly. Unlike many, I have a clear conscience.'

43

Tench seemed to sigh. 'Are you married, Mr Bebbington?'

'Forty years last November.'

'I presume your wife will corroborate what you say.'

'She's a Christian woman. She would never tell a lie.'

Tench bit his lip hard. He changed the subject again.

'You said that you and the Major didn't get on.'

'It would be lacking in truth to say that we were close.'

'You disliked him?'

'I did.'

'Why did you dislike him? It was hardly his fault that he wasn't born around here.'

'He was not a man to my taste.'

'What d'you mean by that?'

'He scorned the word of God.'

'How did he do that?'

'He was a man of pretence. He set himself up as a pillar of the church.'

'And he wasn't?'

'He was not. The pillar was cracked, sir, the stone of it unsound. He was a lecher, and more than that, an adulterer.'

'You know that for certain?'

'Evil makes itself known.'

'Then tell me,' Tench said, 'who was the adulteress?'

'The woman arrayed in purple and scarlet. The mother of harlots.'

'You mean Mrs Reynolds?'

'She that breaks wedlock, let her be judged.'

Tench drew a deep breath.

'Forgive me for saying so, Mr Bebbington,' he said, 'but you don't seem to show any deep regret at what happened to the Major.'

Bebbington looked him straight in the eyes. 'The adulterer shall surely be put to death, sir. Those, if I recall, were the words of the Lord.'

He pulled out his watch.

'I regret,' he said, 'but I can give you no more time. I have a bus to catch. Please see that the registers are returned to the rector without too much delay.'

Tench let him go. He'd had more than enough.

One thing was for sure. Mr Bebbington wouldn't be fleeing the country.

# 2

That was at half-past nine.

There was more to come.

At twenty-five to ten McKenzie arrived. He brought in Velda Reynolds.

A trim, svelte figure with chestnut hair waving round her shoulders, she was wearing a black suit with a white blouse and a small black halo hat. She carried a black handbag and a pair of black gloves: not exactly the ideal outfit for summer in Salleston. Nonetheless she looked decidedly smart. Very fetching, thought Tench.

She sat down facing him, dropped her handbag on the floor, laid her gloves on the table and looked at him expectantly.

'I'm told you want to see me, Inspector,' she said. Her voice was low and lilting.

Tench eyed her with guarded appreciation. He reminded himself that he had a job to do.

'Your name's Velda Reynolds?'

'Velda Margaret Reynolds.'

'And you're married to Leslie Reynolds?'

'In a way,' she said.

Tench was plainly puzzled. He hadn't expected such an answer.

'What exactly does that mean?'

'We share the same cottage . . . from time to time.'

Tench made no comment.

'How long have you been married?'

'About seven years.'

'Don't you know precisely?'

'Seven years last week,' she said. '22nd June.'

'You said you shared the same cottage from time to time. What d'you mean by that?'

'What I said, Inspector.'

'You mean there are times when you don't live together?'

She laughed. 'That's one way of putting it.'

'Then how would you put it?'

'He comes and he goes.'

'The marriage is in trouble?'

'No, I wouldn't say that.' She was calm, quite unruffled. 'We have an arrangement. He has his own friends and I have mine.'

'Men friends?'

'Mostly. I'm a woman, Inspector.'

'I was hardly in any doubt about that, Mrs Reynolds,' Tench said drily. 'Was Major Tremellen one of these friends?'

She looked down, and then up at him.

'Yes, he was,' she said.

'A close friend?'

'Yes.'

'Then his death must have come as a considerable shock.'

'Yes, it did.' Apart from biting her lip, she showed no distress.

Tench sat back in his chair.

'We're anxious', he said, 'to trace the Major's movements in the twenty-four hours before he died. That is, from early last Monday morning. Can you help us with this?'

'Monday? I think so . . . I only know what he told me.'

'And what was that?'

'He said he'd spent the day at his office in Norwich.'

'When did he tell you this?'

'When I saw him at the Circle meeting that evening.'

Tench made a note. 'D'you know what he did once the meeting was over?'

'Yes, he came home with me.'

'To your cottage?'

'Yes, Inspector. We walked there together.'

'He came in?'

'Of course.'

'And how long did he stay?'

'He left at four o'clock.'

If Tench was mildly shaken, he showed no surprise. 'You mean four o'clock on the Tuesday morning?'

Mrs Reynolds seemed amused. 'That's right,' she said.

'Then he spent the night with you.'

'Yes, till four o'clock. He always left at four.'

'So it wasn't the first time he'd stayed the night.'

'No. There had been others.'

'You slept together?'

46

Velda Reynolds raised her eyebrows. 'Naturally, Inspector. Why else would he have stayed?'

'You admit that?'

'Why not? You must have been told. It's common knowledge in Salleston.'

'And that doesn't bother you?'

She shrugged: just a graceful lift of the shoulders. 'Why should it?'

Tench wasn't prepared to speculate. He simply moved on. 'You say he always left you at four o'clock. Why?'

She was perfectly frank. 'Because Les gets home at five.'

'Your husband?'

'That's right. He works nights in Norwich. A van brings him back, drops him off in the village . . . if he troubles to come.'

'How d'you mean, Mrs Reynolds? "If he troubles to come."'

'If he doesn't get the driver to drop him at Marsham.'

'Why should he do that?'

'Well, he sometimes stays there.'

Tench stared at her. 'You mean . . .?'

'Oh, yes, Inspector. I told you before. He has his own friends. He has, in particular, one little friend.'

'You mean that he sleeps with a woman in Marsham?'

She was bland, almost casual. 'Yes, quite often.'

'You know that for sure?'

'For positive, Inspector.'

'You know her name?'

'Yes.'

'What is it?'

'Minty Rogers.'

'Minty?'

'Araminta.'

'And you know where she lives?'

'Yes. St Mary's Close. She's a widow, she's fat and she thinks he'll divorce me.'

'But he won't?'

'Of course he won't. He's perfectly happy.'

Tench closed his eyes. He seemed to be in pain. Then he opened them again.

'Mrs Reynolds,' he said, 'did your husband know about you and the Major?'

She looked straight at him. 'Yes, of course he did.'

47

'And didn't he resent it?'

'No. Why should he?'

'I'd have thought that was obvious.'

She gave a little sigh. 'Are you married, Inspector?'

Tench admitted that he was.

'Happily married?'

'Yes, I believe so.'

'So am I,' she said. 'Let's leave it at that, shall we?'

Tench breathed deeply. 'Unfortunately, Mrs Reynolds, we can't leave matters there. Major Tremellen's dead. He may well have been murdered, and, as far as we know, you were almost the last person to see him alive. Added to which, by your own admission, he was sharing your bed . . . Did your husband come home on Tuesday morning?'

'No, Inspector, he didn't.'

'He stayed at Marsham?'

'I haven't asked him. I presume so.'

'When did he get home?'

'At five o'clock this morning.'

'Not yesterday?'

'No.'

'So where is he now?'

'I should think he's still in bed. That's where I left him.'

'Did you tell him that Major Tremellen was dead?'

'At five o'clock, Inspector? No, I was asleep.'

'Didn't you wake up?'

'No.' She shook her head. 'We have separate rooms.'

'So he still doesn't know.'

'He could have heard, I suppose. Marsham isn't that far. It's only five miles away.'

'But you haven't told him.'

'No. How could I? I haven't had the chance to speak to him since he went to work on Monday.'

Tench seemed to be wondering where to go next.

'Tell me, Mrs Reynolds,' he said. 'On Tuesday morning. What did you do after the Major left?'

'I went back to sleep.'

'Till when?'

'Till about eight o'clock.'

'Then you got up?'

'Not immediately, no.'

48

'When did you get up?'

'Somewhere round about nine.'

'You knew the Major had to put up the flag that morning?'

'Yes, of course. He told me.'

'When you got up, didn't you notice it wasn't flying?'

'I never bothered to look. I sleep at the back, the opposite side to the church.'

'So when did you hear about Major Tremellen?'

'Not till I went down to the village shop.'

'And what time was that?'

'Oh, round about ten.'

Tench paused for a moment. 'How were things between you when Major Tremellen left?'

Velda Reynolds crossed her legs and drew up her skirt. Tench glimpsed a tantalizing spindrift of lace.

'What exactly d'you mean by that question, Inspector?'

'Where you on good terms?'

'Yes, we always were.'

'What was the last thing he said to you?'

'He said he'd see me again that evening at the usual time. Then he kissed me.'

'And after that?'

'I kissed him.'

'Then he left?'

'Then he left, Inspector, yes.'

Tench frowned. He tapped the table. 'I find all this very hard to believe.'

She opened her eyes wide. 'You do?' she said. 'Why?'

'You've been having an affair with the Major for how long?'

'I suppose . . . oh, six months.'

'Yet you seem to accept his death as a matter of course. No tears. No sign of grief.'

She gave another little shrug. 'Let's just say that tears don't come easily to me . . . And after all, he was just a friend.'

'Just a friend. Nothing more.'

'He was a man. I wanted one and he wanted me. We settled for that.'

'And now he's dead, Mrs Reynolds.'

'So what am I supposed to do? Go into purdah?'

'No, but . . .'

She stopped him. 'Look, Inspector. Chris was good for me.

49

Yes, I'll miss him, but there'll be others. Men aren't exactly scarce.'

Tench looked her straight in the eyes. Her gaze didn't waver. He told himself with an effort that he needed time to think.

'You've no intention', he said, 'of leaving the village in the next few days?'

'No, Inspector, I haven't.'

'Good. Please don't. You may be needed again.' He stood up and pushed his chair back under the table. 'I'd like you to make a statement about Monday night to Detective Sergeant Gregg. He's the one over there. After that, you're free to leave.'

She picked up her bag, and after that her gloves.

'Thank you,' she said and smiled.

Then she turned, tossed her hair back and walked across to Gregg, her heels tap-tapping on the floor of the annexe.


Tench watched her go, then he jerked his head at McKenzie and they both went outside.

The sergeant hadn't merely been watching; he'd been listening.

'An attractive bitch,' he said.

Tench was thoughtful. 'Maybe.'

'Oh, come on. She's a natural. I'll bet she's already got two or three in line to take Tremellen's place.'

'OK, she's attractive, and what's more she knows it. But whether she's the bitch she makes herself out to be, that's another matter.'

McKenzie was scathing. 'What d'you reckon she is then? Little Nell in disguise?'

'Not quite,' said Tench, 'but I reckon as an actress she's a good yard ahead of your friend Rita Hayworth.'


# 3


'So what's the next move?'

'Get over to Marsham and check with the widow. Araminta Rogers, St Mary's Close. Find out just when Leslie Reynolds was there . . . I'm going to roust him out of bed while Gregg's taking that statement.'

'That's not going to please him. He'll have been up all night.'

'Too bad,' said Tench. 'He's had five hours to snore his head off. He can get up and greet me with a smile on his face.'

'You'll be bloody lucky.'

'You never know, Mac. He could be full of the joys of summer. If he isn't, hard cheese. I want to hear what he's got to say. I've a pretty good idea it'll be a different tale from the one that his darling Velda's just told us.'


The trouble was that it wasn't.

Roused from his morning sleep by Tench repeatedly drumming on the door, Reynolds peered out bleary-eyed at the intruder. A heavy, square-built man, he was wearing a pair of old trousers and a rumpled shirt that was still unbuttoned. He needed a shave, and his greeting was just as rough as his appearance.

'What the hell do *you* want?' he said. He was all belligerence.

Tench gave him no chance to assert himself. He produced his card.

'Detective Inspector Tench. Norwich,' he said. 'Are you Leslie Reynolds?'

'Yes, that's me.' The admission was grudging.

'Then I'd like a few words.'

'What about?'

'Perhaps we could go inside, sir,' Tench said smoothly. 'Better than letting the whole village know.'

Reynolds stepped aside reluctantly, and then closed the door.

'Back room,' he said. 'Second down on the right.'

It was clearly a woman's room. Tench took in at a glance the flowered curtains, the chintz covers, the knick-knacks arranged on the mantelpiece, the water-colours hung discreetly on the walls.

Reynolds lowered himself on to a high-backed chair and motioned his visitor to a chintz-adorned pouffe.

'Now,' he said, 'what is it? It'd better be good. Is it post office business?'

Tench decided that in this case a dose of shock tactics might well be beneficial.

'I'm inquiring into the death of Major Tremellen.'

Reynolds' response was one of mild unconcern. 'Dead, is he?'

'I'm afraid so.'

'So what's it to do with me?'

'You don't sound very surprised, Mr Reynolds.'

The man scratched his armpit. 'Couldn't care less.'

'Isn't that a rather callous attitude to take?'

Reynolds threw the question back. 'Is it?' he said.

Tench declined to answer. He was beginning to wonder how two such ill-assorted mortals as Leslie and Velda Reynolds had managed to link themselves together for life.

'You knew that your wife was having an affair with the Major?'

Reynolds raised his eyebrows. 'So that's what it was, was it?'

'What did you think it was?'

'I thought he was sticking it up her most nights.'

Tench eyed him with a barely concealed distaste. 'What did you feel about it?'

'About what?'

'This affair.'

Reynolds shrugged. 'Not much.'

'Didn't it make you angry?'

'Why should it? She can do as she bloody well likes.'

'You *are* married, Mr Reynolds.'

'What difference does that make?'

'Apparently,' Tench said, 'none.'

'Right enough. So why all the questions, now, at this time? Blast it, the birds aren't bloody well awake.'

Tench said nothing. He just looked.

Reynolds made to move.

'Well, if you've got nothing more to ask,' he said, 'I'm off back to bed.'

'Sit down, Mr Reynolds.' Tench spoke quietly, but there was sufficient authority behind what he said to make the man pause. 'Sit down,' he repeated.

Reynolds gave a sigh and sat down again. 'What d'you want now?'

'Just a little information . . . Where were you between three o'clock and eight o'clock last Tuesday morning?'

'Tuesday? On night shift.'

'Where, Mr Reynolds?'

'Post office. Norwich. Why the hell d'you want to know?'

'I'm asking the questions. Just answer them,' Tench said. 'What time did the shift finish?'

'Always finishes at four.'

'Then what did you do?'

'Waited.'

'What for?'

'The van, of course. What d'you think?'

'And what van would that be?'

Reynolds breathed noisily. 'The one that brings me home.'

'You waited for transport. What time did it arrive?'

'Where?'

'At the post office.'

'Quarter past four, like it always does.'

'And then?'

'I got in.'

'Were there other men with you?'

'Yes, a couple.'

Tench pulled out his notebook. 'Who were they?'

'Will Grimes and Tom Stormer.'

'And where do they live?'

'Grimes lives at Stratton Strawless. Stormer at Hevingham.'

'So both of them got out of the van before you did.'

'Had to, hadn't they?'

'After Hevingham, then, you were alone with the driver.'

'That's right. Just the two of us.'

'What's his name, this driver?'

'Archie Cobban. It's always Archie does the driving. What the hell does it matter?'

Tench ignored him. 'Whereabouts in the village did he drop you off?'

'You mean here in Salleston?'

'Yes.'

'He didn't.'

'Then where did he drop you off?'

'At Marsham.'

'Why there?'

'Look,' said Reynolds. 'How much more d'you want to know?'

'Everything,' said Tench. 'Everything you did right up to eight o'clock . . . Why Marsham?'

'That's my business.'

'Then you'd better make it mine, Mr Reynolds, and fast. If you can't account for your movements, I may have to take you back to Norwich for further questioning.'

Reynolds peered at him suspiciously.

'Hang on a minute,' he said. 'What's all this about?'

'We think Major Tremellen may have been murdered.'

Reynolds stared, then he laughed. 'And you think I did him in, just because of Velda? You must be bloody well joking.'

'Far from it, Mr Reynolds. As far as suspects go, you're the head of the list.'

'Then you and your pals in Norwich must be loose up top. I wouldn't soil my hands on the smarmy little bugger.'

'You'll have to do better than that, Mr Reynolds. You'll have to prove to me that you weren't in Salleston early on Tuesday morning.'

'I've told you I wasn't, haven't I?'

'You claimed you were in Marsham. I can see no reason for Mr Cobban to drop you there.'

'Well, he did.'

'Then I think it'd be better if you told me why.'

'All right, all right. I went to see someone.'

'Who did you go to see?'

'Her name's Minty Rogers.'

'Mrs Araminta Rogers, St Mary's Close?'

'Yes, if you've got to know.'

'Oh, I have to, Mr Reynolds . . . You went to see Mrs Rogers. What time did you get there?'

'Round quarter to five.'

'And what did you do between then and eight o'clock?'

'I was there with her, wasn't I?'

'Where was that?'

'In bed.'

'You went to bed with Mrs Rogers. For how long?'

'That's a daft question.'

'Daft or not, you'd do well to answer it, Mr Reynolds.'

'How do I know? Till ten o'clock maybe. Could have been eleven.'

'And you never left the house at all during that time?'

'What do you bloody think?'

'I don't know, Mr Reynolds. I'm asking you.'

'Course I damn well didn't.'

'Mrs Rogers will confirm that?'

'She'd be lying if she said she couldn't.'

Tench returned his notebook and pen to his pocket.

'Well, thank you,' he said. 'That'll be all for the moment. But if you've any intention of going beyond Norwich, or possibly Marsham, I'd like to be informed.'

'Don't worry. I'll not be shifting that far.'

Tench gave a nod and turned towards the door.

Reynolds followed him along the hall.

'If someone really did for that smarmy creep,' he said, 'I reckon you've got a job on.'

'Why's that?'

'Reckon you'll be finding out soon enough.'

'Then suppose you tell me now and save me the trouble.'

Reynolds opened the door.

'I'm only saying this,' he said. 'From what I've heard, there's plenty round here that wouldn't have wept if they'd found him with a knife sticking out of his back.'

# 4

Tench made his way thoughtfully back to the annexe. Constable Grenville was hovering by the door.

'Miss Tremellen, sir,' he said.

'The sister?'

'That's right, sir. She's just arrived. I told her you'd want to see her. She's waiting inside.'

Tench pushed the door open. His immediate impression was that Miss Tremellen was younger than her brother, perhaps in her late twenties. Her hair was dark and cut short. She wore a white jacket and skirt, and a blue high-necked blouse. She was slim, not very tall, and sat on a folding chair with her ankles crossed and a white handbag at her feet. She looked, he thought, a little lost amid the clatter of the incident room.

'Miss Tremellen? Grace Tremellen?'

'Yes.' She stood up. 'You're Inspector Tench?'

'Correct.'

'You wanted to speak to me before I went to the cottage?' Her voice was soft and husky, and Tench detected a West Country burr.

'If you can spare the time.' He moved her chair closer to the table, and she sat down again and crossed her ankles as before.

'I don't know that I can be of any help to you,' she said. 'You see, Inspector, I didn't really know my brother very well.'

'Believe me, I'm very sorry about what's happened, Miss Tremellen.'

'Thank you,' she said. The words were quiet, controlled.

'You were in Switzerland, I was told. On holiday?'

'Partly.' She gave a faint smile. 'I was there with a friend. He was attending a medical congress in Lausanne.'

'A doctor?'

She nodded. 'We're engaged to be married. I met him at the hospital.'

'The hospital?'

'In Truro. I'm a nurse, Inspector.'

'Oh, I see. And you heard about your brother . . .'

'From the consul in Geneva. I came back straight away.' She looked at him and smiled again. 'Though I'm afraid there's very little I can do.'

'Tell me about him,' said Tench.

'Chris?' She frowned. 'What do you want to know?'

'As much as you can tell me. And about you. You were both born in Cornwall?'

'Yes, at St Just-in-Penwith. It's a little grey stone town close to Land's End. A rather bleak place. Dad was a tin miner. He worked at Levant. Chris was born in 1912. I came six years later.'

'Levant? Isn't that on the edge of the cliffs?'

'Yes. Some of the workings, the Forty Backs they called them, ran out under the sea. Dad was killed there by a roof fall the year after I was born. And three years later Mum died of TB.'

'So you were orphaned, both of you, at a very early age?'

'Yes, Chris was ten and I was only four.'

'What happened then?'

'We were sent to an orphanage in Truro and later to foster parents. I went to a family in Helston, and Chris to a couple who lived in Redruth, but soon after that they moved away to London. I lost touch with him completely. In fact, I never knew whether he was alive or not until four years ago.'

'How did you hear?'

'He was wounded,' she said, 'in Normandy. He'd given me as his next-of-kin, as of course I was. All the War Office knew was the address of the orphanage, but by that time it was closed. The police in Truro traced me.'

'And he hadn't been in touch with you for more than twenty years?'

'No, but he'd been abroad for part of that time. He wasn't happy with the family he went with to London. He was moved here and there, and at last he ran away and joined up in the army.'

Tench nodded. 'You went to see him?'

'Yes, he was in a military hospital in Devon. Near to Moreton-hampstead . . . I think he was glad to see me.'

'It must have been quite a reunion, meeting a brother you'd never really known.'

'Oh, yes, it was.' When she smiled, she seemed to glow. Then the smile disappeared. 'But it was difficult, too. Like strangers meeting for the very first time.'

'I can imagine,' said Tench. 'Have you seen him often since?'

'Not very often, no. About three or four times. He wrote and told me he'd bought this cottage in Norfolk. We met twice in London, and I came here and stayed for a few days last year, but then . . .'

She seemed to hesitate.

'What, Miss Tremellen?'

'Well, we didn't really seem to hit it off together. His life had been so very different from mine, and in a way it still was. You see, Inspector, I was lucky with my foster parents. I had a happy childhood. Chris never settled, according to what he told me. And it showed, even twenty years later. I was content; I'd put down some roots; but he seemed to be always restless, always searching for something he knew he'd never had. Something he'd missed in life. It was a strain, staying with him. I felt I was intruding.'

'Neither of you was adopted, legally I mean?'

'I was, yes.'

'But you're still Grace Tremellen.'

'Yes, I'm still Grace Tremellen. I don't know whether you realize, Inspector, but legal adoption wasn't possible in this country till 1926 – the Adoption of Children Act. By the time

57

my foster parents got around to thinking about it, I was already ten years old. I'd got used to my name, and they didn't think it right that I should change it so late. The court confirmed their wish. As for Chris, he was shuffled from one lot of foster parents to another – with intervals in children's homes – till at last he ran away . . . Perhaps he was just unlucky, or perhaps he remembered too much about Mum and Dad to be able to settle. I don't really know.' She smiled again sadly. 'Can I ask a few questions?'

'Of course,' said Tench.

'Well, I wasn't exactly prepared for all this. I was simply told in Switzerland that Chris was dead. It wasn't till I spoke to your constable here that I knew what had happened. He said you suspected that things weren't quite as straightforward as they seemed. Can you tell me why?'

'Yes, you've every right to know, Miss Tremellen. And apart from that, you may be able to help us . . . We think your brother was threatened by someone before he died.'

'Threatened?'

'That's right.' Tench opened a file and handed her the photographic copies of the letters. 'These were addressed to him, and delivered to the cottage in the week before his death.'

She glanced through them quickly and then looked up at him.

'But who would do such a thing?'

'That's what we need to find out, Miss Tremellen . . . Did your brother ever mention the word Baradari?'

'No,' she said. 'What is it?'

'We don't know yet. It could be someone's name or it could be a place . . . Did he ever speak about his time in the army?'

'Not much,' she said. 'I know he was in the Middle East. North Africa, then Italy.'

Tench was suddenly alert. 'When was he in Italy?'

'He didn't mention any dates, but I suppose it must have been back in '43. He was in England before the Normandy landings.'

'You don't know what unit he was with?'

'No. He was in tanks.'

'The Desert Rats?'

'It's possible. He never talked much about it. What he did have to say was mainly about the landings and the time when

58

he was wounded. That was at some place in Normandy near Caen. He had nightmares about it.'

'Nothing about Italy?'

'I think he felt he was lucky to get out when he did.'

'Did he mention any places?'

'Not that I remember. Do you think Baradari . . .?'

'I'm only guessing, Miss Tremellen.'

'It does sound Italian, doesn't it?' she said.

'It's just a lead. We'll have to check . . . Whereabouts are you staying?'

'I've booked in for three nights at the Maid's Head in Norwich. I like a bit of comfort, and somehow I didn't want to stay at the cottage.'

'That's natural,' said Tench. 'Well, I'll keep you in touch and let you know when you're free to arrange the funeral . . . Just a couple more questions before you go. D'you know of anyone – anyone at all – who might have wanted to kill your brother?'

She shook her head decisively. 'No one, Inspector. I was never close enough to him to get to know his friends, let alone his enemies.'

'But you think he may have had some?'

'I honestly don't know.'

Tench nodded slowly. 'Last question. D'you know if your brother made a will?'

'Yes, he did,' she said. 'He told me about it when I was here last September. He'd just had it drawn up.'

'Did he tell you the terms?'

'Oh, yes, Inspector. He said for the moment he'd left everything to me.'

'For the moment?'

'Well, he might have got married. There was always the possibility. In that case he'd have changed it. He'd have had to, wouldn't he?'

'I suppose he would, yes.'

She waited. 'Is that all, then?'

'I think so,' said Tench. 'Thank you very much. You've been very co-operative.'

'But not very helpful.' She smiled at him again, and then suddenly she was serious. 'Will you want me to see him?'

'To identify the body? No, Miss Tremellen, I think we can spare you that. It's already been dealt with.'

'I'm glad,' she said quietly. 'It wasn't something that I really wanted to do. As a nurse you get used to looking at death. But it's different, isn't it, when it's one of your own?'

Tench followed her to the door.

'If you need any help,' he said, 'you know where we are.'

'Yes, thank you.' She paused, looking out across the village. 'Why did he come here? I've often wondered about it.'

Tench shrugged. 'It's close to Norwich, and his business was there.'

She tossed her head. 'No. I didn't mean that. I meant why come here at all?'

'Why shouldn't he?'

'Well, he'd already bought a cottage.'

'You mean . . . somewhere else?'

'Yes, he'd moved in. He wrote and told me it was just what he'd always wanted. He seemed settled for once.'

'So what happened?'

'He upped and left. It was all quite sudden. He couldn't have been living there more than a few weeks. Next I heard, he was here in Salleston.'

'He didn't tell you why?'

'No. When I asked him, he shied away from the subject. But something must have happened, something unexpected, to make him change his mind.'

'He probably just decided he didn't like it after all. Where was it, this cottage? Can you remember?'

'Oh, yes,' she said. 'It was a place with a very peculiar name. A little village called Stow-cum-Quy. He said there was a very old priory near by.'

'That's right,' said Tench. 'Anglesey.'

'Anglesey?' She looked puzzled. 'But surely, Anglesey's in Wales.'

Tench explained. 'Anglesey Abbey. It's a few miles from Cambridge.'

By mid-afternoon, with the threat of Maitland's prompt return
hanging over him like a thundercloud, he was beginning to
wonder, surveying the mass of evidence, just what it all meant
and whether he'd made any headway at all.

The house-to-house had produced very little, except to confirm what he already knew: that Major Tremellen wasn't exactly
the most popular of Salleston's residents; that most of them
regarded him with a narrow-eyed mistrust and a resentment
that was natural in a close-knit community banded together
against a brash intruder. Among all those questioned, while a
few had professed a careless indifference, only one had
appeared to be genuinely pleased at the Major's all too visible
presence in the village. This lone dissenter from the general
opinion was George Alfred Starling, who for many years had
toiled up and down the tower steps to raise and lower the flag.
As far as he was concerned, the Major had been a welcome
addition to Salleston's force of voluntary workers. His assessment of the job and the Major himself was refreshingly forthright. 'Bloody tirin' it were,' he said, 'climbin' they steps. Glad
to be rid of it. If he wants to do it, let him get on wi' it, that's
what I said. He could have stayed here till kingdom bloody
come if he'd liked.'

The lab report on the letters had been equally unhelpful. The
only fingerprints on them, apart from Tremellen's, had been
those of Lubbock and Tench himself; whoever the writer was,
he'd taken good care to avoid leaving any; and the envelopes
bore so many overlaid prints as to make them virtually indis-
tinguishable. The notepaper was a common brand manufac-
tured by Dickinsons at the Croxley Mills, Rickmansworth and,
as Lubbock had guessed, it was obtainable from stationers all
over Britain. The ink was common enough, too: Waterman's
blue; and the writing had been done with an ordinary metal
nib, probably new.

Tench had spread the photographic copies on his table, and
spent a full half-hour looking first at them, and then at the

entries in Bebbington's registers; but, as far as he could see, there was no resemblance at all between them. In fact, though no handwriting expert himself, he found it difficult to imagine that, under oath in a court of law, any such expert witness would be rash enough to claim that Henry Bebbington's hand, apparently somewhat erratic with age, could possibly have penned the firm and flowing copper-plate found in the letters.

Nor had other inquiries proved any more productive. No one had seen anything unusual around the church on Monday evening or during the hours of darkness, while it seemed that half the village had noticed Mr Bebbington hard at work in his garden at the side of Maple Cottage all through the morning and most of the afternoon.

Added to which, Detective Constable Lock, sent back to Norwich to check with the Major's business employees, had reported that the firm – Tremellen Publicity – was a small one: the staff a mere half-dozen, three men and three women, all of whom appeared to be above reproach. They were suitably dismayed by the news of his death, and none could do more than confirm what Velda Reynolds had already said: that he'd been in his office the whole of Monday, and had left, as usual, round about six o'clock. On leaving, he'd casually mentioned to his secretary that he was going to a meeting of the Salleston Circle that evening, but no, she said, he'd never mentioned any letters and she didn't know anyone who might have wished him harm. He was a generous employer. He'd established the business, and built it up from nothing. It was doing very well. After the wartime bombings, firms in the city were branching out again. They needed publicity; there was a good deal of work for a firm such as theirs, and everyone on the staff realized how much depended on the Major. No, he hadn't seemed worried. As far as she'd known, there was no reason why he should have been. All was running smoothly, though goodness knew what was going to happen to them now.

It was while Tench was pondering all this negative information that Dave Ransome, the crime reporter for the *Eastern Daily Press*, had appeared, without warning, at the door of the annexe. Ransome had been helpful on a number of occasions, giving them space in his columns when they'd needed information, and keeping quiet when they'd decided, for reasons of their own, that silence was likely to prove the better option. Because of that, and in spite of Maitland's blasphemous intolerance of anyone who approached him with a notebook and pencil, Tench hadn't been prepared to turn him away without offering him at least a snippet of news. He'd given him just enough for a preliminary report, saying, without divulging the contents, that Tremellen had received a number of threatening letters; promising to keep him abreast of events; and hinting, with his tongue very firmly in his cheek, that the Chief Inspector, once he got back from Ipswich, would doubtless be holding a press conference as soon as he had something tangible to report.

Ransome had only just disappeared – to do a bit of nosing on his own, as he put it – when a rattle like an approaching mobile machine-gun signalled the return of McKenzie from Marsham on the vintage Norton that he swore had once, in the distant past, won a TT race in the Isle of Man.

He blundered into the office, his black mane of hair in tempest-tossed disorder, and slumped down on a chair.

'Well,' said Tench, 'what tidings from the outback? Did you see the widow Rogers?'

McKenzie gave a sniff. 'Mrs Araminta Rogers isn't someone you can miss. Sixteen stone if a pound, and fifty round the bust. How big's Reynolds?'

'Solid,' said Tench.

'He'd bloody well need to be. If you took her on, you'd be lost between her tits.'

'So what did she have to say?'

'Oh, he was there all right. Let himself in at a quarter to five, like he normally did.'

'With a key?'

'Oh, yes. She's always tucked up in bed. He just goes up and joins her.'

'And she folds herself round him.'

'That's the general idea.'

'And how long did they stay there locked in each other's arms?'

'He'd be lucky to get his arms round her,' McKenzie said.

'Right. I'll rephrase the question. What time did they get up?'

63

'Ten past eleven. She was sure about that. She looked at the clock.'

'Any special reason?'

'Yes, they were late. She had to catch a bus at quarter to twelve. Hair appointment in Aylsham.'

'Then why were they late?'

'I asked her that. Thought she'd simply say that they'd just overslept, but she was a bit miffed about it, so I got the whole tale.'

'Which was what?'

McKenzie grinned. 'Seems he hadn't had much sleep the morning before. Velda had had some of her pals in for coffee, and they'd chattered like starlings for a couple of hours. He was so shagged out when he got to Minty Rogers' he just rolled into bed, and in less than half a minute he was snoring his head off. She was very rightly miffed.'

'So she didn't get her oats.'

'Not till ten o'clock. That's why they were late. "I always have to have a little sleep," she said, "after."'

'So, if we believe her, that puts Leslie Reynolds out of the reckoning.'

'Looks like it, yes . . . So where do we stand?'

'At the moment,' said Tench, 'nowhere much at all . . . As soon as the squad's finished over at the church, I think we'd better go and take a look at that tower. How d'you feel about climbing a hundred and forty steps?'

McKenzie closed his eyes.

'Revolted,' he said.

# 6

Tench unlocked the door and pocketed the key. Then he let McKenzie through and followed him in.

The steep flight of stairs rose up ahead of them, winding out of sight.

Tench examined the treads.

'Badly worn,' he declared. 'If they're like this higher up, it wouldn't take much for a man to lose his footing.'

'Just a push. That's all.' McKenzie looked up at the curving walls. 'How many stages did the rector say there were?'

'Four, so he told me. There's a landing every thirty-five steps . . . OK. Shall we go?'

'You go first.' It was clear that McKenzie wasn't viewing the climb with any great relish. 'If you find I'm not behind you, don't worry about it. I'll be taking a nap on one of the flat bits. Just expect me at the top before it gets dark.'

'Oh, come on,' said Tench. 'If George Starling could make it, then I'm damned sure we can.'


They did, though it took a little longer than he'd intended. McKenzie flatly insisted on taking what he called a short siesta every thirty-five steps, and when they reached the third landing he sat down, wiped his brow with the back of his hand, and complained that the rector was distinctly lacking in financial astuteness.

'Should have had a beer-stall half-way up these bloody stairs,' he said. 'He'd have made enough in a summer, if he'd opened them up to visitors, to build a parapet on that tower like the Walls of Jericho.'

By the time they reached the top he was bluntly dismissive of flags, campanology, medieval builders and the Major's intelligence.

'Mad,' he said. 'Must have been. Plain bloody mad. You wouldn't catch me climbing these stairs to raise a flag, not for a hundred smackers, let alone for nix. Why the hell did he do it?'

'Perhaps he needed to prove something.'

'Who to?'

'Himself.'

'Inadequate. Had to be. No other explanation.' McKenzie leaned against the wall. 'You'll have to open that door,' he said. 'I'm knackered.'

It was set into an arch and made of solid oak, with wrought-iron hinges that splayed out across it and a pendant iron ring that lifted the latch. Tench turned the ring, put his shoulder to the door and pushed. It opened with a groan like some demented spirit bewailing its fate.

If the stairs had been dim, the bell-chamber itself was positively sombre. The only light from outside was filtered through a series of slanting louvres that pierced the walls, and it seemed to Tench that he was stepping from twilight into shadowy dusk.

He put out a hand to hold McKenzie back.

'Hang on,' he said. 'There must be a light switch somewhere.'

'Think so?' McKenzie sounded less than hopeful.

'Has to be, yes. Bell mechanisms have to be greased now and then. You can't do that in the dark. And Blake said there were lights.'

He fumbled along the wall and at last found the switch, but when he pressed it, the result barely lessened the gloom. The single sixty-watt bulb – McKenzie swore it was forty – did little but throw even deeper shadows from the beams of the bell-cage, the spokes of the wheels and the yawning black mouths of the silent bells.

'Nice place for a murder,' McKenzie said.

'Someone must have thought so. But who? That's the question.'

'What did the crime squad find up here?'

'Nothing.'

McKenzie nodded. 'Well, there wouldn't be anything, would there?' he said. 'No signs of a struggle. All he needed to do was wait behind the door, and when the Major came in, give him one good shove.'

'That's true,' – Tench frowned – 'but if he was lying in wait for Tremellen, how did he get up here in the first place? The door at the bottom was always kept locked, and only Blake and the Major had keys.'

'Well, one thing's for sure, he couldn't have done it from outside. The walls are sheer to the top. Not even a Barbary ape could get a grip.'

'Then that means one of two things. Either there was a third key floating around somewhere, or else he picked the lock.'

McKenzie thought for a moment.

'He could have followed Tremellen up. All he'd have to do would be to stow himself away somewhere here behind the bells.'

'You mean wait for him coming down from the top of the tower?'

'Why not? If Tremellen was making for the stairs, he'd have his back to anyone waiting in here.'

66

'But he'd already have raised the flag, and we know it wasn't raised.'

'Do we?' said McKenzie. 'It wasn't flying when the rector got himself out of bed, but whoever was intent on killing our friend Tremellen could have pushed him down the stairs and then climbed up again and lowered it.'

'He could,' said Tench, 'but why would he do that? There wouldn't be any point. No, Mac, I reckon he either had a key or else he nobbled the lock.'

McKenzie shrugged. 'We're just guessing, aren't we? So why hang around? The crime squad's pretty thorough. If they say there was nothing up here, fair enough. That's good enough for me.'

'We've still got to go all the way to the top.'

Beyond the bell-frame was the ladder that led to the trap. McKenzie jerked a finger towards it.

'Up there?'

'That's right.'

'You mean out on the leads?'

'Someone's got to go. We need to get the whole picture.'

McKenzie shook his head. He was quite decisive.

'Not me, Mike,' he said. 'I never was any good at heights. Get me up there and you'll need a bottle of brandy and a stretcher to get me down.'

'OK. You stay here.'

'You're not going up on your own?'

'Why not?' said Tench. 'Tremellen did. More than once.'

'Tremellen was mad.'

Tench gave a grin. 'Maybe he was. In a sane sort of way.' He set his foot on the ladder. 'We're all a bit mad,' he said. 'It's got to be done.'

'Bloody hell,' said McKenzie. He stood for a second, irresolute. Then he took a step forward. 'Hang on,' he said, almost in desperation. 'Wait there for me.'

But Tench was already at the top of the ladder, pushing at the trap. It fell with a clatter on the lead-covered roof, and he heaved himself up on to the top of the tower.

McKenzie stared at the square of light above his head. He gripped the sides of the ladder, raised a foot and let it fall.

'What's the view like?' he called.

67

Tench was staring out across what seemed to him like the whole of Norfolk.

'Wonderful,' he said.

McKenzie seemed to hesitate. 'You reckon it's worth the risk?'

'There isn't any risk. It's safe enough up here.'

'Can you see them pulling pints in the Norwich pubs?'

'Almost. Come on up.'

McKenzie took a deep breath and set his foot on the ladder. Half-way up he stopped, and wiped first one hand, then the other on the seat of his trousers. When at last he reached the top, he struggled through the gap, took one look at the skyline and fell on his hands and knees.

'I'm not standing up,' he said. 'I'm not even crawling as far as that flagstaff. It's blowing a bloody gale.'

'There's bound to be a breeze. We're a hundred and twenty feet up.'

'On a roof with no wall.'

Tench flexed his arms. 'So what? Taste the air. It's as sweet as a nut.'

'You taste the air,' McKenzie said sourly. 'This child's going down. The last time I was as far from the ground as this was on Blackpool Tower. I threw up in the lift.'

He shuffled back to the trap and lowered himself out of sight.

Tench wasn't prepared to admit it, but he wasn't feeling any too safe himself. The breeze was whipping the cords on the flagstaff, and though he was well away from the edge of the tower, he suddenly felt that perhaps, after all, McKenzie was right. But he hadn't toiled up a hundred and forty steps and twelve rungs of a ladder simply for the view and a breath of fresh air.

He crouched down and moved as close to the edge as he dared. Lying flat, he gripped the rim of the tower with his fingers and dragged himself forward till he could see over the verge. Then he lay there, staring down. The drop was a sheer one to the paving stones at the foot of the tower, and squinting to left and right he could see the double buttresses rising, as Blake had said, all the way from the ground to form the projecting corners at the top.

He pushed himself back, and still crouching made his way to the nearest corner. There he stretched out again and looked straight down the buttress, and, not satisfied with that, repeated the process at each of the three remaining corners.

After that he lay still for a moment or two, gazing out across the fields to the short, squat tower of the church at Clunch with its crenellated parapet. Then he eased himself up, took one last look at the village below, walked slowly and thoughtfully back to the trap, lowered himself on to the rungs of the ladder and, gripping the iron ring, heaved the door up and let it fall above his head.

McKenzie was leaning on the bell-frame, staring at the bells.

'Hell of a size,' he said, 'aren't they? Remind me of that film about the one-eyed hunchback.'

'Quasimodo?'

'That's the chap. Rode them like a jockey. Deaf as a post, had to be.' He straightened up. 'Sorry about the tower,' he said. 'Vertigo. Always had it.'

'You're not alone, Mac,' said Tench. 'It's just one of those things. Forget it. Some people feel the same way about crowds.'

'See anything worth seeing?'

'Thought I did. Once. Way down below. One moment it was there, and then it was gone.'

'What was it?'

Tench was solemn. 'Couldn't be sure,' he said, 'but it looked to me a bit like a Barbary ape.'

There was silence for a second.

'Did you say an ape?'

'Yes, a Barbary ape.'

McKenzie eyed him narrowly. 'Now that's really something. What was it doing?'

'Trying to climb. Then it fell. Beat its head on a buttress.'

'Frustration?'

'Seemed like it.'

'And then?'

'It just vanished.'

'Was there a puff of smoke?'

'Now you mention it,' said Tench, 'yes, I think there was.'

McKenzie showed the right amount of concern.

'It's the height,' he said soothingly. 'Shortage of oxygen. It fuddles the brain.'

Tench glanced towards the bells. Then he turned back and grinned. 'Come to think of it, of course, it could have been Quasimodo.'

McKenzie took him by the arm.

'Let's get out of here,' he said. 'We both need a pint at the Cow and Heifer.'

## 7

They didn't get them for quite a while.

Near the bottom of the steps, McKenzie suddenly stopped and sniffed.

'I can smell smoke,' he said.

Tench stopped as well. 'Where?'

'Down below,' said McKenzie. 'Look. You can see it. Something's burning down there.'

Tench looked. Wisps of smoke were drifting up the stairs.

He sniffed. Then he laughed.

'Relax, Mac,' he said. 'If there's anything burning at all, then it's Lubbock. I'd know the scent of that corroded old pipe if it wafted across me in the middle of a skunk farm. Come on. Face the fire. We could do with some new ideas.'

The ex-Chief Inspector was squatting in the doorway, lighting his pipe and examining the steps.

He blew out the match and stuffed it in his pocket.

'What did the crime squad have to report?' he asked.

'Only their preliminary findings,' said Tench. 'Nothing at the top. Nothing in the belfry. Blood on the stairs, presumably Tremellen's.'

'Whereabouts on the stairs?'

'All the way down, at irregular points.'

'How close to the top?'

'Six steps down. That was what they said.'

'And no signs of a struggle?'

'Apparently not.'

Lubbock heaved himself up and jabbed the air with his pipe-stem. 'What about the door?'

'Nothing to indicate contact with the body.'

'Looks like I was right then, doesn't it, laddie? Someone was waiting for him up among the bells. There's no light switch outside. He'd open the door and step into darkness. He'd be taken by surprise. One good shove with the flat of a man's hands – or even a woman's – and he'd fall backwards down the stairs.'

'And hit his head on the sixth one down.'

'It'd be about the right distance, wouldn't it?' said Lubbock. 'Then the killer nudged him further down the steps as many times as it took, and laid him out neatly like a cross at the bottom.'

McKenzie looked up the stairs. 'It's a logical theory. But let's suppose it's right. It wasn't exactly a foolproof method of murder, was it? What if the fall hadn't killed him?'

'Who knows? Perhaps it was never the killer's intention to kill. Fact remains, Tremellen's dead, and it's your job to lay hands on whoever did him in.' He looked across at Tench. 'What have you got so far?'

'To be honest,' said Tench, 'nothing much at all. Just a series of negatives.'

'Well, that's a start. Never forget that negatives always print positive. What about suspects?'

'None very convincing.'

'Let's be hearing them.'

'For what they're worth.'

'They may be worth a good deal more than you think. Remember what Holmes implied, though not in so many words. First eliminate the impossible. Then what's left is the possible. Who are they?'

'Well, there has to be Blake. He was the only one who had a key to the tower, apart from the Major.'

'Motive?'

'None at all, as far as I can see. Unless he had some clandestine ambition to raise the flag himself.'

'Clandestine ambition?' Lubbock bit hard on his pipe-stem. 'What the devil's that?'

'A secret desire.'

'Then say it, laddie, say it. Short words are the best.'

'Right, sir,' said Tench. 'He may have wanted to raise the flag.'

71

'Not likely, from what I know of the Reverend Mr Blake . . .
Who's next?'

'Henry Bebbington.'

'Why?'

'First of all, he's an intolerant bigot. Second, he told me the
Major was a lecher who'd committed adultery with the mother
of harlots. He said he deserved to die.'

'That doesn't mean that he killed him.'

'No, it doesn't.'

'And the man's a rabid pacifist. Wasn't he a conchie back in
the first war?'

'So he claims.'

'Hardly the best of suspects,' said Lubbock. 'Who else?'

'Well, there's Velda Reynolds. She was having an affair with
Tremellen.'

'Not too likely she'd want to murder him then, is it . . .?
You've spoken to her?'

'Yes, we both have.'

'When was that?'

'This morning.'

'So what's your opinion?'

'If you want mine,' McKenzie said, 'she's a cold-blooded
bitch.'

Lubbock looked at Tench through a cloud of tobacco smoke.
'That your impression, too?'

'Not entirely,' said Tench. 'True, she didn't seem very upset
by his death, but then again . . .'

'What?'

'I don't think she was telling us the whole of the truth.'

'She was lying.'

'No,' – Tench seemed troubled – 'I wouldn't say that.'

'What would you say then?'

'I'd say she was determined not to show her true feelings.'

'You mean she really was upset, but she wasn't telling you.'

'Possibly, yes.'

'But why should she do that?'

'I haven't the faintest idea,' said Tench.

Lubbock drew on his pipe.

'I'd have thought,' he said, 'that her husband was a much
more likely candidate.'

72

'He was, but he's got an alibi. He was tucked up in bed with a widow from Marsham called Minty Rogers.'

'And, of course, she corroborates what he said.'

'Every single word.'

'Means nothing,' said Lubbock. 'When it comes to an alibi, never trust a wife, and still less a mistress. Women are quite illogical. I've known them be married to violent criminals who've beaten them senseless, and they've gone into the box and perjured themselves just to keep them out of gaol. It happens time and time again . . . Where does Velda say he was?'

'Not with her, so she reckons he must have been at Marsham.'

'Is there anyone else who might vouch for his alibi?'

'Three of his workmates. We're checking it with them, but it looks pretty solid.'

'You think he's telling the truth.'

'Frankly, yes,' said Tench.

Lubbock stroked his chin. 'No one else in the frame?'

'Not so far, no.'

'Nothing from the house-to-house? No one seen around the church?'

'Nobody you wouldn't expect to be there.'

The ex-Chief Inspector pulled a folded sheet of paper out of his pocket and handed it to Tench.

'Visitors' book,' he said. 'Here in the church. I've written down Monday's names and addresses. Four from Norfolk, and another four from outside. Might be worth making an effort to trace them. They could have seen something.'

'It's worth a try,' said Tench. 'I'll put Gregg on it. He's thorough.'

Lubbock tamped down his pipe and dropped it in his pocket.

'You haven't got very far, laddie, have you?' he said.

'Not yet, but it's early days.'

'The first forty-eight hours are vital. I've told you that before.' He paused. 'Want some advice?'

'Be our guest,' said McKenzie.

'Why not?' said Tench. 'You're going to give it to us anyway.'

Lubbock gave a chuckle. 'That's right enough, laddie.'

'So what are we doing wrong?'

'You're looking in the wrong place,' Lubbock said mildly. 'Your murderer's not here. He's somewhere out in the wide blue yonder. The key to this case is that word, Baradari. Unless you can link it to someone in the village, you may as well forget all your fancy suspects and Salleston as well. So let's go and do what you should have done first. Let's take another good look at those letters.'

## 8

They spread them out on Tench's table.

'Now,' said Lubbock, 'let's see what we can glean from these gems of scripture. Remember that we're looking for three different things: what they tell us about the writer, what they tell us about Tremellen, and what, if any, was the link between the two. Let's look at the writer first.'

'Well, the first thing', said Tench, 'is that he seems to know his Bible.'

Lubbock chewed his pipe.

'That's the obvious deduction, but it may be too obvious. It's easy enough to look up a pack of quotations. He might be just as irreligious as Tremellen himself.'

'There is the point that young Grenville picked up.' McKenzie laid a finger on one of the letters. 'This bit here: "as long as I am in this tabernacle". That suggests that he's one of the congregation.'

Lubbock was still sceptical. 'A tabernacle isn't always a fixed place of worship. It's one that can be moved. The phrase could simply mean that he'd arrived from somewhere else and didn't intend to stay. Look at this sentence here: "Behold, I come quickly".'

'They do at least imply some connection with the church,' said Tench. '"The time is come for judgement to begin at the House of God."'

'And', McKenzie added, 'most of the quotations are taken from St Peter.'

'All right. He may be a member of the church here in Salleston. But the references are vague and could be contrived.

They may be just a trick to throw us off the scent . . . What else about him?'

'He knew what he was going to do. He mentions falling more than once. Look at this.' Tench pointed. ' "Beware lest ye fall". And in the last one he talks about "falling headlong". Then there's this piece here: "they stumble at the word". And in the same extract, "a stone of stumbling".'

'So he planned in advance to push Tremellen down the steps. Is that what you mean?'

'Looks like it,' said Tench. 'And he wasn't bothered about keeping it a secret either.'

'What about this last bit? "This man obtained a field with the reward of his iniquity".'

'Someone with a grudge?'

'Someone who was jealous? Who thought Tremellen had done him some wrong?'

'That's what the words imply. Seems the writer felt much as Henry Bebbington did: that Tremellen was a bad lot, a flourishing bay tree that needed cutting down. There are all sorts of references: "them that do evil"; "them that obey not the gospel of God"; "being carried away with the error of the wicked". Then he talks about "cleansing from old sins" and "putting you in remembrance".'

'And', said McKenzie, 'there's all this business about walking in lasciviousness in time past, and this list of things that follows: "lusts, winebibbings, revellings" and the rest.'

'So, someone who knew Tremellen in the past and disapproved of his conduct.'

'And suffered because of it.'

'Right . . . Now what about the letters themselves? Did the lab come up with anything?'

'Nothing helpful,' said Tench. 'All very negative. No distinguishable fingerprints apart from Tremellen's – and, of course, yours and mine. Common type of notepaper. Common type of ink.'

'So that leaves us with the writing.'

'Copper-plate.'

'Yes. That could provide a clue. Who in these days writes copper-plate?'

'Someone', McKenzie said, 'who was taught to write that way.'

'But where?'

'In a church school?' said Tench. 'But not recently. It must have been some time ago.'

'He's no stripling then. Has to be getting on a bit.'

'Looks that way, yes. He could well be someone with dual writing skills. Taught copper-plate at school, but now writes a normal hand. Used it here as a disguise.'

'Effective, too,' said Lubbock, 'unless we can link a church school education with someone who knew Tremellen in the past and bore him a grudge.' He picked up the photographic reproductions of the envelopes. 'There is another odd thing,' he said. 'I don't know whether you've noticed, but look at the places where these letters were posted. The first came from Newmarket. Now look at the sequence. Ely's the next one, then Diss and Thetford. After that you get Beccles, Wymondham and Norwich, and the last two are from East Dereham and Aylsham . . . Anything strike you?'

'Yes,' Tench nodded. 'The places get closer and closer to Salleston. I wondered about that.'

'It's worth noting,' said Lubbock. 'He starts off at Newmarket, fifty miles away. Then the distance narrows down. Thetford's thirty, Wymondham about fifteen, and he ends up at Aylsham which is almost on the doorstep. It's as if he were telling Tremellen that he was closing in on him, the threat was getting nearer with every day that passed . . . You know something, Mike? I reckon I'm right. This is someone from outside, someone who had a score to settle with Tremellen; and that means, as I said, that the key must lie in that word, Baradari. That's the link between them . . . Any ideas?'

'Only a vague suspicion that it might be Italian.'

'Well, you're the expert.'

'I can't claim to be that.'

'You were in Italy during the war.'

'Not for very long.'

'And you can speak Italian.'

'Just about enough to make myself understood.'

'You underestimate yourself, laddie. When I sent you to Naples on that Elsdon Hall case, you cracked it wide open . . . In what way Italian?'

'Well, it could be someone's surname, say Giuseppe Baradari. Or it could be a place . . . And Tremellen did serve in Italy.'

Lubbock showed more than a flicker of interest. 'Who told you that?'

'His sister.'

'She's here?'

'Yes, she's over at the cottage, sorting things out.'

'She told you he was in Italy? I thought he was in Normandy.'

'That was later on. He was in Italy before that. In tanks, so she said. He was probably with the Desert Rats, Seventh Armoured Div. They were there from the start.'

'In the south, where you were?'

'Had to be, yes. They drove up from Sicily.'

Lubbock leaned back in his chair.

'Think back a bit, Mike, to that Elsdon case. Colonel Wilder was murdered, and he served in Italy. Got himself tangled in all that vendetta business, and it followed him home. D'you think this might be the same kind of thing?'

'You mean another vendetta killing? The Lex Talionis?' Tench was doubtful. 'I wouldn't have thought so. It's possible, of course. But twice in eighteen months? In the heart of Norfolk? That's stretching things a bit.'

'I suppose it is,' said Lubbock, 'but the war could well have followed him, like it did Wilder. Something could have happened while he was out there . . . You think this Baradari might be a place?'

'It could be, sir, yes. We simply don't know.'

'That professor chap would know. The one who helped you in Naples.'

'Visco?'

'That's him. Get on to him. Find out. He'd be willing to help, wouldn't he? You struck up quite a friendship.'

'Oh, he'd help, yes,' said Tench.

'You see, Mike,' – Lubbock shifted restlessly, took out a penknife, loosened the dottle in his pipe and knocked it out on a sheet of paper – 'it all boils down to what I've told you before. When you're faced with a murder, the first thing to do is find out as much about the victim as you can. More often than not it'll lead you to the killer. There's nearly always some connection except in random killings, and this isn't a random killing. There's clearly a connection between Tremellen and the person who sent those letters. There must be, because he said he had a pretty fair idea who'd written them. The word Baradari must

77

have meant something to him. The trouble is we can't ask him what it was, nor can we ask whoever it was wrote them. So it's our job, somehow, to make the connection. Baradari – whether it's a person, a place or something very different – lies buried somewhere deep in Tremellen's past, and there's only one possible way to root it out. We've got to find out whether he ever met anyone named Baradari, whether he ever passed through a place called Baradari, or even if he ever slept with a girl in Italy who used a scent called Baradari.'

He dragged a pouch from his pocket and began to fill his pipe.

'It's a tall order, laddie, so let's make a start. What have we got on him so far?'

## 9

Tench gave him a summary. Father was a tin miner. Orphaned at ten. Farmed out with his sister to foster parents. Never settled. Ran away and joined the army.

'I don't think you need bother about his early years,' said Lubbock. 'This is something more recent, since he joined up. How much do we know about his army career?'

'Only sketchy details up to now,' said Tench. 'Served in North Africa and Italy with an armoured division, probably the Seventh, but could have been the First. Then in Normandy. Military Cross near Caen – you told me that. Wounded, part of his jaw shot away. Invalided out. That must have been late '44 or early '45, because you said he bought the cottage here three years ago.'

'That's all?'

'At the moment.'

'Not much, laddie, is it? You'll need to contact Army Records. What about that fellow Clyde that I sent you to see when we were dealing with the Wilder case? Is he still there?'

'As far as I know.'

'Then he's the one to ferret out Tremellen's army record. I'd get on to him right away.'

McKenzie leaned forward. 'What about that invitation I found in his cottage?'

'Invitation?' Lubbock frowned.

'Hell's bells,' said Tench. 'I'd forgotten about that. Haven't had time to look in the envelope yet. Where is it?' He fished it out of a wire tray and emptied it on the table. 'Mac found an invitation to an army reunion.'

McKenzie reached out.

'That's the one. The card with the gilt edge.' He pulled it clear and glanced at it. 'Royal Tank Regiment.'

'Seventh Armoured,' said Tench. 'The RTR were with them. Who's invited to this do?'

McKenzie read it out. 'All commissioned ranks of the First and Fifth Royal Tank Regiments who served in North Africa and Italy between 1942 and 1944.'

'Where's it being held?'

'Army and Navy Club. That's in Pall Mall.'

'When?'

'18th September.'

'RSVP?'

McKenzie peered at the card. 'Yes, so it says.'

'Who to?'

'A Colonel Chandler.'

'Does it give his address?'

'Reply to Rushmere Lodge, Great Bealings, Suffolk.'

'There you are then,' said Lubbock. 'That's a lead to begin with. Get someone down to see him . . . And it might be worth checking whether anyone here in Salleston saw service in Italy.'

'We'll do that,' said Tench, 'but we're working on an assumption we've still got to prove. The Baradari connection may not be Italian.'

'That's true, but it's the only valid clue this case has so far thrown up. When it comes to murder, all you can do is follow a trail and hope it won't peter out; and as of now, laddie, the only one in view points towards Italy. If I were you, I'd follow it.'

'This Military Cross,' said Tench. 'D'you know how he came to get it?'

'Never mentioned it to me. It was Reg Denstone told me. Said he heard he got it for disabling a tank.'

'There must be more to it than that. A lot of men disabled tanks, but they didn't get MCs.'

'Reg said it was a Tiger. Is that any help?'

'Could well be,' said Tench. 'From what I saw of Tigers, it must have been quite a feat to put one out of action.'

Lubbock struck a match and blew clouds of pungent smoke up into the rafters.

'You'll have to explain, lad,' he said between puffs. 'I'm not up in the business of military hardware. What was a Tiger?'

'The biggest of the German panzers. Over fifty tons and heavily armoured. Almost impenetrable. Had a gun with a barrel like a telegraph pole. Fired a shell that pierced our own tanks at over half a mile. Picked off Shermans and Churchills like sitting ducks . . . How on earth did he do it?'

Lubbock gave a shrug. 'Reg didn't know any details, but I think Tremellen told him it was just a lucky shot.'

'It'd have to be, I reckon.'

'Doesn't his sister know?'

'I doubt it. They lost touch for twenty years. She seemed to know very little about his life in the army.'

'Well, the citation'll be in his army records. We'll just have to wait. Not that it's going to help with this Italian business.'

'Maybe not,' said Tench, 'but you never can tell.'

'France isn't exactly Italy.'

'No, but Corsica's French and most people there have Italian names.'

'It's an improbable link,' said Lubbock, 'but I suppose it might be worthwhile keeping in mind . . . Anything yet from Ledward?'

'Not at the moment.'

'Well, he always takes his time. I'd give him a ring, if I were you. Let him know you want results . . . Didn't Tremellen's sister come up with anything at all?'

'Very little. She gets his money, but I wouldn't think that that's got any bearing on the case.'

'No sinister plots to be rid of her brother?'

'From what I've seen of her, no. Not the slightest chance.'

'She said nothing at all that might give us a lead?'

Tench hesitated, tapping a finger on the table.

'Only one thing,' he said, 'and whether it's a lead I wouldn't really know.'

'What was it?'

'She mentioned the fact that Tremellen bought a cottage.'

'Well, we know that already.'

'No, not this one here. Another, at a place called Stow-cum-Quy. It's a mile or two from Cambridge.'

Lubbock's eyes glinted.

'Go on,' he said. 'Tell me.'

Tench explained, and the smoke from Lubbock's pipe grew thicker and more pungent.

'You say he bought this place, and then just took off?'

'Apparently so.'

'And all within weeks?'

'That's what she said.'

'And she didn't know why?'

'No, when she asked him, he just changed the subject. She got the impression that something had happened that he didn't want to talk about.'

'Intriguing,' said Lubbock. 'Did she give you the address?'

'No, she didn't know it. Just the name of the village. He wasn't there long enough to send her a letter. The next one she had was posted here in Salleston.'

Lubbock laid down his pipe.

'Follow it up,' he said. 'I would. If I were running this case, I'd want to know what made him leave.'

Tench gave a wry grin. 'The trouble is I'm not running it. Maitland is, and he's due back tonight. So it won't be up to me.'

'He'll probably send us out tomorrow to count the steps in the tower,' McKenzie said drily.

'That's his privilege,' said Lubbock. 'He's the DCI. But let's put it this way. If he doesn't get someone down there first thing tomorrow to ask a few questions, just let me know. I could do with an outing.'


# 10


But not even Lubbock could dictate every move on the chequer-board of Fate.

At 4.45 that same afternoon, Police Constable Roger Winford, answering a call in his police car, approached a crossroads in the centre of Ipswich. As he did so, a taxi-cab, travelling at speed, swung across his path. He braked hard, swerved to the left and stopped, but the cab, also veering away to its left, mounted the pavement and slewed into a lamp-standard.

Winford got out and raced across the road. The cab had hit the lamp-post broadside on, snapping it off at the base, and it had fallen across the rear of the vehicle. The driver, though shaken, appeared to be unhurt, but the passenger in the rear was trapped by the legs. He was conscious, but dazed.

Winford dived into the nearest shop, and phoned his headquarters for an ambulance and a fire crew with cutting equipment. Then he set about doing what little he could to help.

The man in the rear seat was groaning and writhing from side to side.

'Don't try to move, sir,' he said. 'Just lie still and we'll have you out of there as soon as we can.' He eased the man back into what seemed to be a more comfortable position; then he turned to the driver who was slumped across the bonnet, led him inside the shop and sat him down on a chair. 'Water,' he said to the girl assistant behind the counter, 'and a cup of hot tea. Make it very sweet.'

He squatted down beside the man.

'Where did you pick up the fare?' he asked.

The driver closed his eyes. He was clearly in a state of some shock.

'Assize courts,' he said.

'And where were you taking him?'

'Told me to get him to the station fast. He had to catch a train.'

Winford pushed his way through a gathering crowd back to the cab. The passenger – middle-aged, flecks of grey at his temples – was still lying as he'd left him. He seemed to be unconscious.

The constable reached inside his jacket and took out a wallet. He flicked through the contents.

Then he pulled out a card.

'Jesus!' he said.

*

82

At half-past five the desk sergeant in Norwich received a call from Ipswich.

He took the message, whistled softly to himself and then made his way upstairs to the Chief Super's office.


In Salleston they were locking up the incident room when the telephone rang.

Gregg covered the receiver. 'It's the Chief Super, sir. He wants to speak to you.'

Tench took the phone. 'Yes, sir. Inspector Tench.'

He listened.

'Oh, no,' he said. 'Right, sir . . . Yes . . . Yes, of course. I'll be back right away.'

He dropped the receiver on its hook, and stood staring at the others.

'Well?' said McKenzie.

Tench blinked and shook himself. He took a deep breath.

'It's Maitland,' he said. 'Took a taxi to Ipswich station and rammed a police car . . . He's fractured his leg.'


# 11


The Chief Super, Detective Chief Superintendent Hastings, was, in Lubbock's view, a good man to work with: one who could be trusted, who never pulled rank but argued his case with a gentle brevity that was, in the end, completely disarming. He'd served as his Chief Inspector for more than ten years, and during that time an odd kind of intimacy had grown up between them.

Hastings, for his part, had taken to this stolid, slow-moving, unemotional figure, and though he'd never placed any trust in intuition, he'd been forced to admit that, at least in Lubbock's case, something very similar had always been at work with considerable success. Where murders were concerned – and there'd been plenty in Norfolk in the years they'd spent together – he'd seemed to have a kind of built-in compass that invariably turned him in the right direction: towards the killer and the motive that had led him to kill. Even without the visible evidence to support him, he'd more often than not pursued the right trail.

He'd respected Lubbock for that and, face to face with him, had been prepared to listen with a good deal more patience than he might have granted to others. He'd known how much his monthly crime statistics owed to his Chief Inspector's uncanny knack of solving the most intractable of crimes, and he'd valued his opinions, forthright as they'd been, and irrational as, on more than one occasion, they'd seemed. Most of all he'd valued his character assessments. When it came to appraising his junior officers, Lubbock had almost always proved to be right, which was why, as he now sat facing Mike Tench, Hastings looked at his young Detective Inspector with some serenity.

He remembered the day, some eighteen months before, when Lubbock had suggested that Tench, then merely a fledgeling sergeant, should be packed off to Italy to deal with a particularly difficult case.

He'd demurred.

'Surely, John,' he'd said, 'he's far too inexperienced.'

But Lubbock had had his own, very different views.

'He's bright, he's conscientious and he won't let us down. He knows that part of Italy. He was stationed there at the end of the war. And he speaks a certain amount of Italian. He's equipped to do the job and if, as you say, he lacks the experience, then what better way of giving him what he needs?'

He'd still had his doubts.

'You think he's up to it?'

'Oh, yes,' – Lubbock had been firm – 'he's up to it all right. Believe me, sir, Tench is going to climb fast. In another six months you'll be ready to put him up for DI. In another twenty years he'll be sitting in the chair that you're sitting in now; if not here, then somewhere else. And, at this early stage, it might be worth gambling on a future Detective Chief Superintendent.'

Well, he'd gambled. Tench had gone, and he'd wrapped up the case; and six months later, almost to the day, he'd put him up for promotion. He'd been an inspector now for all of nine months, and in that time he'd matured out of all recognition. Hastings, as he watched him, had few, if any, misgivings. In the present emergency, given the support, he was worth another gamble. He'd fill the gap while Maitland was away. He was capable enough and, as Lubbock had said, what better way was there to give him experience?


He leaned back in his chair.

'So,' he said, 'the Chief Inspector's out of action for at least six weeks, if not a couple of months. It'll mean a lot of extra sweat. How d'you feel about that?'

What Tench felt, above all, was a sense of liberation, but he thought a little caution might be in order.

'Oh, we'll all pull our weight, sir. I'm sure we can cope.'

'You were working together on this Salleston case.'

'That's right, sir, yes.'

'You've got everything set up?'

'Yes, sir, I think so. It's all running smoothly.'

'Have you got any leads?'

'No firm ones yet, sir. One or two ideas.'

'Well, it's in your hands, Mike. Has to be, I'm afraid.'

'Thank you, sir.'

Hastings looked down his nose. 'Don't thank me just yet. You may wish you'd never been lumbered with the job . . . You'd better keep me posted, and if you need any help you know where to come. I've no doubt you'll deal with it capably enough . . . D'you think it's purely local?'

'Not entirely, sir, no.'

'That may complicate things. You'd better give me an out-line.'

Tench summarized the details. Hastings made the odd note.

'Cambridge,' he said. 'And Great Bealings is Ipswich. Will you be thinking of spreading men around?'

'I think we'll have to, sir, as resources allow.'

'Well, don't forget that other forces can help. There are times when it's better for them to do the leg-work. Sending men outside the area's difficult nowadays. Petrol's the snag, and it's likely to be a problem for some time to come. I know it's a temptation to see things for yourself, but trains and buses are time-consuming. It's a choice of two evils, I'm afraid, as things stand . . . You're not thinking of swanning off to Italy this time?'

Tench smiled. 'I don't think so.'

'Good. I'll ring up Cambridge and Ipswich and ask them to give you all the help they can. In any case, if we're working on their patches we'll have to let them know, and they may be able to provide some short-distance transport.'

'Thank you, sir. That could be useful.'

'Well, the best of luck.' Hastings clipped his pen back inside his pocket. 'Oh, by the way,' he said – he was, Tench thought, just a little bit too casual – 'I had a phone call the other day from an old friend of mine. Reg Denstone. You wouldn't know him. Chief Super at Ipswich until he retired.'

'Oh, yes, sir.'

'Bought a cottage at Salleston.'

Tench nodded. 'I've heard his name mentioned, sir. I haven't met him yet.'

'Told me he was giving a talk to some local society about his years in the force. Rang me because he wanted to check a few details . . . He mentioned John Lubbock was staying there with him . . . Isn't still there, is he?'

'As a matter of fact, sir, yes.'

'I somehow thought he might be.' Hastings' eyes narrowed. 'He wouldn't have any interest in this Tremellen case, would he?'

Tench coughed discreetly. 'Well, you know Mr Lubbock . . .'

'We both know him, Mike.'

'Yes, sir.'

'We've worked with him.' Hastings paused. 'You feel you owe him a great deal. I'm right about that, aren't I?'

'He taught me a lot, sir.'

'He was a good DCI. Had a nose for a murder. And he wasn't often wrong . . . You've talked to him about the case?'

'Once or twice, sir, yes.'

The Chief Super pushed back his chair and stood up.

'Well, use his experience by all means, Mike,' he said. 'But be careful.'

'Sir?'

'Don't let him use you.'

'No, sir,' said Tench. 'I can promise you that.'

\*

86

Back at his desk, he called in McKenzie.

'Get the team in here, Mac,' he said. 'We've got to make plans.'

# III

## HESITANT STEPS

And Elijah came unto all the people, and said, How
long halt ye between two opinions?

I Kings: 18.21.

# 1

He stood on the first floor of an estate agent's office on King's Parade, gazing out at the familiar silhouette of the chapel with its towers and pinnacles, its great east window and the massive buttresses that supported the wonderful fan-vault inside. It was a prospect he viewed with nostalgic affection. He'd spent two years in Cambridge, reading history, until the war and the army had wrenched him away; and though, once demobbed, he'd chosen not to return but to train in the police, that decision had been one of the head, not the heart.

He still had a fierce, pervasive love for the town. It was here that he'd begun to grow from a boy into a man. It held memories that would stay with him for the rest of his life: boating on a summer afternoon up to Grantchester; wrestling with pointless examination papers as the flashes of war lit the Dunkirk beaches; nights spent talking with friends as the shadows lengthened and night closed down upon the age-weathered stones; and sunlit days on the Backs, watching the clouds as they drifted across those same pinnacles at King's . . . And there were other reminders, too: the wistaria hanging in purple cascades from old college walls; the silence of ancient courts deep in the snow; and the sound that still for him held everything of Cambridge: the bells ringing out from innumerable towers on a Sunday morning . . .

'Inspector Tench?'

He turned and dragged himself back into the present. An elderly, grizzle-headed man with a straggling moustache was holding out his hand.

'Mr Parfitt,' he said. 'I'm the manager here. What can I do for you? Do please sit down.'

'Thank you, sir,' said Tench. 'I don't know whether you can

help me, but I'm trying to trace the agents who dealt with the sale of a certain piece of property, and so far I don't seem to be having much luck. I've already been to Hockey's and Grain and Chalk's, but I've drawn a blank at both.'

Mr Parfitt drew a sheet of paper towards him, took a pen from an inkwell and clipped a pair of pince-nez on to his nose.

'We can only do our best, Inspector,' he said, 'but if you give me the details . . . When was this sale?'

'I don't know for sure, but I suspect it was early in 1945.'

'And where was the property?'

'Out at Stow-cum-Quy.'

Mr Parfitt looked up sharply. 'You wouldn't by any chance be talking about The Hermitage?'

'I'm afraid I don't know the name. It was a cottage. It was bought by a man called Tremellen.'

'Ex-army?'

'That's right. Did you deal with the business?'

Mr Parfitt sniffed. 'Oh, yes, Inspector, we dealt with it all right. The purchase and the sale, both within a fortnight. It was most unusual. That's why I remember it. Most extraordinary. I never did get to the bottom of it, no.'

'Can you tell me what happened and give me the dates?'

'Oh, yes, without doubt. It'll all be on file.'

He rang a handbell on his desk, and a trim young woman in a white blouse and black skirt appeared in the doorway. She had her arm in a sling.

'Sally,' he said, 'you remember the trouble we had over The Hermitage at Stow? Can you find me the file?'

'Right away, Mr Parfitt.' She flashed him a smile and disappeared on the instant.

Parfitt took off his pince-nez and cleaned them with a handkerchief.

'Sally Merivale,' he said. 'Daughter of Sir Marcus at Shelford Hall. Broke her collar-bone last week riding point-to-point. Can't understand these girls, trusting themselves to horses. She's a perfectly good car.' He replaced his pince-nez. 'Would it be injudicious to ask what your interest is in this cottage?'

'We're not so much interested in the cottage, sir,' said Tench. 'We're making inquiries about Major Tremellen.'

Mr Parfitt tut-tutted. 'He's in some sort of trouble?'

'Not the kind, I'm afraid, that you have in mind. He's dead, Mr Parfitt. We think that perhaps he may have been murdered.'

Parfitt pursed his lips. 'I see. Yes, of course.'

'You're not surprised?'

'Shocked, Inspector, yes, but hardly surprised. Nothing that Major Tremellen did would surprise me in the slightest. He acted in a most irrational manner.'

'In what way, Mr Parfitt?'

Miss Merivale reappeared with a buff-coloured folder. She laid it on the desk.

'Thank you, Sally,' he said. 'No, please don't go. Pull up a chair . . . This is Inspector Tench. He's come all the way from Norwich to ask some questions about Major Tremellen and the cottage he bought. You may be able to help.'

'Yes, Mr Parfitt.' Miss Merivale flashed another smile, this time at Tench, and sat down on one of the spindle-backed chairs.

Parfitt opened the folder.

'The Major first came to see us in February '45. He told me he'd just been discharged from the army and was thinking of setting up a business in Cambridge. He said he had his eye on some offices to let in St Andrew's Street, but he wanted to live outside. He was looking for a small property, perhaps in a village, but not too far from town. I asked him whether he had a car. He said not at that moment, but he intended to buy one . . . As it happened, I knew that The Hermitage at Stow had just come on the market. The vendor was a widow who was moving to be closer to her children in Kent. I suggested the property and showed him some photographs. He seemed enthusiastic, so I drove him out to look at it.'

'And was he impressed?'

'Very much so.' Parfitt turned over a sheet in the file. 'The asking price was, I felt, a little high, and I was doubtful whether he'd accept it without a quibble. But he did. The whole transaction was completed in a matter of days.'

'He moved in?'

'Apparently. He said of course he'd have to buy some utility furniture, but that was all he needed. I advised him to go and see Eaden Lilley.'

'And did he?'

93

'I can only assume that he did, Inspector. There was furniture in the cottage when I drove out to see him a few days later.'

'And why did you do that?'

Mr Parfitt smiled sourly. 'Because, Inspector, he phoned me to say that he wanted to sell.'

Tench furrowed his brow. 'That seems, as you say, very strange, Mr Parfitt.'

'It was more than strange. He'd already told me he was delighted with the cottage: it was just what he'd been looking for. I could hardly believe that he'd changed his mind so soon.'

'Did you ask him why?'

'Naturally. I had to. I felt that perhaps we might have been at fault: that he'd discovered some defect that we'd overlooked.'

'And what did he say?'

'Simply that he'd decided not to set up in Cambridge. He thought Norwich would be better. He was moving out right away and he wanted the cottage sold.'

'Did he move out?'

'He did, Inspector. Within forty-eight hours the place was empty. I was led to understand he put the furniture into store.'

'Did he say where he was going?'

'No, but a fortnight later I had a letter from him with a Norfolk address.'

'Salleston?'

'I believe so.' Parfitt flicked through the file. 'Yes, here it is. The Larches, Cawston Road.'

'And that's all you can tell me?'

Mr Parfitt laid his pince-nez down on the file.

'No, not entirely.' He turned to Miss Merivale. 'Sally,' he said, 'please tell the inspector about the Blue Boar.'


2


Tench switched his gaze towards her. Early twenties, slim, undeniably attractive, bags of confidence cushioned by family wealth. Probably Benenden and some finishing school in Switzerland.

'Before I start,' she said, 'I'd like to make one thing plain. I'm

94

not a good-time girl. I don't accept invitations from every strange man who pokes his nose inside the office. Not even you, Inspector, could drag me out on a first acquaintance.'

'Oh, I believe you, Miss Merivale,' Tench said smoothly.

'Jolly good,' she said. 'Well, now that that's clear. I'll tell you what happened . . . It was two or three days after the Major and Mr Parfitt had finalized the sale. I was in the office, typing. It was brass monkey weather – you know what I mean – and I'd turned on both bars of the electric fire. He came in – trench coat and muffler – stripped off his gloves, and bent down to warm his hands. Then he suddenly looked up. "Any boyfriends," he said, "Sally?" Well, I took it for granted that all he was doing was making conversation, so I thought I'd play along. "Scores of them," I told him. "They queue up to take me out. I'm a great believer in playing the field." He straightened up at that. "Ditch them all," he said, "and I'll take you out to dinner."

'Well, I stared at him. Not that he wasn't dishy, but I'd met his type before: lots of smooth talk, a sports car at the door, and half-way down the drive they've got a hand up your skirt.'

Mr Parfitt coughed. 'I think the inspector has a vivid enough picture, Sally,' he said.

She ravished him with yet another of her smiles.

'Just explaining,' she said cheerfully. 'I wouldn't want him to get hold of the wrong idea. We're not all of us breathless to lose our little treasure.'

Tench had the feeling that when Miss Merivale lost hers, she'd do so with a calculated zest that would leave her lucky partner struggling for breath. He reflected that it might be quite an experience.

He smiled at her. 'But you accepted the invitation?'

'Not right away. I hummed and ha'd a bit. Well, you've got to, haven't you? Couldn't have him thinking he was God's own gift to women. So I asked him why he wanted to take me out, and he said why not, did there have to be a reason? I told him yes, there did, and he gave me a lot of guff about how he thought it'd be fun for both of us, how I'd made a deep impression and he'd like to know me better. I'd heard it all before – I could see I was going to need a chastity belt – so I told him no thanks, I wasn't into rutting on the spur of the moment . . .'

Mr Parfitt coughed again, and Tench suppressed another smile.

'But you did go out with him?'

She laughed. 'Oh, at last I said yes. I strung him along a bit, and got it out of him that he was stuck on his own in Cambridge and wanted to celebrate buying the cottage. So I thought why not? It'll be a free meal, and if he gets a bit fresh I know enough about men to turn him off at the stopcock . . . So he said he'd pick me up at the Hall at seven o'clock.'

'And did he?'

'Oh, yes. Turned up in a sporty number that he'd hired for the night: one of those low-slung, twin-seater MGs. Sal, I said, be careful. Watch his hairy hand when he goes for the gears. But he didn't try anything. Seemed to be full of beans. Chattered like a corncrake all the way into town. Told me how thrilled he was, getting the cottage. Stow was the sort of village he'd always wanted to live in, and it was going to need an earthquake to make him move out. He kept turning towards me and yelling in my ear above the noise of the car. Drove like a maniac . . . He'd booked a table at the Blue Boar – that's in Trinity Street – and I was glad to be still in one piece when we got there.'

'Sally,' said Mr Parfitt, 'I don't think the inspector . . .'

'No, please.' Tench raised a hand. 'I'd like to hear it all.'

'Well, there isn't much more to tell,' she said, 'except for the end. We had a couple of drinks. He had a beer; I had a pink gin. He was still in good form, still rattling on like a can full of pebbles. I didn't need to say much. He seemed a bit self-conscious about his face. He'd lost a piece of his jaw in France, and it made him look a wee bit lop-sided. I said it didn't matter: he'd still got all the important parts, and he'd have to learn to dodge a bit faster next time. We had a laugh about it . . . The head waiter came and we ordered the dinner. Then he went for a tinkle, and that was it.'

Tench stared at her. 'You mean he didn't come back?'

'Someone came back,' she said, 'but I still find it hard to believe it was him. He was only gone for a couple of minutes, but when he got back he was altogether different. I haven't seen many men who were scared, but I'd swear that he was. All the colour had gone from his face, and his hands were trembling. It was just as if he'd bumped into Dracula in the corridor. He didn't even sit down. "I'm sorry," he said, "but I've got to go. You stay and have dinner"; and before I could ask him why, he simply walked away and left me sitting in the bar.'

'And as soon as the office opened next morning,' Parfitt said, 'he rang me up and told me he wanted to sell.'

Tench looked blank. 'He just walked out and left you? What did you do?'

Miss Merivale laughed.

'What would you have done?' she said. 'I swore good and hard. If he'd still been around I'd have poured the rest of the gin on his head . . . I called the waiter and ordered the stiffest cocktail he'd got on his list. Then I went and had dinner, and took a taxi home. What with that and the meal, it cost me a mint.'

She laughed again. Then suddenly she was serious.

'Bloody man,' she said. 'If he'd come back next morning, I'd have kicked his shins and run a nail-file right along the side of his car.'


## 3


Tench lolled in the rear seat of the car as the constable drove him back into town.

His trip out to Stow hadn't exactly been productive. He'd located The Hermitage and spoken to the owners, a retired couple from London. He'd talked with the neighbours and the landlord of the pub, but no one could add anything to what Parfitt and Miss Merivale had told him earlier. Tremellen, in the few days he'd been there, seemed to have kept himself very much to himself. People remembered seeing him go in and out, but apart from that they knew nothing about him. He had, it appeared, avoided all contact with the residents of Stow.

That meant that his behaviour remained enigmatic. What had happened at the Blue Boar to make him suddenly change his mind about the cottage? It must have been something that had shaken him rigid. Hadn't he told Miss Merivale that nothing but an earthquake would move him from Stow? What had he seen in those few brief moments when he'd left her alone? Someone he hadn't expected to see? Someone he had to avoid at all costs? Somebody surfacing out of a past that they'd still got to fathom?

Was it Baradari, and if so, then who the hell was he? What was his connection with this British army officer who'd fought his way through the desert, across the mountains of Italy and on to the plains of France? Where and when had he crossed Tremellen's path?

Tench closed his eyes and tried to imagine who this mysterious figure could be, but he knew it was hopeless. He hadn't the facts to work on, and facts, as Lubbock had told him often enough, were what counted in the end . . .

He heard the driver's voice.

'Where d'you want me to drop you, sir?'

He pulled himself up. They were passing the airfield on the Newmarket road.

'Put me down at the bottom of Jesus Lane,' he said.


He walked from there to the college and turned down the Chimney, the broad, high-walled passageway that led to the Tudor gatehouse. As he did so, the memories flooded back again. He remembered the wet December evening ten years before when, as a lonely sixth former from a Lancashire grammar school, away from home on his own for the very first time and with the threat of exam papers looming on the morrow, he'd lugged a heavy suitcase down that same path and through the narrow gap in the massive wooden door. He'd felt at that time that he was entering a world that was dauntingly unfamiliar, far removed from the cotton mills and tall smoking chimneys that surrounded him at home.

He hadn't known then that he was walking down the Chimney. To him it had been no more than a path that led to a dark, forbidding tower. If he'd known what it was called, the name might have struck a chord, brought a smile to his lips, made the place seem less of an alien prison; but it had only been nine months later, when he'd taken his place as a first-year undergraduate, that he'd learnt to call it the Chimney, as everyone else did. He'd thought then that people had given it the name because, enclosed by brick walls, it resembled one. It was only by delving into college history that he'd discovered it was simply a corruption of a French word – *cheminée*: a path – and dated from the time, seven hundred years before, when the site had been a nunnery . . .

He stepped through the wicket-door and into the porter's lodge. Mallender, the head porter, lean and keen-eyed – tail coat, piped trousers and black silk hat – stood behind the counter as he had done that evening ten years before.

'Mr Tench, sir.' He smiled. 'Glad to see you back.'

'I'm one of those, Mallender, who'll always come back.'

'I'm sure you're right, sir. What can we do to help you?'

Tench rested both hands on the counter.

'I've just popped in to see Dr Summers,' he said. 'He knows I'm coming. You might give him a ring and warn him I've arrived.'

'We'll do that for you, sir.' Mallender flicked a finger, and a bowler-hatted acolyte sitting behind him picked up the phone. 'You know where to find him?'

'Same rooms?'

'That's right, sir. Over in Chapel Court.'

As he crossed the cobbled courtyard and entered the cloisters, Tench reflected that, in spite of all the cataclysms born of world conflict, some things didn't change. Mallender was still there – razor-sharp as ever: never forgot a name – still dressed in the familiar trappings of his office. He found that strangely comforting, while admitting to himself that the head porter's deference was almost anachronistic. Mallender had won the Military Medal as an NCO at Passchendaele in the First World War and, rejoining his regiment in 1939, had ended up as a captain with a DSO at Arnhem. Three years ago, passing him in the street, he'd have had to salute him. Mallender would have been the one giving him orders . . .

He felt a sudden impulse to see his old rooms, and, turning on his heel, he walked back across the cobbles and into Second Court. He stood at the foot of the staircase and looked at the names painted up on the wall. For a moment he half expected to see his own – '3 M. B. Tench' – and those of his friends; but they were all unfamiliar. The staircase now bore a cosmopolitan aspect. There were two Chinese students, and his own rooms were occupied by an Indian.

He gave a little laugh, and then turned away and made for the arch that led to Chapel Court.


Alan Summers, a Medieval History scholar of high reputation, had been Tench's personal tutor for the whole of the time he'd spent at the college. A squat, sandy-haired man, heavily freckled, he was now Senior Tutor and, like most of his kind, was possessed of enduring patience and an infinite courtesy. Having greeted his former student with genuine warmth and plied him with sherry, he sat back in an ancient wicker basket-chair and surveyed him thoughtfully.

'So,' he said, 'the Old Library. You want to take another look at the Carlotti maps. Are you off again to Italy?'

Tench sipped his sherry.

'No, not this time, Alan – too busy in Norwich – but I need to do some checking, and the Carlotti maps are better than any others I've seen.'

Giuliano Carlotti, the only son of a motor manufacturer based in Turin, had arrived at the college as a freshman in the same year as Tench. He'd been a brilliant Modern Languages student, tipped to get a first; but, like so many others, the war had cut short his Cambridge career, and four years later he'd been killed in Northern Italy fighting with the partisans up in the mountains. His father, in his memory, had gifted the college with a magnificent set of Italian maps and a handsome gazetteer, all leather-bound, from the library of his own spacious villa in Tuscany. They'd been placed in the Old Library, and Tench had consulted them once before when, eighteen months earlier, he'd been sent by Lubbock to seek out Professor Visco in Naples.

His tutor gave a nod. 'I'm quite sure that's true . . . Are you following another trail?'

'It could be a dead end. That's why I need to check. I've got to make sure it isn't before we go too far.'

The wickerwork creaked as Summers heaved himself up.

'And time in Norwich', he said, 'moves faster than here. I know what you mean . . . All right, Mike.' He pulled open a drawer in his desk and took out a bunch of keys. 'Let's go and open up.'

*

100

Twenty minutes later, between the high banks of shelves, with the heavy volumes of maps spread out on a table, Tench screwed the top on his fountain-pen and closed up his notebook.

There was a Baradari. It was in the Southern Apennines, roughly a dozen miles from the town of Benevento, and, as far as he could see, it was the only place of that name in the whole of Italy.

When he got back to Norwich early that evening, confirmation was waiting. There was a cable from Naples lying on his desk.

'BARADARI,' it read. 'HILL VILLAGE. 18 KM SE BENEVENTO. SUI GENERIS. CIAO. GIOVANNI VISCO.'

# 4

Tench assembled his forces and made his report.

'So,' McKenzie said, 'there is a place called Baradari.'

'Just one, so there can't be any mistake about it.'

'Then we need to find out if Tremellen was ever there and, if he was, what happened.'

'I rang up the War Office when I got to Cambridge,' said Tench, 'and had a word with Clyde. He's sending us the details of Tremellen's army career. In the meantime we can check with this Colonel Chandler. See what he knows about the Major's movements.'

'The inquest's fixed for ten o'clock tomorrow,' McKenzie told him.

'That means I'll have to be here.' Tench turned to Sergeant Gregg. 'Looks like your job, Andy. First thing tomorrow. The Chief Super's already had a word with Ipswich. They'll provide you with transport out to Great Bealings. It's only five miles. See Colonel Chandler and ask him if he knows who was Tremellen's CO when he served in Italy. He may be able to give you a name and address.' He pushed a map across the desk. 'And take this with you. I've marked Baradari. You want to know whether Tremellen's unit was anywhere near there, and if so, when. And any other relevant facts about him . . . It's a

101

gamble. Chandler may not know much at all. A division's pretty big. Anything from twelve to sixteen thousand men. It could be that to him the Major's nothing more than a name on a list. Anyway, do your best.'

'Right, sir.' Gregg made a note.

'What about Salleston? You were doing some checking. Is there anyone living there who served in Italy?'

'Only one, sir,' said Gregg. 'Chap called Algar. Works on a farm at Brandiston. He was with the REs. Spent most of his time rebuilding bridges, from what I could gather.'

'Give his name to Grenville. Ask him to find out whether he was anywhere near Baradari . . . Did we get that list of church helpers from the rector?'

'Dropped it in this morning,' McKenzie said. 'Not exactly a bombshell. Most of them seem to be women, apart from Bebbington and old George Starling. From what Grenville says, they're all knocking on seventy. They'd have a job to get half-way up that bloody tower, let alone reach the top.'

'What about the postal workers, Reynolds' pals? Have they been questioned?'

'I saw them, sir,' said Rayner. 'They confirmed what he said. Times and places. Looks like we can rule him out.'

'Anything more on Tremellen Publicity?'

'Nothing that would give us a lead,' said Lock. 'The business seems to have been doing pretty well. I checked with the accountants. And no one on the staff seemed to have any grudges.'

'No competitors who might have wanted him removed?'

'Not really possible to say for certain, sir. But no indications up to the present. According to his secretary, he didn't concern himself much with what other firms were doing. Had his own set of clients, and simply put his mind to keeping them happy.'

'And were they?'

'Yes, sir, those I spoke to. Seemed very impressed with the standard of service.'

Tench turned back to McKenzie. 'Nothing more on the letters?'

'No. They've gone to Dalkeith. Spurgeon took them.'

Angus Dalkeith was the most reliable of the graphological experts used by the police. A dour Scot from Pollokshaws, he sniffed perpetually and lived out at Swaffham.

102

'Right.' Tench pulled a file from his basket-tray. 'Now this report that's in from Ledward.' He read it through swiftly. 'Doesn't seem to help us a great deal, does it? Broken neck, abrasions, general bruising. Injuries consistent with a fall down the steps. No conclusions at all about how it might have happened.'

'Well, you'd hardly expect any, would you?' McKenzie said. 'Not from Reg Ledward. He always says conclusions are our affair, not his.'

'It *would* still be useful to know what he thinks.'

'He thinks it was murder, but no one's going to get him to say so in open court.'

'You've spoken to him?'

'Thought I'd better,' McKenzie said. 'The report came in just after you'd left this morning, and then the coroner's office rang to tell us the time of the inquest. We needed to know what he really thought, and it was a pretty safe bet you wouldn't be able to catch him before the hearing tomorrow. He's not given to early rising, isn't Reg. Doesn't sleep well, and tends to show his fretful side before ten o'clock. So I went along to see him this afternoon.'

'Good thinking, Mac,' said Tench. 'What exactly did he say?'

'Nothing exactly. In fact, at first he said nothing much at all except to wonder aloud why it happened to be me, and not you or Maitland. So I thought the best thing was to act a bit devious. Creep up on him from the rear. I said we had a theory that Tremellen had stumbled and fallen when he'd all but reached the bottom of the tower. Did he think the man's injuries squared up with that? Well, he looked at me as though he didn't quite believe me, and said how close to the bottom did I mean? When I told him maybe ten or twelve steps, he tightened his lips. Then he gave me to understand – guardedly, of course: you wouldn't expect anything else from Reg – that whoever subscribed to such an outrageous theory had to be out of his tiny mind. No, he said, all very sanctimonious, he thought he could assure me that Tremellen had fallen much further than that. I asked him how much further, and he made a few non-committal noises. He's an awkward old sod. So I reminded him that this was a spiral stair – after ten or twelve steps the body would have lodged itself against a wall; and to cut a long story short, he didn't need much persuading to admit what we'd suspected.

If he had to make a guess, he said – and it wasn't something he'd be prepared to state openly at an inquest – it seemed much more likely that the deceased had fallen somewhere near the top, and had then been kicked from there to the bottom.'

'Kicked?'

'Yes, that was the word he used. Kicked. And not just once.' McKenzie gave a grin. 'Well, I reckoned up to then I wasn't doing too badly, so I pushed him a bit more. Was it possible to say just when Tremellen fractured his neck? No, he said, it wasn't. What did I think he was? A pathological wizard? He turned quite frosty. The atmosphere in the lab dropped a good ten degrees. So I said no, sir, of course not, but was that all he could tell us? That seemed to rile him. I'll tell you one thing for nothing, Sergeant McKenzie, he said. Wherever your man was when he fell down those steps, he fell backwards, not forwards. Then he went off into a lot of medical stuff that was double Dutch to me, but the gist of it was that there was only one wound of any real consequence, and that was to the back of the head. He reckoned that Tremellen had gone over backwards and cracked his head against one of the steps.'

'So,' said Tench, 'it looks as if Lubbock was right.'

'Dead right, it seems to me. Someone was lying in wait at the top, gave him a shove, and then helped him with a foot all the way to the bottom.'

'Not just helped him. Kicked him . . . Did Reg say what the foot that kicked him was wearing?'

'I asked him that. Didn't think I'd get an answer.'

'But you did.'

'Half an answer,' McKenzie said. 'He told me we'd have to wait for the boffins to finish their job, but from what he'd seen of the bruising and abrasions to the body, he'd just a suspicion – no more than that – that it could have been a boot. A heavy boot, too, with nails in the sole.'

'Hobnailed boots.' Tench breathed a sigh. 'That's all that we need. We're tracking down a murderer in the middle of rural Norfolk, and we find that the prime suspect wore hobnailed boots! Hell's bells, Mac, every farm labourer in East Anglia wears them. And if Tremellen saw someone inside the Blue Boar, and that someone was his killer, then where on earth's the logic? It hardly makes sense for a chap with hobnailed boots to be tramping all over a classy place like that.'

104

'Simple,' said McKenzie. 'He wasn't wearing them at that time. He put them on specially to kick Tremellen to death.'

Tench gave a hollow laugh. 'Very funny,' he said.

McKenzie raised his eyebrows. 'It was meant to be serious. You wouldn't expect a chap to wear hobnailed boots if he was having a drink in the Blue Boar at eight o'clock at night.'

'And if he was going out in the small hours to kill Tremellen, you wouldn't expect him to put on a pair. He'd choose something quiet, like rubber running shoes.'

'True,' McKenzie said, 'but look at it another way. There aren't many farm labourers who clomp down a Cambridge street and turn into the Blue Boar for a noggin of ale . . . What I'm saying is this. We're looking at two sets of evidence, and they're inconsistent.'

'More like irreconcilable.'

'Then we've got to find some way of reconciling them.'

'Can you think of a way?'

'Well, it seems to me', McKenzie said, 'that we're faced with two alternatives, and we've got to choose one. That's assuming that whatever scared Tremellen off his dinner was a person, not a thing.'

'I've got nothing to prove it, but I'm sure he saw someone.'

'A person then, unknown.'

'That'd be my guess.'

'OK. Then either it was a different person from the one with the hobnailed boots, or whoever kicked Tremellen was no farm labourer. Which do you prefer?'

'Could be either,' said Tench. 'That's the whole trouble. What would your guess be? It can only be a guess. We've no sound evidence yet to make a choice.'

'I'd go for the second alternative. For a start, I can't believe that a woman would put on a pair of hobnailed boots, climb up that tower and kick Tremellen down. It's got to be a man. And if he's a man who frequents the Blue Boar, then he was wearing those boots on the night of the murder for some special reason.'

Tench gave a shrug. 'They could just as easily be two different people . . . Oh, I think you're right about it being a man, but whoever it was that Tremellen saw may have no connection at all with the murder.'

'Not likely,' said McKenzie.

'No, not likely, but possible . . . The key to the whole thing, as Lubbock said, is this word Baradari. We know now it's a place in Italy, but it could still just as well be the murderer's name. We need facts, and until we get them there isn't a great deal more to be said. We're waiting on Chandler and we're waiting on Clyde. At the moment they're our only two sources of information.'

'So what d'you suggest we do?'

Tench closed all the files and dropped them in his in-tray. 'Did you ever see *Gone with the Wind*?'

McKenzie stared at him. 'Who didn't?'

'Tomorrow's another day,' said Tench. 'Let's go home.'

# IV

## UP THE CHIMNEY

This is the way, walk ye in it
Isaiah: 30.21.

# 1

Late the following morning, Tench knocked on the door of the Chief Super's office.

Hastings laid down his pen.

'Come in,' he called. '. . . Yes, Mike?'

'Reporting, sir, as promised. The Salleston case.'

'Any further progress?'

'Some, sir, but things are moving pretty slowly. We're waiting for other people.'

'What happened at the inquest?'

'Adjourned, sir. The coroner refused to release the body. I've told Miss Tremellen to go back to Truro. There's no point in her hanging around up here till we get things sorted out.'

Hastings leaned back. 'You said you were waiting for others. Who exactly?'

'Sergeant Gregg, sir, first of all, and then the War Office.'

'You'd better sit down and tell me.'

Tench pulled out a chair.

'The trouble, sir,' he said, 'is that this doesn't seem to be a purely local case. We've eliminated all the obvious suspects in Salleston, and the signs seem to point to the killer being someone from outside the area.'

'No luck on the handwriting?'

'Not on the samples we provided, sir. I've just been talking to Angus Dalkeith. He's quite adamant there's no comparison at all with anything in the registers.'

'Right. So what makes you think the murderer lives outside the area?'

'A combination of facts, sir. First of all the letters. They were posted from a number of different places as far away as Newmarket. Second, Tremellen bought that cottage at

Stow, and then put it on the market within two or three days . . .'

'Was he perhaps out to make a quick profit?'

'No, sir. He sold it for a good deal less than he paid. Seemed to want to get rid of it as soon as he could, though he'd told the agent it was just what he needed. Said it'd take an earthquake to shift him from there.'

'So there must have been an earthquake.'

'Looks like it, yes.'

'Then the problem is to find out just when it happened and what form it took.'

'Well, we think we may have a lead on that, sir. Apparently he saw someone quite by chance in a Cambridge hotel, and it seems to have scared him off.'

'But you don't know who it was.'

'Not yet, sir, no, but it seems more than likely the same person pushed him down the tower steps at Salleston. We've had Ledward's report and he pretty well confirms that that was what happened. Tremellen was pushed from the top and then kicked down the stairs. And whoever did it was wearing a pair of hobnailed boots.'

'Sounds like a farm worker.'

'Yes, sir, it does, but I don't think it's quite as straightforward as that . . . There's this word Baradari that appeared in the letters.'

Hastings tapped his fingers together beneath his chin. 'Point taken, Mike. Anything more on that?'

'Well, there is a place in Italy called Baradari. We had an idea there might be. It's a hill village in the south, close to Benevento. And Tremellen served in the army in Italy.'

'You think there's a connection.'

'We're hoping there may be. That's what we're waiting for just at the moment. If you remember, sir, when we searched Tremellen's cottage, we found an invitation to an army reunion. It came from a Colonel Chandler. I've sent Gregg down to see him, and Army Records have promised to let us have details of Tremellen's career. We're hoping that between them they may provide us with a link.'

Hastings seemed doubtful. 'Well, you could be right, Mike. The answer could well lie somewhere in Italy, but I wouldn't be

110

too quick to dismiss the idea that the murderer comes from Salleston . . . You're still manning the incident room down there?'

'For the time being, yes, sir.'

'I think that's wise. Keep all your options open. Before this case is sorted, you may find you need to move back there again. You know what often happens in these murder inquiries. What seems to be the best of all possible leads turns out to be the deadest of all dead ends. Then you have to start again. If I were you, I'd be tempted to get a couple of lads out there to ask a few more questions about Monday night. It's amazing what people see and don't bother to tell you. Somewhere in the village there may be the one vital clue that you need.'

'Grenville – he's the local man – he might help, sir. And I could send out Rayner.'

'I would, Mike, and the sooner the better. Memories fade fast . . . Let's come back to this Baradari. You had the idea that it might be someone's name. Have you thrown that one out?'

'No, not entirely, sir, but we've checked the telephone directories and the electoral rolls. There doesn't seem to be a Baradari anywhere in the area.'

'That's not surprising.' Hastings thought for a moment. 'What about the possibility that it might be an Italian prisoner-of-war? There was a camp out at Cley. Some of the men were freed to work on the farms, and one or two of them stayed on here after the war was over . . . It could link up with the hobnailed boots.'

'I hadn't thought of that, sir, but it might be a line that's worth following up. I'll make some inquiries.'

'Have a word with John Lubbock. I know he had some dealings with the prison camp commandant. There were odd occasions during the war when we found it was necessary.'

'I'll get on to him, sir.'

'Can't remember the chap's name, but John'll know what it was. He's got a memory like a set of cross-indexed files . . . When did Sergeant Gregg leave?'

'This morning, sir. Early.'

'Then you're likely to have some news this afternoon.'

'Before that, hopefully. I told him to give me a ring from Ipswich.'

'And the Army Records Office?'

111

'Well, it's Saturday, sir. Unless we get something by the afternoon post, it looks like we're going to have to wait until Monday.'

Hastings picked up his pen. 'Well, let me know what develops.'

'Yes, sir, I will.'

'And don't be discouraged. Some murder cases take longer than others. You can't expect to solve them all in a matter of days . . . What else have we got on our plate at the moment?'

'Nothing too pressing, sir. Minor incidents in the main. Thankfully, things are pretty quiet just now.'

'Then let's hope tonight doesn't throw up a crop of those mindless stabbings . . . Maybe Gregg'll come up with the right result.'

'I hope so, sir.'

'Yes. Keep your fingers crossed.'

'I'll do that, sir,' said Tench.

The trouble was, he thought, as he closed the door behind him, that you could never keep your fingers crossed for long enough. It was a physical impossibility.

Unless you were double-jointed or a devotee of yoga.

And he wasn't either.

2

Detective Sergeant Andrew Gregg was a tall young man, soft-spoken, thoughtful and always circumspect. Having telephoned Colonel Chandler the evening before to make sure he'd be at home, he picked up his police car and driver in Ipswich, and then sat back and relaxed as they threaded the Suffolk lanes. The day was clear and sunny, the trees and hedges were green, and this was the kind of assignment he enjoyed. All he had to do was ask a few questions, get the right answers, and after that take a leisurely train back to Norwich.

Great Bealings was little more than a hamlet with a scatter of cottages, but Rushmere Lodge was a large Georgian mansion set on a rise and commanding a view across the fields as far as Woodbridge, two miles away. The drive to the house was long and twisting, the grounds extensive, and Gregg, who lived in a poky little flat near the centre of Norwich, felt a brief twinge of envy as he raised his hand to the front-door bell.

It was answered by a smart, middle-aged woman in a green silk dress. She smiled at him.

'Sergeant Gregg?'

'That's correct, ma'am.'

'Please come through,' she said. 'The Colonel's out on the back lawn, savouring the sun . . . You must have had a hot journey. Would you like a cool drink? Or can I offer you a coffee?'

'Coffee would be splendid.'

'This way then,' she said. 'I'll bring it out on a tray.'

The lawn spread downwards from the house, and some fifty yards away was a man in a wheelchair. He sat side-on to a white garden table surmounted by a gaily striped parasol.

The woman ushered Gregg forward.

'Sergeant Gregg, dear,' she said.

Colonel Chandler was, as far as Gregg could judge, in his middle forties: a slight, slim man with a touch of grey at the temples and a neatly trimmed moustache. He had a shawl across his knees. He held out his hand.

'Glad to meet you, Sergeant. Sorry I can't get up. No legs to speak of. Still waiting for tin ones. Blasted Jerry mine blew up beneath the tank . . . Please take a seat.'

Gregg took the remaining garden chair. Mrs Chandler – he assumed it was she – disappeared towards the house.

The Colonel swivelled his wheelchair.

'Now, what can we do to help you . . .? You wanted to talk about Chris Tremellen. Don't tell me he's in some sort of trouble?'

'I'm afraid, sir,' said Gregg, 'that Major Tremellen's dead.'

'Good God!' The Colonel seemed genuinely shocked. 'When did this happen?'

'Last Tuesday morning.'

'But how and where?'

'A little village called Salleston in Norfolk, sir. The Major was murdered.'

'Murdered!' Chandler stared at him. 'Hell and damnation, how did he manage that?'

'Pushed down a flight of steps in a church, sir.'

113

'Who by?'

'We don't know yet, but there are just one or two fragments of evidence. We're following them up, sir. That's why I'm here.'

'Well, damn me!' Chandler gripped the arms of his wheel-chair. 'I often told Chris that he'd get himself killed, but that was out at the front. Never even dreamed he'd get knocked off in civvy street.'

Gregg felt he was making progress.

'You knew him well, then, sir?'

'God, yes! He was in my squadron. We were together all through the scraps in the desert.'

'And in Italy?'

'And in Italy, Sergeant. All the way beyond Rome.'

'Then you may be able to help us, sir.'

'Any way I can . . . What the devil was Chris Tremellen doing in a church? He was always a bloody atheist.'

'Putting up a flag, sir.'

'Oh, well, that explains it. Couldn't picture him down on his knees in prayer . . . Well, Sergeant, what do you want to know?'

Gregg took a deep breath. 'Does the word "Baradari" mean anything to you?'

'Not a thing,' said the Colonel. 'Should it? And if so, why?'

'The Major received some threatening letters before he died. They all ended with the words "Remember Baradari".'

Chandler shook his head. 'Means nothing to me, Sergeant.'

'Well', – Gregg unfolded his maps – 'there's a place called Baradari in the south of Italy. We wondered if it had any connection with Tremellen.'

'Never heard of it,' said Chandler. 'Whereabouts is it?' He leaned forward as Gregg spread the maps on the table.

'We've marked it, sir. It's here. Close to Benevento.'

The Colonel peered at the map. 'The squadron was never that close to Benevento, and certainly not there. We were well to the west.'

'Can you show me exactly where, sir?'

'I can't show you exactly. I can show you roughly, Sergeant. It was a devil of a mess, and we rarely knew to half a dozen miles just where we were. But we were never less than twenty miles from Benevento, and when you're fighting a war, that's a hell of a way . . . We landed here, at Salerno. Then we pushed

114

up behind Naples and on towards Capua. I remember one little place. It was called Grazzanise. Where the devil is it?'

'Here, sir,' said Gregg. He put his finger on the map.

'That's it. West of Capua. Then we swung towards the coast. Nowhere near Benevento. That was the Yankee sector. General Clark's mob. Some of Monty's lot went east of there up to Foggia, and then on to Termoli. But they'd be even further from Benevento than we were.'

'Then there's no chance that Tremellen was ever near Baradari.'

'None at all, I'm afraid.'

Gregg folded up the maps.

'Then it looks like we've reached a dead end, sir,' he said.

'Seems like it, Sergeant. Sorry about that.'

'What kind of a man was Major Tremellen?'

'Chris? He was the sort of bloke you were glad to have with you when the going got tough. Tremendously loyal. Wouldn't let you down. He had bags of guts. It didn't surprise me to learn that he'd clicked for an MC. Once he got the bit between his teeth on the battlefield, nothing was going to stop him.'

'And off the battlefield?'

The Colonel threw up his hands. 'Oh, well, off the field I suppose you'd have to say he was very much a wild card. Quite unpredictable. Irresponsible on odd occasions. Fond of the women and fond of the booze. We used to say his tank would never run out of juice because it ran on Chianti . . . He was a captain when I knew him. Must have been promoted after he cut such a dash in France.'

'You liked him, sir?'

The Colonel seemed to muse.

'Yes,' he said. 'Immensely, in a way. He was a free spirit, was Chris. Oh, he had his frailties. He womanized and drank. But he was a damn good soldier.'

Gregg knew that he had to tread softly.

'These frailties, sir. Did they get him into any kind of trouble in Italy?'

The Colonel frowned. 'Trouble? What sort of trouble?'

'Well, I'm told the vendetta still rules in Southern Italy. Did he rouse any enmities while he was out there?'

'I should think we all did, Sergeant. We smashed up their villas, we brought down their churches, and there were times when we had to kill them. It was difficult to know which side the Wops were on.'

'But he wasn't involved in any particular incident?'

'No, Sergeant, he wasn't. We didn't rape the signorinas or pillage the works of art. We were all too damn busy dodging Jerry shells.'

'Well, thank you, sir,' said Gregg. 'Just one more question. Were you ever in contact with him after the war?'

The Colonel shook his head. 'No. Lost all touch with him once he left us in Italy. This do in September was to be our first get-together. I was hoping to meet him, have a good natter. Now I never will . . . Who the hell could have had it in for him?'

'I don't know, sir,' said Gregg, 'but whoever he is, we'll find him.'

'String the bugger up,' said Chandler. 'That's what he deserves.'

A green silk dress brushed by Gregg's elbow. A coffee tray slid into place on the table.

'White or black, Sergeant?' a voice said sweetly.


Gregg made his way slowly back to the car.

The driver was cheerful. 'Get what you wanted, Sarge?'

'No. Drawn a blank.' Gregg wasn't too happy. 'I can't think the boss is going to shower me with ticker-tape.'

'Do any of 'em, ever?' The driver started up. 'Ours is a right bastard.'

'Stop at the first phone box,' Gregg told him sourly.


## 3


Tench put the phone down and swore to himself softly.

Turn again, Whittington.

What had the Chief Super said? 'What seems to be the best of all possible leads turns out to be the deadest of all dead ends. Then you have to start again.' Lubbock had once said something very similar. 'We strike out in one direction, think we're on the

116

right track, and then the trail peters out. We have to turn round and start again from scratch.'

Turn again, Whittington.

Well, there wasn't the slightest chance that he'd be once Lord Mayor of London, let alone thrice, but he certainly had to turn. The question was, where? If Italy was the deadest of all dead ends, and it seemed that it was, then where did he look next?

Perhaps, as Hastings had suggested, there was only one possible place to look. He'd have to turn back to Salleston.

But where was he to look in Salleston, and who in God's name was there in the village who could have pushed Tremellen down that flight of steps?

He ran through the list of names in his mind. Blake, the rector? He was the only other person, apart from Tremellen, who had a key to the tower. He locked and unlocked the church. A man of strong convictions, no doubt about that. And likely to be intolerant of other people's views. He was a big man, too, possibly six foot five, and heavily built. But why on earth would he want to kill the Major? If, as he said, Tremellen had done a great deal for the church, he'd have less reason than most to want him out of the way. And he was a man of God. Likeable or not, he was a Christian pastor. No, it wasn't feasible. Rule out the Reverend Eustace Blake.

Henry Bebbington? Even less likeable. A narrow-minded bigot. Almost a fanatic. And hadn't someone once said – was it Bernard Shaw? – that an honest fanatic was far more dangerous than the worst of scoundrels? He clearly detested the sight of Tremellen. A foreigner, he'd said, an interloper, a man of pretence who scorned the word of God. And an adulterer, too. 'The adulterer shall surely be put to death. Those, if I recall, were the words of the Lord.' But could he possibly have done it? A man of sixty-two, climbing those hundred and forty steps to the top of the tower? In hobnailed boots?

Velda Reynolds? He shook his head. Try as he might, he could never imagine that trim, svelte figure, so conscious of what she wore, tramping through Salleston in a pair of heavy boots.

Her husband, then? Theoretically, he had the strongest motive of anyone in the village. Jealousy. The green-eyed monster. 'O! beware, my lord, of jealousy. It is the green-ey'd monster which doth mock the meat it feeds on.' The trouble was that Leslie Reynolds didn't seem to be jealous. 'She can do as she bloody well likes,' he'd said. He was happy with his widow, Minty Rogers in Marsham. And they'd checked out his movements on the morning in question. His statement stood confirmed by four separate witnesses, three of them without any axes to grind. He hadn't been anywhere within pushing distance of Salleston church.

Who else? Old George Starling? Not even a chance. He'd been only too glad for Tremellen to take on the raising of the flag. No resentment there. And the very last thing he'd have wanted to do was climb up the tower. Amy Bedwell, the neighbour who'd accosted McKenzie? No. She was just a compulsive curtain-twitcher, nothing more than that. Algar, the engineer who'd spent his time rebuilding bridges? No, not after what Colonel Chandler had said. If Tremellen had never been near Baradari, they could forget the man completely.

Who then?

Someone who'd entered the church, got into the tower, climbed to the top and confronted Tremellen at five o'clock in the morning. That, according to Ledward, was roughly the time of death.

Tench struggled with the logic. Blake locked the church at dusk, and he'd locked it, so he said, on the Monday night. Visitors were never allowed up the tower, so the door to the steps would be locked as well. That meant that when Tremellen arrived at the church to put up the flag, he must have used two keys: one to open up the church, and the second to unlock the door to the tower. That matched the evidence: both keys had been found in the pocket of his trousers. What had happened next? He'd left both doors unlocked and made his way up the tower. After that there were three alternatives. Either someone was waiting for him up in the belfry; someone followed him in and caught him as he reached the top of the steps; or else that same someone followed him up, hid in the bell-chamber, waited for him to raise the flag and then attacked him as he made for the stairs to go down.

Now, suppose he was followed. The killer wouldn't have been likely to attack him on the stairs. He'd have been at a disadvantage: behind his victim, and on a lower level. That left the landing at the top, or the belfry itself. What evidence there was, was against the landing: the belfry door had been found wide open; but then again, the crime squad had detected no signs of a struggle inside the chamber.

Was it possible that the man, whoever he was, had done as McKenzie said: followed Tremellen up, hidden in the belfry, and then attacked him at the top of the stairs going down? Yes, of course it was, but here again there was a flaw. If the Major had already climbed up to the roof and raised the flag, why hadn't it been flying when Blake had looked out of his bedroom window?

Had someone then been waiting for him up in the belfry? That, too, was possible, but if so, how the devil had he got up there? Even if he'd hidden in the church overnight, he couldn't have got into the tower because the door would have been locked. The walls outside were sheer. As McKenzie had said, not even a Barbary ape could have climbed them. There was nothing to provide a foothold: no lightning conductor, not even a drainpipe. The rain-water spouted through gargoyles' mouths at the corners of the tower . . .

What was left that might provide him with the clue that he needed?

He pulled out a writing-pad from a drawer, unscrewed the top of his fountain-pen and began to make a list.

1. Clyde's letter with the details of Tremellen's army career. It didn't look now as if he'd get it before Monday, but even if it arrived by the afternoon post, what help would it be? The Italian theory was dead. Chandler had effectively killed it off. Tremellen had never been near Baradari, so what could a bare account of his progress in the army be expected to offer?

2. Hastings' idea that everyone in Salleston should be questioned again about Monday night. Well, he could do that. He intended to do it, but they'd already been questioned once. Was it likely that a second interrogation would produce anything more revealing than the first?

3. Dave Ransome from the *Eastern Daily Press*. He'd kept him happy so far with snippets of information, but was it time now to enlist him as an ally? Get him to print a public appeal for help? He thought long and hard about this, and decided it wasn't. Not for the moment. The key to the case still lay with those two enigmatic words: Remember Baradari; and he'd deliberately not mentioned them so far to Ransome. It wasn't

time yet to let the killer know exactly what steps the police were taking. Better that he be left completely in the dark.

4. Lubbock's list of names that he'd taken from the visitors' book in the church. He shrugged. They were making efforts to trace the people concerned, but the addresses were mostly incomplete. They just gave the name of a town and a county, like 'Mr and Mrs Smith, Bromley, Kent'. One couple had already been traced with no result. The odds were just as long against any of the others.

5. The Chief Super's notion that the word Baradari might be connected with an Italian POW still working on a farm. Worth investigation? He shrugged again. It might be. He'd get on to Lubbock, but God only knew where the commandant of the camp was now. He might have retired to the other end of Britain. Might even be dead. A better bet would be to contact the farm workers' union. They had offices in Norwich.

Any more ideas?

He tapped the desk with his pen.

There was one thing he'd had at the back of his mind.

6 (he wrote). The letters.

Whoever had written them had posted them from a wide variety of places. He'd moved around quite a bit in the week before the murder. How had he got from one place to another? By car? No, hardly. The petrol restrictions were far too tight. Even Tremellen had found it impossible to travel by car every day into Norwich. He'd never had one at Salleston. He'd cycled into Cawston and caught the Norwich train. Then how had the murderer travelled? Had he cycled, too? Tench shook his head. The distances were too great. Then he must have moved about either by bus or train. Was it worth questioning ticket collectors or bus conductors . . .?

No, he told himself, it wasn't. Not as things stood. Once they discovered who the man was, and could work on a description, then perhaps it might be. It was something to bear in mind if they needed corroborative evidence later. But as for providing an immediate clue, not a ghost of a chance . . .

He stared at the paper.

He wasn't getting anywhere.

What was it that Hastings had said? 'Don't be discouraged. Some murder cases take longer than others. You can't expect to solve them all in a matter of days.'

The trouble was, he was in a tunnel without a speck of light. At the present rate of progress, the case seemed likely to drag on for months. If he ever managed to solve it at all . . .

He felt a sudden yearning to lock everything up, take a day off and forget it all completely. Murders were very like crossword puzzles. You got stuck in a groove and tossed them aside, and when you picked them up next morning, the answer would be there. You didn't even need to think.

He remembered once at Cambridge, racking his brains for the answer to a clue: 'Daisy's twin.' Six letters, ending in 'm'. It had seemed simple enough. He'd run through all the flowers he could recall, but none of them would fit. He'd even ambled across to the college library and borrowed a book on the flora of Britain. All to no avail. Then, next morning, as he was walking up the Chimney towards Jesus Lane, he'd seen the ranks of bicycles propped against the walls . . . 'Tandem', of course.

Perhaps he ought to sleep on the Salleston case; forget all about it, get out into the country and look at it again with a fresh mind on Monday. Then it might just be like walking up the Chimney . . .

Strange phrase, that. Walking up the Chimney. It'd make a good question for a topographical quiz. 'Where in England can one walk up a chimney?'

He could imagine the pundits trying to work it out. Walk up a chimney? It wasn't possible, was it? Unless there were steps . . .

He stiffened suddenly . . .

Think, he said. Think.

He sat for a moment, staring at the writing-pad on the desk, not even seeing it, staring through it, trying to recapture an image that he'd lost.

Then suddenly he seemed to reach a decision. Glancing at his watch, he picked up the phone and dialled a number.

His fingers drummed on the desk till he heard a voice answer.

'Inspector Tench,' he said. 'I need a photographer . . . Yes, Sergeant, now . . . What the bloody hell does it matter if it's Saturday? Get me a photographer. He's to meet me at the incident room at Salleston. I'll be there in half an hour. And tell him he'll need a long-focus lens.'

121

# 4

The photographer was an acne-pitted, tousle-headed youth who'd seen it all before. Or thought he had.

He offloaded his equipment on the boarded floor of the incident room.

'Right, sir,' he said. 'Where is it?'

'Where's what?'

'The body.'

'No body,' said Tench.

'That's a pity.' The young man was visibly aggrieved. 'I'm an expert on bodies. What are we here for, then? Footprints? Window frames? Long-distance shots of the victim's place of residence?'

'None of those. I want you to photograph the church.'

'A church. That's something new. Well, anything for variety, that's what I say. Forensic, architectural or just plain picture-postcard?'

'Architectural,' Tench told him. 'I need some prints of the tower.'

The youth hoisted his equipment on to his shoulder.

'Lead the way, sir,' he said.


They stood at the foot of the tower, looking up.

'Never been here before,' the photographer said. 'It sure is some height.'

'Second highest in Norfolk.'

'That a fact?'

'It's a fact.'

'What's the highest, then?'

'Cromer.' Tench was somewhat terse.

The young man gazed up again. 'It hasn't got a parapet.'

'No,' said Tench. 'Stolen.'

'Stolen?' The youth was predictably baffled.

'The stones for it were stolen by the people of Clunch. That's the next village.'

'You're kidding.'

'Far from it.' Tench appeared to be deadly serious. 'They used them for the battlements on their own tower. Climb up to the top and you can see it from there.'

'Doesn't look very safe.'

'Oh, it's safe enough. You'll see. Once we get up there.'

'We're going up?'

'Later.'

The young man looked doubtful. He dumped his equipment down on the flags and, shading his eyes, peered up at the tower.

'How do we get up?'

'There's a spiral stair. A hundred and forty steps.'

'What about all this gear?'

'Oh, we'll just have to take what we need,' said Tench. 'I'll be around to help.'

'But we're starting down here?'

'I should think so, yes. Do the easiest bit first.'

'OK. If you say so.' The photographer ran a hand through his tousled hair. 'What d'you want taken?'

'Everything,' said Tench. 'Full view, first of all, from the three open sides. Then the same from the fourth. After that I want some vertical shots up the double buttresses.'

'Which are they?'

'These.' Tench laid his hands on them. 'Then I need some close-ups, picking out the stonework. All the way up. And the gargoyles at the top.'

'You mean the gremlins up there?'

'That's right. The water-spouts.'

'Used 'em at one time for boiling oil, didn't they?' the youth said cheerfully. 'Ever see that film about the hunchback? Kwazi something? Good movie, that was. Loads of boiling oil.'

He gave a passable imitation of a one-eyed Charles Laughton. Tench suffered in silence.

'It was lead,' he said, 'not oil . . . Come on. Let's get started. I want these films developed and printed today.'


He got them at six o'clock, delivered to the office in a brown cardboard box.

They were good. They were what he needed.

123

He drew the phone towards him, dialled the operator and asked for a Cambridge number.

If nothing else, he thought, he now had a plan of action that might just possibly yield up a clue.

He crossed his fingers on the phone. Heard Mallender's voice.

'Mallender?' he said. 'Is Dr Summers in college? Put me through to him, will you? Tell him it's Mr Tench.'


# 5


Why, he thought, did it always rain on Sunday?

Cambridge needed sunlight to gild the towers and pinnacles, to pick out the colours in the gatehouse coats of arms, to sparkle on the river and to cast contrasting shadows in the cloistered courts. But the weather had broken, the sky was sombre, thunder rolled and crackled across the rise and fall of roof-lines, and water streamed down the leaded panes of the window.

He heard the clink of the sherry bottle as Summers returned it to its place in the cabinet.

'Here you are, Mike.'

Turning from the window, he took the glass that was offered.

'Now,' Summers said, 'it's confessional time. Sit down and tell me all. What's so urgent that you dash here from Norwich first thing on a Sunday morning?'

'I need some help, Alan.'

'Help as in helping the police with their inquiries?'

'Help as in calling an expert witness.'

'Would this be the case you were working on last Friday?'

'Yes, it's still the same.'

Summers set his sherry glass down on the floor. 'I'm no expert on Italy.'

'It's not Italy,' said Tench. 'Italy's gone for a Burton.'

'Dead end?'

'Very much so.'

'Then what am I supposed to be an expert on?'

Tench seemed to pause. 'A strictly amorphous group that's known as The Night Climbers?'

124

Summers picked up his glass, walked across to the window and stood there, staring out at the rain.

'Damned weather,' he muttered. 'I was going to picnic on the river.'

'The Night Climbers, Alan?' Tench repeated gently.

Summers turned. 'They don't exist.'

'I know they don't, officially. But both of us know that unofficially they do. They're a functioning non-existent society.'

'You're wrong,' said Summers. 'They're just a handful of men, changing from year to year, with interests that happen to coincide.'

'And those interests are frowned upon by the authorities.'

'Of course they are, Mike. Every college stands *in loco parentis* to its students. We can't have young men climbing all over Cambridge, breaking their necks . . . Not that any of them ever have.'

'But they do climb,' said Tench.

'Yes, so I've heard.'

'And you've done your share.'

'A long time ago.'

'Not so very long. What about the chamber-pot?'

'What chamber-pot would that be?'

'Oh, come off it, Alan. Jack Longhurst had the rooms next to me in Second Court.'

'Oh, you mean the jerry.'

'On the chapel at King's. Lodged on top of one of the pinnacles. Don't tell me you and Jack didn't put it up there.'

Summers gave a chuckle. 'Created quite a stir, didn't it? They got a porter to try and shoot it down with an airgun. At last they had to call in the fire brigade . . . Am I to understand that Jack turned apostate when he was in his cups?'

'He may have dropped the odd hint . . . Don't worry. I've said nothing.'

'I should think not,' said Summers. 'Nobody climbs in Cambridge. You should know that well enough.'

'But I still need some help.'

'Blackmail?'

'No. Wouldn't dream of it, Alan.'

'I didn't think you would.'

'If I wanted to consult that log-book of yours, I could always get a warrant.'

125

There was a moment of silence.

'So . . . you think there's a log-book.'

'I know there's a log-book.'

Summers looked down his nose.

'All right,' he said. 'What is it you want to know?'

'No names. Nothing secret. Just an expert opinion.'

'What on?'

'Possibilities. I don't know enough about the techniques of climbing. You've made a hobby of shinning up buildings. I need your opinion.'

'Go on, then. Ask away.'

Tench cradled his glass. He looked at the sherry, and then he looked at Summers.

'First of all,' he said, 'I want a definition. I want to know about chimneys. What exactly, in climbing parlance, is a chimney?'

'It's a fissure between two walls.'

'I thought it was. And it can be used for climbing?'

'It is used for climbing. If you want to climb a building, then look for a chimney. If you can chimney up a face, it's far less tiring than any other way.'

'Why's that?'

'Simple. You're using legs and not arms, and legs can support the body with far less strain than arms. In chimneying you use a leg-push, rather than a hand-pull.'

'There's a technique to chimneying?'

'Oh, yes, there is.'

'Then explain it to me. How do you climb a chimney?'

'In essence, you walk up it.'

'You make it sound easy.'

'It is, if you're a climber.'

'OK. Then how's it done?'

'You want it step by step?'

'If it isn't too much trouble. You're dealing with a novice.'

Summers gave a sigh. 'Rest your back on one wall with the right leg stretched out and the toes of the foot pressing against the opposite wall. Bend your left leg double underneath your body with the sole of the foot on the wall behind you. Lean slightly forward, just clear of the wall, and straighten your left leg. As you do that, your body rises. Then lean back firmly, and place the left foot on the opposite wall just above the right.

126

You'll then have both your feet on the opposite wall. After that bring the right foot under your body, the sole against the wall behind. Then straighten it again, and just repeat the process. You will, in effect, be walking up the wall.'

'And you don't need to use your hands.'

'You can use them if you like to press on the wall behind. It can help you to rise. But in a suitable chimney – one that isn't too narrow, with vertical walls – you can climb all the way with your arms crossed in front of you. Climbing up a chimney's just a rhythmic action. Mountaineers do it.'

'Is it easier on a mountain than it is on a building?'

'That depends.'

'On what?'

'Well, sometimes it can be easier, sometimes it's harder. Most mountain chimneys are set on a slope. That makes them less difficult. And you can get better footholds because a stonemason hasn't smoothed out the surface. On the other hand the walls may converge or widen out, and the stone may crumble. I'd sooner climb chimneys in Cambridge any time.'

Tench thought for a moment. 'You say it's easy. How fit do you need to be?'

'Reasonably fit. Not a super athlete. Nine out of ten young people could do it. If they had a head for heights.'

'And the nerve?'

'Well, that goes with a head for heights, doesn't it, Mike? If you've got the one, the other's not going to trouble you.'

'Could I do it?'

Summers eyed him up and down.

'Yes,' he said, 'given the proper training. And if heights don't worry you . . . Why? Are you thinking of giving it a try?'

'Not unless I have to, thank you very much.'

'Then why all the questions?'

Tench opened his briefcase and took out a bulky envelope.

'I want you to look at some photographs,' he said.

# 6

He spread them out on the floor.

Summers leaned forward, elbows on his knees, and studied them carefully.

'Needless to say, it's a church. Whereabouts is it?'

'A little village in Norfolk. A place called Salleston.'

'Ah, yes,' said Summers. 'Thought I recognized it. Hasn't it got a double hammerbeam roof?'

'With angels,' said Tench.

'I remember it.' Summers nodded. 'Went there once with a party. There was a chap called Betjeman. Bit of a poet. Seemed to know all about it . . . What is it you want me to look at in particular?'

'The double buttresses running up the tower. I take it the spaces between them are chimneys. Could they be climbed?'

Summers picked up a couple of the prints and examined them more closely.

'They look reasonable enough. They're regular, and they stretch from the ground to the top of the tower. There aren't any overhangs. The stonework appears to be well maintained . . . What's the distance between one buttress and the next?'

'Roughly three feet. Would that be the right sort of breadth?'

'How long is a piece of string? Depends how tall the climber is, and how long his legs are. It's a fair enough breadth . . . How high's the tower?'

'A hundred and twenty feet.'

'No drainpipes?'

'No, just gargoyles.'

'Well, they can be useful when you get to the top. Is there a lightning-conductor? I can't see one anywhere.'

'No, there isn't. Is that a drawback?'

'Not necessarily. They're often quite useless. Unless the staples provide a handhold, they need to stand out quite a way from the wall. They can be a help if you can get your fingers behind them, but many are almost flush . . . In any case, these seem to be good chimneys, so it doesn't matter much.'

'Then you think they could be climbed?'

'Oh, yes, they could be climbed . . . There's no parapet to the tower?'

'No, just a ledge, a couple of inches high.'

'Enough to get a grip on?'

'Yes, I'd say so.'

'No problem then,' said Summers. 'They're tall chimneys, true, but they look to be straightforward.'

'Could you climb one yourself?'

'You mean now? No, I couldn't. I'm out of condition. But I could have done ten years ago . . . Anything else you want to know?'

Tench collected up the photographs.

'One more thing,' he said. 'If you were climbing such a chimney, what would you wear on your feet?'

'Rubber shoes,' said Summers without hesitation.

'Because of the grip?'

'Partly. Not wholly. Climbing in Cambridge is a clandestine pursuit. It needs to be done quietly. Rubber shoes are silent, or virtually so.'

'What about boots with nails in their soles?'

'Climbing boots? No. Not to be recommended. They make too much noise, and apart from that they scratch and damage the stonework. Climbers like to leave no traces behind them . . . That isn't to say that some people don't prefer to wear boots.'

'Who would they be?' said Tench.

'Mountaineers. They're used to them. They like to keep to what they know.'

'Are there many of them? Mountaineers?'

'Here in Cambridge? Very few. The odd one every year. Most regular mountaineers never take up roof-climbing. They think it's too easy. Something like climbing wall-bars in a gym. They're wrong, of course. It isn't. Those who do take it up, soon find it's a bit more tricky than that . . . On the other hand, the finest roof-climber I've ever known never climbed a mountain in the whole of his life. The two sports are quite distinct.'

'But some men do choose to climb in nailed boots?'

'Yes, they do.'

Tench leaned back in the chair and took a sip of his sherry.

'OK. A last question. Which is the easiest chimney in Cambridge?'

'Difficult to say. Climbers don't go for the easiest ones. They're usually not in the places where they're needed . . . I can tell you one of the most popular.'

'Which one's that?'

'It's on the north-east corner of the Fitzwilliam Museum. Directly above one of the stone lions. Ideal breadth, and vertical grooves that stop you slipping sideways.'

'You've climbed it?'

'More than once. It's known as the Lion Chimney.'

Tench drained his glass. 'And what's the most difficult building to climb? King's College Chapel?'

'That's the Everest, yes. A hundred and sixty feet.'

'Just as a matter of interest, when was it first climbed?'

'We don't really know. The first recorded instance was during the '14–'18 war. One of the dons did it. He was an ardent pacifist. I suppose he could have done it to prove he wasn't a coward.'

'But it could have been climbed before that?'

'It could have been. Who knows? It's done nowadays by using the lightning-conductor. I doubt if it was ever climbed before that was installed.'

'And when was it installed?'

'At a guess, sometime late in the eighteenth century. Franklin invented the lightning-rod in 1752, but the first of them wasn't set in place in this country till 1769. That was on St Paul's Cathedral.'

Tench frowned. 'You honestly think someone could have climbed it that early?'

'Why not? Folk have been climbing since the apple-tree grew in the Garden of Eden. And there is a scrap of evidence, for what it's worth. A coin was found on one of the ledges a few years ago. Twenty feet below the pinnacle. The date on it was 1760.'

'A gimmick?'

'It might have been.'

'One of your protégés? A numismatist with a dry sense of humour?'

'Might have been that, too . . . But then again,' Summers said, 'it could have been a seaman trained to shin up a mast in a howling gale. One of Nelson's brave lads paid off with a shilling. Or one of the Spithead mutineers intent on thumbing his nose at authority. As I said before, who knows?'

Half an hour later, Tench stood outside the Fitzwilliam Museum, staring up at the chimney behind the stone lion.

The rain had stopped, and the sun was already threatening to break through the clouds.

He stayed there some time, then he walked back past King's, and on Market Hill took a cab to the station.

# V

## TOWARDS THE LIGHT

And the driving is like the driving of Jehu the son of
Nimshi; for he driveth furiously

II Kings: 9.20.

# 1

The village of Salleston, early that Monday morning, presented a scene of unaccustomed activity. At eight fifteen, the Reverend Eustace Blake strode up the church path, his cassock swinging round his ankles, and unlocked the south door. At half-past eight a contractor's lorry rattled down the main street and parked in the shadow of the old lich-gate. A couple of men in overalls then descended from the cab, lowered the tailboard and unloaded a strange wooden contraption, which they carried up the path and dumped at the very foot of the tower. At eight thirty-five, Henry Bebbington emerged from the door of Maple Cottage, and under the pretence of searching for errant weeds, peered at the men with a growing suspicion. At eight forty-five, the first of the police cars stopped behind the lorry. Two men got out and, burdened by what appeared to be a mass of photographic equipment, made their way up the path and entered the church. Then, five minutes later, a second police car with Tench and McKenzie and the two detective constables, Rayner and Spurgeon, drew up at the village hall, and all four climbed the path to the incident room.

For the next ten minutes, Salleston reverted to its Monday morning calm. Then, shortly before the church clock struck nine, the door of the annexe opened and Tench and his three assistants stepped out with some purpose towards the main street. Once there, Rayner turned towards the bottom of the village, Spurgeon towards the top, and McKenzie made for the police house where Constable Grenville was waiting to meet him.

Tench walked towards the church.

*

At ten o'clock he stood at the foot of the tower, gazing up at one of his forensic team suspended in a cradle between a double buttress.

'Any signs?' he called out.

The man leaned over.

'Reckon you're right, sir,' he said. 'Definite marks of scuffing at intervals on the stonework. Seem to be all the way up to the top.'

'Right,' said Tench. 'Get them to haul you up and make room for the photographer. We're going to need some close-ups . . . Will that cradle hold two?'

'I should think so. At a pinch.'

'Collect him from the top, then. Point out the scuff marks and get them on film. I'll see you both back at the incident room.'

He gave one last look and turned away down the path.

Lubbock was leaning on the gate at the bottom, puffing at his pipe. He straightened up as Tench reached him.

'What's going on?' he said. 'Don't tell me you've spotted a Barbary ape.'

Tench grinned. 'Not exactly.'

'What's afoot then?'

'New developments.'

'You've been busy this weekend?'

'You could say that, yes.'

Lubbock clamped his teeth together hard on his pipe.

'Then it might be a good idea to bring me up to date.' He waved a hand towards the tower. 'Why all the frenzied activity up there?'

Tench swung the gate open and closed it behind him.

'Come up to the annexe,' he said. 'I'll explain.'


Lubbock pushed aside the files on the trestle-table.

'Now,' he said. 'Tell me.'

'It's simple enough, really.' Tench picked up the files and dropped them in a tray. 'It was always your idea that when Tremellen climbed those steps, someone was waiting for him up at the top.'

Lubbock gave a grunt. 'It seemed the most likely explanation. Still does.'

'Yes, but it leaves a problem. How did the killer get up there? There were only two keys. Blake had one and Tremellen had the other.'

Lubbock leaned back. 'That's simple enough, too. He hid in the church, waited for Tremellen, followed him up, and tucked himself away in the shadows behind the bells. Then he caught him coming down.'

'That was Mac's idea as well. But the flag was never raised.'

'You don't know that, laddie. There's always a chance it could have been. It's an easy enough matter to run down a flag.' He peered closely at Tench. 'You don't think I'm right.'

'Frankly, sir, no. Too many complications. There's a much simpler answer.'

Lubbock nodded sagely. 'You've a vague suspicion that, whoever the killer was, he somehow scaled the tower.'

'I'm pretty sure he scaled the tower.'

'Go on, then.' His old chief blew out a cloud of smoke. 'Put me in the picture.'

'Well, first of all, there's no bolt on that trapdoor that opens from the belfry on to the leads. If a man scaled the tower, all he'd have to do to get down among the bells would be to lift up the trap and climb down the ladder. Once there, he could do exactly what you suggested: hide himself away and wait for Tremellen coming up the steps.'

Lubbock seemed doubtful. 'But he'd have to climb the tower first . . . You said yourself it wasn't possible. Now you're telling me it is. What's made you change your mind?'

Tench gave a shrug. 'I suppose you could call it the Cambridge connection.'

Lubbock sighed. 'To use one of your favourite expressions,' he said, 'that's an enigmatic statement, if ever I heard one. It means absolutely nothing. Are you trying to tell me that two years spent drowsing over books in a college gives you a second sight denied to lesser mortals?'

Tench offered him a smile. 'No, sir, of course not.'

'What then? Let me have it in words of one syllable. No more.'

'It's just that in Cambridge you meet all kinds of people. Some of them can be helpful.'

'Even in murder cases?'

'Even when it comes to scaling unscalable towers.'

'All right then,' said Lubbock. 'Who is he, this person who's given you all the help?'

'One of my old tutors.'

'Seems most unlikely. What's he got to do with climbing up towers?'

'Strangely enough, quite a lot. There's a club in Cambridge, a kind of secret society that's frowned upon by the college authorities. Most of its members aren't known to one another, but they're bound together by one consuming interest.'

'What's that?'

'They climb buildings.'

'In Cambridge?'

'Strictly in Cambridge, and mostly by night. They're known as The Night Climbers.'

'That's original,' said Lubbock drily. 'And what about your tutor?'

'He was one of them. In his younger days.'

'An expert on towers.'

'He's climbed a few, yes.'

'And you spent the weekend with him?'

'Not as long as that. Just a couple of hours. I was keeping Holmes in mind. Eliminate the impossible. I wanted to be sure the tower couldn't be climbed.'

'But you found that it could.'

'It's not difficult, so I'm told.'

Lubbock heaved himself up and crossed to the window. 'It looks one hell of a problem to me.'

'You're not an experienced climber.'

'No, thank God.' He stared at the tower. 'Tell me then, laddie. How would one of your experienced climbers tackle a wall like that?'

'He'd chimney up between the buttresses.'

Lubbock showed a flash of exasperation. 'Damn it all, Mike. That could be Italian for all it means to me.'

'OK. I'll put it simply. In effect, you walk up. Your back against one wall. One foot against the other, and the other foot beneath you. You push yourself up and keep changing feet.'

Lubbock had his gaze still fixed on the church. 'Sounds as if it needs a contortionist to do it.'

138

'Well, according to what I'm told, it's the easiest way to climb.'

'But surely, laddie, you'd need rubber shoes. Our chap wore hobnailed boots. You said so on Saturday when we met at the inquest.'

'Climbing boots,' said Tench. 'Mountaineers prefer to use them.'

Lubbock sat down again.

'So,' he said, 'you think we're looking for a man who's climbed mountains.'

'The signs point that way.'

'And you're examining the tower.'

'Yes. A chap from forensics. He's got a photographer with him. They've already found scuff marks. And the lads are out with Grenville doing another house-to-house through the village. It's only a chance, but they could turn up someone who's done a bit of climbing.'

'Well, I suppose that's the obvious step to be taking.'

'You don't sound convinced.'

Lubbock shook his head. 'I still think you're searching in the wrong place, laddie. What about Baradari? Any more ideas since that colonel in Ipswich put the mockers on Italy?'

'No. No further clues.'

'Did you get that report on Tremellen's army career?'

'Oh, that,' said Tench. 'Yes, it came this morning. It's around here somewhere.' He rooted among the files and brought out an envelope. 'Haven't had the time to take a look at it yet. It didn't seem all that urgent once Italy proved to be just a dead end.'

Lubbock waved his pipe. 'Forget Italy for the moment. Forget Salleston, too. I've a shrewd suspicion this case is going to take us much further afield.'

'How much further?'

'If I'm right, then it could be thousands of miles.'

Tench stared at him. 'What on earth gives you that idea?'

'Oh, let's just say something a little bird told me . . . Well, jump to it, laddie. You've an envelope there. Open it up and let's see what's inside. That's what I came for, not scuff marks on towers.'

'You open it,' said Tench.

139

Lubbock took out the penknife he used from time to time to scour out his pipe, slit the flap of the envelope, pulled out the report and smoothed it down on the table.

There was silence for a moment as he scanned the first sheet.

'Well?' said Tench.

'Just as I thought . . . India.'

'Say that again.'

Lubbock slid the report towards him.

'India,' he repeated. 'Tremellen served in India. That's where the answer is, Mike. Not in Salleston.'

2

There are moments when the earth seems to tilt on its axis.

Tench felt it tilt.

His whole concept of the case seemed to shatter into fragments at Lubbock's laconic words. He looked down at the sheet of paper in front of him, and saw nothing but a jumble of letters and numbers.

'Read it,' said Lubbock. 'Here, pass it back to me and I'll give you a summary.'

He tapped the report with the stem of his pipe.

'It's laid out quite clearly. Tremellen joined up in August 1930. Duke of Cornwall's Light Infantry. Victoria Barracks, Bodmin. He reached the rank of sergeant, was commissioned at Sandhurst in 1934 and posted to India with the DCLI. Served on the North-West Frontier at Razmak. After that the battalion returned to its base. That was at Bareilly. In 1935 he was seconded to Manton's Horse, whatever they were, and stationed at Sarajpur. Between 1937 and the outbreak of war in 1939 he was back with Manton's lot on the North-West Frontier. In January 1940 they were moved to Rosh Pinna on the Syria-Transjordan border. From there he seems to have travelled all over the Middle East – Palmyra, Basra – till the unit was mechanized. It was then incorporated into the Royal Tank Regiment and formed part of the Seventh Armoured Division. That was somewhere near Cairo. I can't pronounce the name.

So . . .' Lubbock paused and looked up. 'He was in India, Mike, for five and a half years.' He pushed the report back. 'See for yourself.'

Tench forced himself to read. He felt a wave of irritation.

'What am I supposed to say?' he said. 'Tremellen served in India. So what does it matter? What the hell's it got to do with a church tower in Norfolk? I just don't get the link.'

'The link's Baradari.'

'What is it then? A place?'

'No, not exactly.' Lubbock crossed to the door and knocked out his pipe on the step of the annexe. 'You've been busy this weekend, laddie. Well, so have I. That word Baradari was niggling at me. I told you long ago it was the key to this case. You thought it might have something to do with Italy. With your knowledge of the place that was logical enough, but it got us no further. As far as I knew, the word had no Norfolk connections at all. But I remembered Holmes, like you. Eliminate the impossible. So I took a train into Norwich and a bus to Newton St Faith, and went to see Lawrence Bell.'

Tench knew all about Bell. He was one of Lubbock's old schoolfriends, a brilliant scholar who'd won a place at Oxford and then taught at Gresham's. In his spare time he'd started to write murder mysteries, all of them set in Norfolk. Their success had given him financial independence and, deciding to write full-time, he'd bought a quiet little cottage at Newton St Faith and devoted himself to a lifetime of fiction. In the course of it, he'd made himself an expert on Norfolk: a man with an extensive library that seemed to cover every aspect of life in the county: its history, its legends, its buildings, its roads, its trade and its landscape.

Lubbock refilled his pipe, slowly and methodically.

'You know I always go to Lawrence,' he said, 'if I find I need any local information. He knows more about Norfolk than any man living. He put us on to that legend about Elsdon Hall, and told us about those smugglers' tunnels that led us to do that search up at Breckmarsh Mill. He hasn't often let me down. Not that I was very hopeful on this occasion. Baradari didn't seem to have anything to do with Norfolk. It was more a negative inquiry than a positive one.'

He struck a match, lit his pipe, tamped it down and relit it.

The whole operation took a good half-minute, filled the annexe with smoke and reminded Tench of a kippering shed he'd once visited in Scotland.

'I told him about Tremellen and the letters he'd received. "Now, Lawrence," I said, "has this word Baradari any Norfolk connotations?" Well, he thought long and hard and then said that, as far as he knew, it hadn't. He'd never heard of it cropping up anywhere in the county. That was just what I'd expected to hear, so I wasn't disappointed. But then he came up with something out of the blue. "I have heard the word," he said, "but not here in Norfolk. It's an Indian word – Hindustani, Urdu, whatever you like to call it. It means a summer-house or a summer palace."

'I don't know whether I ever told you this, Mike, but Lawrence was out in India during the First War. While I was wallowing in the mud of the trenches, he was lounging in one of those pillared bungalows soaking up the sun. But he had a job – intelligence – that took him around the country. Wherever British troops were stationed, Lawrence was there at one time or another. So I pressed him a bit further, asked him had he ever seen a baradari?

'Oh, yes, he said, plenty. There were baradaris dotted all over Northern India. The word was a generic term for a type of building, like mahal which meant a palace, or masjid, a mosque or a house of prayer. There were many mahals, not merely the Taj, and many masjids, and in the same way there were many baradaris. There was a particularly elegant one, so he told me. I think it was in Lucknow. "I'll show you," he said, and he went upstairs and came down with a book half the size of a grave-stone. *Historic Buildings of India*. He showed me the title. "Picked it up off a stall in a Delhi bazaar. You know what I am for collecting books. Had it shipped home wrapped in gunny and sewn up in muslin." Then he looked at the index and flicked through the pages. "Here you are," he said. "That's a baradari, but since they're a kind of glorified summer residence, they could be built in any of a dozen different styles."'

Tench had been listening with a good deal of patience. He knew from experience that when Lubbock was in flow, there was little else to do. Now he intervened.

'What was it like?'

142

'No point in my trying to describe it, laddie. You can see for yourself.'

'You didn't bring the book back?'

'I didn't carry it, that's for sure. But after what Lawrence had told me I was pretty confident that at last we were on the right track, and that Clyde's report would tell us that Tremellen had served out in India. And not only that. It would give us the low-down on where he'd been stationed. I tried to get in touch with you twice yesterday to ask if you'd got it, but you must have been swanning round chimneys in Cambridge. So I gambled on the fact that you'd have it by this morning, and got Lawrence to drive over with the book in his car. He's down at Reg's cottage, waiting for us now. So let's go and see if we can find a baradari somewhere on the line of Tremellen's travels. What were the names of those places in India where he did his service?'

Tench ran a finger down the report.

'Razmak,' he said. 'Then Bareilly and Sarajpur.'

'They mean nothing to me,' said Lubbock, 'but Lawrence is sure to know them.'

He pushed himself up.

'Are you fit, then? Shall we go? I've a feeling, Mike, that the Salleston knot's beginning to unravel. Remember that chap Bruce? What was it he said when he looked at the spider?'

'"Now shall this spider teach me what to do, for I too have failed six times."'

Lubbock gave a chuckle.

'All that, was it? I thought it was something shorter, like "Give it another go, Bob. You never know your luck."'


# 3


Bell, a tall, gaunt man with a mop of ginger hair, was precise in his analysis.

'You can rule out Razmak,' he said. 'It's merely a post on the Afghan frontier, and Bareilly's an industrial city with a railway junction. Nothing much of architectural importance there. Your best bet's Sarajpur. It's close to Lucknow, and Lucknow was the capital of the Kings of Oudh. They had residences in Sarajpur.'

Tench glanced at the heavy tome on the table. 'You think we'll find it in there?'

'Bound to,' said Bell. 'It's a comprehensive guide. No other quite like it. That's why I snapped it up.' He turned to the index. 'Sarajpur,' he said. 'Page 498.' He riffled through the gilt-edged pages. 'Here you are. Here it is. This is what you want. The Lal Baradari.'

Tench and Lubbock leaned over the table. They both read the entry.

'The Lal or Red Baradari takes its name from the colour of its exterior. It stands at a crossroads on the fringe of the city on the main road running from Cawnpore to Lucknow, and was built between the years 1789 and 1814 by Sa'adat Ali Khan, the Nawab of Oudh. It was intended as a throne room or coronation hall for royal durbars.

'The literal meaning of the word baradari is a building with twelve doors, and the Lal Baradari was almost certainly constructed to conform to this plan. The interior was, however, radically altered by the second King of Oudh, Nasir-ud-Din Haider, who ruled from 1827 to 1837. Nasir-ud-Din was obsessed with the Occident and surrounded himself with European artists, one of whom he made comptroller of his household. Because of this, the baradari became a mixture of eastern and western influences. The walls were hung with scarlet and gold tapestries, interspersed with full-length portraits of the royal family, and the windows were narrow, admitting a dim but appropriately dignified light. The throne itself was set at the upper end on a raised platform approached by six steps and protected by a golden railing. It was made of solid silver and ornamented with jewels.

'Overhanging it was a square canopy covered with beaten gold and threaded with precious stones, including, at the front, a magnificent emerald, said at the time to be the largest in the world. Beneath this canopy the nobility of Oudh and English officials gathered at public durbars and state councils to be presented to the King.

'The building is nowadays used as a museum.'

144

There was a somewhat faded engraving that showed a multi-sided structure with eight minarets.

Lubbock stroked his chin. 'When was this published?'

Bell turned to the title page. '1912.'

'And the place is still standing?'

'Why shouldn't it be? It's already stood for what? A hundred and fifty years? The Indians aren't like us. They don't demolish things like that.'

'Must have been worth seeing,' said Lubbock, 'in its heyday.'

Tench seemed uneasy. 'D'you think it's what we're looking for?'

'It's a gamble, Mike, isn't it? Let's just say that it looks a better bet than your village in Italy. It *is* a baradari. It *is* in Sarajpur, and according to Army Records so was Tremellen. He served there for two years with Manton's Horse . . . What kind of an outfit was that, d'you reckon?'

'Obviously a cavalry unit,' said Tench. 'The report said it was mechanized after war broke out. Probably got trucks with Vickers machine-guns, and then Crusader tanks. It sounds to me like one of those irregular outfits recruited to fight the Pathans on the frontier.'

'It was,' Bell told them, 'but in my time it was one of the crack cavalry regiments. Very jealous of its reputation and traditions. I wouldn't think its officers took very kindly to being merged with the RTR.'

Lubbock's eyes gleamed. 'Crack troops, were they? Proud of themselves?'

'Very much so.'

'That makes it even stranger.'

Tench frowned at him. 'What does it make stranger?'

'Tremellen's silence. He never seems to have talked about India. North Africa, yes. Italy, yes. France, all too often. But India, never, as far as I can discover. Don't tell me that's not strange. Have you ever known a man who's spent time in India not talking about it? No, laddie. They all do. It's the magic of the East. They tend to bore the pants off people who've never been there.'

'What makes you so sure that Tremellen never mentioned it?'

'Well, he doesn't seem to have even whispered the word in Salleston. I went around yesterday checking with those who

145

were closest to him. Blake, Velda Reynolds, even Henry Bebbington. None of them had the remotest idea that he'd ever been to India. So why didn't he talk about it? That's what puzzles me. Did something happen there that he wanted to forget? Something that, raked up, might tarnish his new image? Something connected with this building, the baradari?'

'Hang on,' said Tench. 'Let's give it a bit more thought. Let's think about the letters. They all signed off with the words "Remember Baradari", not "Remember *the* Baradari". That means it could still be a place, not a building.'

Lubbock turned to Lawrence Bell. 'I suppose it's no good asking if there's a place called Baradari anywhere in India?'

Bell ran a hand through the flame of his hair. 'Not much good at all. There are literally thousands of villages in India. There could be a Baradari. It's more than possible. But I can't remember one.'

Lubbock gave a brisk nod. 'Then let's stick to what we've got. Look at the facts, laddie. The letters said Baradari. There's a Baradari in Sarajpur. Tremellen was in Sarajpur. That's a firm connection. What more do you want? Mountains? They've got them in India.'

Tench closed his eyes. 'I'm just trying to work out exactly where we stand.'

'Where we usually stand at some point in a case. One trail's petered out and we've got to start again on a different track. But this time the signs aren't leading to Italy. They lead to this place Sarajpur, so I reckon it's time to press your friend Clyde into action again. We need to know about the two years Tremellen spent there. According to Lawrence, he was part of a regiment that was proud of its name. That means that if he got into some sort of trouble, brought the unit into disrepute in some way or other, there'd be hell to pay. It wouldn't be forgotten. And who'd be most likely to remember what happened?'

'His CO?'

'Who else? So let's find out who commanded Manton's Horse in Sarajpur. If he happens to be still alive, he may have the clue we've been searching for.'

'It could be a dead end, just as Italy was.'

'Then all the more reason to check it out,' said Lubbock. 'Come on. Let's get weaving. What have we got to lose?'

Hastings rested both arms on his desk. 'And who is he, this man?'

Tench flicked the pages of his notebook. 'He's a brigadier, retired. Name of Maddox. Ewen Maddox. Lives out in Derbyshire. A place called Winster, sir, up in the Peak.'

'Quite a way,' said Hastings. 'And this isn't a job you'd want to leave to the locals.'

'No, sir. We need someone who knows what he's looking for.'

'Then who were you thinking of sending? McKenzie?'

Tench was remembering what Lubbock had said when he'd packed him off to London to interview Clyde about the Elsdon Hall case. 'I'm sending you,' he'd said, 'not Sergeant McKenzie. Mac's a bulldog. He'll growl and then he'll bite, and I can't see our pin-striped friend, Mr Clyde, taking too kindly to a nip on the ankle. I need someone with tact and diplomatic skills. Mac isn't the man for the job. You are.'

Now, eighteen months on, he reflected regretfully that Lubbock was right. This wasn't Mac's job.

He brought all his diplomatic skills into play.

'I can't spare McKenzie at the moment, sir,' he said. 'I've had to send him out to Attlebridge. Case of malicious wounding.'

Hastings took a deep breath and leaned back in his chair. 'And I can't spare you to go gallivanting off to the Derbyshire hills. Not with Maitland still laid up in a hospital bed. So, who've you got in mind?'

Tench didn't hesitate. 'I'd like to send Sergeant Gregg.'

Hastings, too, was remembering a conversation with Lubbock. History, it seemed, was prone to repeat itself.

'You think he's the right man?'

'Yes. Certain of it, sir.'

'It mightn't be an easy assignment, Mike. You know the reputation these Indian colonels have. Suppose Maddox turns out to be a choleric old soldier with a bristling moustache. It could be a difficult job to prise the facts out of him.'

147

'Gregg's intelligent, sir. He's got patience and tact.'

Hastings had a strange feeling he knew what was coming next. 'A future DCI?'

'That's possible, sir.'

The Chief Super seemed to be weighing all the odds. At last he nodded three times, very slowly.

'Send him then,' he said. 'But remember, Mike, we both of us need results. See you make that clear to him before he sets off.'

'Gregg's reliable, sir. If there's anything to be found, I'm pretty sure he'll find it.'

'Let's hope so. Keep me posted.'

'I will, sir,' said Tench.


He gave Gregg his instructions.

'Andy,' he said, 'you don't need to be told the score, but a word to the wise. Interviews like this can be a dicey sort of business. You may just be chasing shadows like you were with Colonel Chandler, though I hope to God you won't be. It's vital we discover the truth about Tremellen. Did he get caught up in any sort of trouble while he was in Sarajpur? And if he did, what's the link with this Indian building, the Lal Baradari? Now we don't know a thing about Brigadier Maddox, except that he was Tremellen's commanding officer with a mob called Manton's Horse. But if I were you, I'd tread a bit carefully. Be prepared for snags. If there is something there to be winkled out and it reflects in some way on the regimental honour, then Maddox could be awkward. He might be reluctant to give you all the facts. Might even refuse to discuss it at all. So make sure he knows it's a murder inquiry. Keep cool and probe away at him gently. Tactful persistence, that's the name of the game.'

'He may not be a problem, sir. Chandler wasn't.'

'No, but it's always best to be warned in advance. When I spoke to him on the phone, he didn't exactly sound overjoyed . . . Anyway, he's expecting you sometime this evening.'

'Don't worry, sir,' said Gregg. 'I'll winkle something out of him, even if it's only a recipe for curry.'

*

148

His confidence lasted as far as the little wayside station at Darley Dale.

The constable who was waiting there to drive him to Winster greeted him cheerfully.

'Sergeant Gregg?'

'That's right.'

'PC Jackson.'

'Glad to meet you.'

'Elton Court, is it, Sarge?'

'So I'm told,' said Gregg.

'Brigadier Maddox?'

'Yes, that's the name.'

Jackson was terse. 'Then all the best of British. I reckon you're going to need it.'

'Bit of a Tartar, is he?'

'Only spoken to him once. Had to go and see him about a pile-up in the village. Needed his evidence.'

'Did you get it?'

'Not a chance. Refused to say a damned thing. Had his batman show me out by the servants' door . . . What is it you're after?'

'Just a little bit of help with a murder case,' said Gregg.

'You'll be lucky,' Jackson said. 'He's got a mouth like a gin trap.' He started up the car. 'Indian army wallah, wasn't he? Well, that fits. He wouldn't even give you a recipe for curry.'

# 5

Elton Court was a Georgian house. Constructed of ashlar, it stood in its own grounds set back from the village street. It had a pedimented portico supported by what Gregg assumed to be Tuscan columns, and three steps led to its white-painted door.

He climbed them and rang the bell.

There was silence inside, and he was about to ring again when he heard footsteps approaching and the door was wrenched back to reveal a short, wiry man with receding hair and a nose that had clearly at one time been broken. He eyed Gregg with speculation and then with distaste.

149

'Yes,' he said. 'What?'

Gregg produced his card.

'Sergeant Gregg,' he said, 'Norwich. I've an appointment to meet with Brigadier Maddox.'

The man studied the card closely with obvious suspicion, and then handed it back.

'Never said nowt to me.'

Gregg believed in treating retainers with firmness.

'Then you'd better make inquiries, hadn't you?' he said.

The man scowled at him. 'Wait.'

Gregg waited what seemed an unconscionable time. He peered inside the gloomy hall, hung with what appeared to be the heads of wild boar. At last the man returned.

'Says to go in.' The words came out grudgingly. 'Door's over yon.' He jerked his head towards a dark recess at the rear of the hall.

Gregg made his way across to the heavy door and knocked. A harsh, nasal voice ordered him inside.

Brigadier Maddox was a tall, spare man with an over-large forehead, a thrusting jaw and lips so thin they were almost invisible. His feet were planted firmly on a tiger-skin rug. He looked at his visitor with some irritation.

'You're Gregg?'

'That's right, sir. Detective Sergeant Gregg.'

'Sit down.'

It was a command, not a courteous invitation. He gestured towards a hard, high-backed chair that was set behind a massive bulbous-legged table.

Gregg sat down.

Maddox eyed him beadily. 'I take it you're here about Lieutenant Tremellen.'

'Major Tremellen. Yes, sir.'

'He's dead, so I gather.'

'Yes. That's correct.'

'Murdered, I was told.'

'So we believe, sir.'

'In Norfolk.'

'That's right.'

'And you think I can help you.'

'We hope you can. Yes, sir.'

150

'Well, I can't,' said Maddox curtly. 'Never been to Norfolk. Told your inspector so . . . Too flat,' he added, as if the mild slopes around him were Himalayan foothills.

Gregg coughed discreetly. 'The information we need, sir, doesn't concern Norfolk.'

'Where does it concern then?'

'India, sir.'

The Brigadier's eyebrows were thick and bushy. Beneath them his eyes were keen, almost piercing. He fixed them on Gregg.

'India's a big place. A sub-continent, Sergeant, or weren't you aware? It's a couple of thousand miles north to south and again east to west. You'll need to be more precise. Whereabouts in India?'

'I undersand there's a place called Sarajpur, sir.'

'Then you understand right. What about Sarajpur?'

'We believe you were there with Major Tremellen. According to our information, you commanded his regiment, Manton's Horse.'

'I was there with Lieutenant Tremellen, Sergeant. He was one of my junior officers. Try to be accurate. We'll get on much faster.'

Gregg remembered his instructions. Keep cool, Tench had told him.

'Well, go on,' said Maddox testily. 'What about Sarajpur?'

'There's a building there called the Lal Baradari?'

'There is. Carry on.'

'We suspect it may have something to do with the Major's death.'

'And why should you think that?'

'He received a number of threatening letters before he died. They were all unsigned.'

'You mean anonymous, Sergeant.'

'Anonymous, sir, yes. But they all concluded "Remember Baradari".'

The Brigadier selected a large cigar from a carved wooden box. He clipped the end with a cutter, lit it and seated himself at the table.

He blew out two smoke rings.

'And?' he said.

151

'Well, sir, we think there may be some connection between the Major and this building. Something may have happened there . . .'

'Wrong.' Maddox brought his hand down hard on the table.

'Wrong, sir?'

'Yes, Sergeant, wrong. Lieutenant Tremellen had no connection with the Lal Baradari. As far as I'm aware, he never even once set foot inside the place.'

'Then why, sir, was it mentioned?' Gregg was clearly at a loss.

'It wasn't,' Maddox said. 'You're imprecise again, Sergeant.'

'I am, sir?'

'You are. It's a fault. You should watch it. You told me the letters said "Remember Baradari". Take careful note. "Remember Baradari". Not, if I heard aright, "Remember the Lal Baradari".'

'You mean . . . they were alluding to somewhere quite different?'

'That would seem to be the obvious deduction, Sergeant.'

Gregg took a deep breath. 'Then have you any idea, sir, just where that might have been?'

Maddox gave a shrug. 'I can make a shrewd guess.'

Gregg waited. The Brigadier tapped the ash from the end of his cigar.

'In Tremellen's case,' he said, 'I can only conclude that the writer was referring to the Baradari Crossing.'

6

'In Sarajpur?'

'Yes, Sergeant. In Sarajpur. The Lal Baradari stands on a crossroads. Hence the name. Its the busiest traffic intersection in the city. The point where the Lucknow to Cawnpore road crosses the one that leads from the Gymkhana Club to the Sikandra Cantonment. That's the military district.'

'And something happened there to Major Tremellen?'

'Lieutenant Tremellen. Yes, Sergeant, it did.'

'What was it, sir? Perhaps you'd be good enough to tell me.'

'It was nothing more than an unfortunate accident. Not Tremellen's fault.' Maddox paused. He seemed disinclined to go any further. 'I can't see any profit in reciting the details.'

'Maybe not, sir,' said Gregg. He was gently persistent. 'But this is, after all, a murder inquiry. Lieutenant Tremellen's dead and we have to know who killed him. We need all the assistance you can possibly give us.'

'If there's a connection.'

'But surely, sir, there must be a connection. The letters distinctly said "Remember Baradari" . . . This crossing. Was it known just as Baradari? If, say, you were driving from the barracks to the Club, would you describe it as going by Baradari? If you were giving someone instructions, would you simply tell them to go by Baradari?'

The Brigadier didn't hesitate.

'Yes,' he said, 'I would.'

'Then there has to be a connection, sir, hasn't there?' said Gregg. 'Whoever wrote the words "Remember Baradari" must have known what had happened there on the crossing. He was intent on reminding Tremellen of the fact. He, too, had some connection with whatever occurred. It's vital that you tell us what happened there, sir, believe me.'

The Brigadier raised his eyebrows.

'It isn't vital that I tell you anything at all, Sergeant. I'm not the only person who knows about the incident. There must be another couple of dozen people you could contact.'

'You'd be saving police time, sir, and time in a murder case is always important.'

Maddox swung himself up, crossed to a corner cabinet, and took out a bottle of Scotch and two glasses. He set them down on the table.

'Not for me, sir,' said Gregg.

'Nonsense.'

'I'm on duty.'

'You're not on duty, Sergeant. You're a guest in my house. I need a drink if I'm to tell you about Tremellen, and you'll be civil and join me.'

'If you insist, sir.'

'Oh, I do insist, Sergeant.' He poured two large tots. 'I'm a very determined man. I'm also a reactionary. Let's drink a toast, shall we? Death to all liberals.'

Gregg began to wonder where the interview was heading. It seemed suddenly to be veering out of control.

'Drink,' Maddox ordered.

Gregg duly drank, consoling himself with the positive thought that he had little alternative.

The Brigadier spread his hands flat on the table.

'Tremellen,' he said. 'A regrettable business. The whole affair created more than a little trouble. Needn't have done, but by God it did. Personalities, Sergeant. Personalities and politics clashing together with a din that could be heard from Bombay to Calcutta . . . I take it that you've never driven in India?'

'No, sir.'

'Think yourself lucky. Driving a car through an Indian city's like flying a Spitfire through a sky full of drifting barrage balloons. Gharries and ekkas; tongas and rickshaws; screeching bullock-carts and creaking taxis; dilapidated lorries and lopsided buses; cows and pye-dogs; piles of rubbish and thousands of men and women clogging the roads. And Indians are the worst drivers God ever made. Sikhs are the very devil. They just grip the wheel and charge. I remember once, coming down from the hills . . .'

He stopped himself abruptly.

'No,' he said. 'Not relevant. Just an old soldier's tale. You want to hear about Tremellen.'

He tossed off his Scotch and pushed the glass aside.

'He was driving to the mess from the Gymkhana Club. From there to Baradari's about half a mile, and the road's dead straight. The crossing's controlled by an Indian constable. He stands on a wooden platform in the middle of the road and operates a set of red and green lights. It was late August, about half-past eight in the evening, and the road runs east to west, so he was driving straight into the setting sun. The light was showing green, but when he was almost on top of the crossing, the constable for some reason switched it to red. He couldn't pull up in time and rammed another car. There were two Indians in it, a man and a woman. The woman was injured. The police charged him with negligence.'

Maddox poured himself another, larger tot.

'The charge', he said, 'was passed to the District Magistrate. He sentenced Tremellen to three months' imprisonment.'

## 7

Gregg frowned. 'A bit harsh.'

'Harsh?' Maddox said savagely. 'Of course it was damned well harsh. But that wasn't the point.'

'No, sir?'

'No. It was quite inadmissible. To send a serving British officer to jail in India! Just for running down a wog! And for a British official to inflict such a sentence! It was unheard of, Sergeant. It just wasn't done. More than that, it was something that the military in Sarajpur weren't prepared to tolerate. Not with conditions as they were in the country. Gandhi stumping around, demanding that we leave. The liberals back at home whittling away at British authority. Witless maniacs who'd never set foot in India encouraging sedition . . . Oh, we knew it couldn't last. The old life, I mean. It was cracking at the seams. But to yield to such elements meant courting disaster. And we couldn't allow an officer from Manton's Horse to submit to such treatment. Apart from the slur on the regiment, if Tremellen went to prison, it'd mean he'd be cashiered. That'd be the end of his army career, and he was a damn good soldier.'

'So what did you do, sir?'

'We hired the finest advocate in India, and paid his fee out of mess funds. He filed an appeal. The case went to the High Court and the prison sentence was cancelled. Tremellen was fined a thousand rupees. It went in compensation.'

'To the woman?'

'I believe so.'

'How badly was she injured?'

'She had a fractured pelvis, so I was told.'

'But she recovered?'

'I assume she did.'

'You don't know for sure, sir?'

'No, Sergeant, I don't. A fortnight after the sentence was reversed, we were posted back to Razmak. Trouble on the frontier.'

Gregg was thoughtful. 'How much, sir, is a thousand rupees?'

'Roughly seventy-five pounds. Quite a substantial sum.'

'To an Indian.'

'Of course.'

'And I'd be right in assuming that Tremellen's conviction was never recorded on his army documents?'

'Yes, Sergeant, you would be.'

'Would it be presumptuous, sir, to ask you why not?'

'More than presumptuous, Sergeant. Inquisitorial. But I'll give you an answer. It wasn't deemed to be necessary . . . Don't press the point.'

'No, sir.'

'The affair was short and sharp, but it raised a lot of hackles. Tempers got frayed. Once it was over, we felt it was best forgotten.'

'For the sake of the regiment?'

'That and other reasons.'

'Which you don't want to discuss.'

'Which I refuse to discuss, Sergeant . . . Now, anything more?'

'Just one or two points, sir. The Indian who was driving the other car involved. What was his name?'

'His name was Surendra Singh. He was, I believe, a student. At Lucknow University.'

'And the woman?'

'Was his wife.'

'Can you recall her name?'

'No, Sergeant, I can't.'

'Did you ever hear, sir, what happened to them afterwards?'

The Brigadier shook his head. 'I was six hundred miles away. So was Tremellen. We were caught up with the Mahsuds in Waziristan. They'd ambushed a convoy. We had to sort them out.'

'And the District Magistrate?'

Maddox gave a sour grin. 'They promoted him, Sergeant. Made him Excise Commissioner.'

'But who was he, sir?'

'The DM? A blasted liberal, that's what he was. Chap called D'eath. Giles D'eath. He pronounced it Dee-ath, but we called him Death.'

156

'D'you know where he is now?'

'I haven't the faintest idea,' said Maddox, 'and what's more, Sergeant, I don't want to know.'


If the Brigadier didn't, Gregg certainly did.

It was close to midnight when he stepped from the train in Norwich, and with great good sense he went straight to bed; but next morning, before reporting to Tench, he spent a fruitful five minutes in the public library.

There, in *Who's Who*, he found the following entry.

'D'eath, Sir Giles, Kt 1945; ICS, retired; b 23 Sept. 1896; s of late Jeremy Salvin D'eath, Tunbridge Wells, Kent and Winifred Macilvenny; m 1920 Elisabeth (decd.) e d of James Holdsworth and Dorothy Joan Reid, no c. Educ: Eton, Trinity Coll., Cambridge. Midshipman, Sub-Lieut, Lieut, RN 1914–18. Passed into Indian Civil Service 1921; various administrative apptmts. inc. District Magistrate, Chandabad 1934–36; Sarajpur 1936–37; Excise Commissioner, Sarajpur 1937; retired, 1938. RNVR and Admiralty, 1940–45. Publications: *Annie Besant and the Growth of Indian Nationalism*, 1945; *In the Steps of the Mahatma*, 1946. Address: Chalk Hill Lodge, Burnham Market, Norfolk.'

He thumped the table, much to the disapproval of the bespectacled librarian.

'Gotcher,' he said.


# 8


It was Tench who drove out to Burnham Market.

'You think there's another side to this tale?' he asked Gregg, once the sergeant had finished making his report.

'Has to be, sir, hasn't there? D'you want me to run out and see this D'eath?'

'No, Andy. Leave him to me. You've done pretty well, but this one's mine.'

'Sir Giles D'eath. Sounds a bit of a stiff-necked bastard, doesn't he? He'd need to be if he had to face up to Maddox.

157

Probably six foot five and bristling with self-importance. A bit snooty, isn't it, Burnham Market?'

'Can be,' said Tench. 'Handsome village street. Lots of big Georgian houses. He may have bought one of those.'

As it turned out, he hadn't.

Chalk Hill Lodge was a surprisingly modest affair: an eighteenth-century creeper-covered cottage on the fringe of the village; and Sir Giles D'eath wasn't exactly the dominating figure that Gregg had assumed. He was a small, slim man with a neatly trimmed moustache and an air of studious reticence that Tench at first found difficult to penetrate.

He explained about Tremellen, the threatening letters and his need to know precisely what had happened at Sarajpur.

D'eath was guarded.

'Tell me something, Inspector. How did you come to connect me with the case?'

'We spoke to Tremellen's commanding officer, Brigadier Maddox.'

'And he gave you my name.'

'Reluctantly, sir, I think.'

Sir Giles seemed to smile.

'I can imagine he might be reluctant,' he said.

'We felt that we ought to check the facts with you before we accepted his version of events.'

'You were probably wise. There are always two sides to a story, Inspector.'

'Then we need to hear yours, sir.'

'I appreciate that. But I should warn you beforehand. My version may be very different from his.'

'I'm prepared for that, sir. The Brigadier described it as a conflict between personalities and politics.'

Sir Giles took his time to reply.

'Not strictly true, I'm afraid, Inspector. It was far more a conflict between the past and the present, between emotion and logic.'

'How was that, sir?'

They were seated in a couple of leather armchairs in a room that D'eath clearly used as a study. There was an open roll-top desk that was scattered with papers, and he leaned across and pulled out a drawer by the side of the knee-hole. Then he handed Tench a heavy blue-backed file. On the front in gilt letters was 'Office of the District Magistrate, Sarajpur.'

'That, Inspector,' he said, 'is a transcript of the evidence given in the case. It's all there, every word that was spoken in court. Perhaps you'd better read it before you ask me any questions. It shouldn't take you long to absorb the essentials. You've been trained to sift fact from fiction, I'd imagine.'

'It's something we have to do from time to time, sir,' Tench acknowledged.

'Good.' D'eath stood up. 'Then I propose to leave you alone to do it. There's nothing more destructive of mental application than reading while somebody waits for you to finish. Solitude, I've found, always aids concentration. So, Inspector, I intend to pay a visit to the bank. I'll be back in half an hour. In the meantime, make yourself at home. There are drinks in the cabinet.'

He took a cheque book from the desk, walked out of the room and closed the door behind him.


If Tench was momentarily disconcerted by his host's sudden exit, he didn't allow it to distract him for long.

Reminding himself that he'd come for a purpose, he shrugged his shoulders in mild amusement, opened the file and settled down to read.

He didn't need more than a couple of minutes to appreciate the truth behind D'eath's warning. The facts in the case differed on a number of material points from the version that Maddox had given to Gregg.

Tremellen had left the Gymkhana Club at around half-past eight. The evening was fine, visibility good, and the road to the Lal Baradari broad and straight. He'd driven down it at some considerable speed, overtaking two other cars on the way.

The Baradari was known to be a dangerous crossing, and was invariably busy at that time of evening. Having this in mind, the Commissioner of Police had posted there, to control the traffic, the most experienced of his constables: a Muslim from the Punjab, Mohammed Akram. It was his job to operate the red and green lights.

The evidence was incontestable, and supported by a number

159

of reliable witnesses. When Tremellen was still some distance from the crossroads, Akram had given the green light to a cyclist and a car on the main Lucknow road, but, facing the red light, the officer had made no attempt to reduce his speed. He'd ignored the warning and rammed the other car on the crossing broadside on.

The Indian driver, Surendra Singh, had been waiting for the lights to change, and he was, according to witnesses, travelling at only some ten miles an hour. He had his wife with him, a girl of nineteen, and Tremellen's car made impact at precisely the point where she happened to be sitting. It was a violent collision. The Indian's car was sent spinning across the road, and the girl was thrown out. She suffered not merely a fractured pelvis, but a ruptured bladder. Singh was cut about the face. Tremellen was unhurt, apart from being shaken.

Next day he was arrested and charged under Section 338 of the Indian Penal Code: 'causing grievous hurt by an act endangering the life or personal safety of others.' The words of the charge were that 'he did inflict grievous hurt on an Indian woman, one Kamala Singh, by rashly and negligently driving his car over a crossroads against a red light.' Such an offence was punishable with imprisonment for any term up to two years, or with a fine that might extend to a thousand rupees, or with both.

At the hearing, his advocate, Mr Drummond, maintained that it was the constable who was at fault. He'd switched the lights too late to give Tremellen time to stop. He made play of the fact that there was no intermediate yellow light at the constable's command, merely a red and a green. It was well known, he said, that on other occasions around Sarajpur, such lights had been switched without due consideration.

D'eath had apparently rejected this plea on a number of grounds. The constable, Akram, had long experience of operating such lights, and there was ample evidence from witnesses that he'd shown the red light when Tremellen was a considerable distance from the crossroads. This was borne out by the relative speeds of the cars, the presence of Surendra Singh's car in the position it was, and the fact that the cyclist had already cleared the crossing when the accident occurred.

D'eath had accordingly registered a conviction, passing a

sentence of three months' imprisonment and a fine of four hundred rupees to be paid in compensation.

Drummond had immediately filed an appeal and the case had been passed to the High Court, where the Acting Chief Justice had given his judgment. He declared that the District Magistrate was right: there was ample evidence to convict; but since imprisonment meant cashiering and it was his belief that no officer should be deprived of his career for criminal negligence, however gross it might be, he felt impelled to cancel the sentence of imprisonment, while imposing the maximum fine permitted – a thousand rupees – to be paid to the injured party.

The facts were clear enough. Tremellen had driven through the red light at speed. He'd made no attempt to slow down. What puzzled Tench was why.

There was nothing in the evidence to explain his quite irrational behaviour; no mention of the fact that the setting sun might have been in his eyes.

# 9

'You were overruled, sir,' said Tench. It was a statement, not a question.

'I expected to be,' Sir Giles replied smoothly. 'It came as no surprise.'

'Then you were, in effect, passing sentence on yourself.'

'Yes, I realized that only too well. The Chief Secretary took great care to inform me that the conviction was right, but the sentence was wrong.'

'Then why didn't you simply impose the maximum fine, sir? Wouldn't that have been easier?'

'Undoubtedly it would.'

'I'm not being critical, sir. I'm just curious. Weren't you perhaps just a bit too conscious of Indian opinion?'

'No,' said Sir Giles. 'Not in any way. The Indians would have accepted a fine and compensation. I think most of them understood my predicament. They wouldn't have demanded that I immolate myself . . . No, Inspector, the truth was that if I

161

hadn't passed the sentence I did, I'd have been violating all my own principles. Imprisonment was right. It was the only correct sentence. I believed it then, and I still believe it now.'

'It must have been a difficult decision to take.'

'Excessively difficult.' Sir Giles picked up the file and returned it to the drawer. 'The hearing was on a Friday, and I gave myself the weekend to think things over. But however many times I read through the evidence, I came to the same conclusion. Justice, if it were ever to survive in India, had to be impartial. I asked myself what I would have done if the case had been reversed. If it had been the Indian who'd driven through the lights and smashed into a British officer's car. If he'd grievously injured the officer's wife. What sentence would I have passed? What sentence would any magistrate have passed? What punishment, indeed, would the British community have demanded in such a case? Imprisonment, Inspector, without any doubt. I had to be true to my own convictions. Justice had to be seen to be done. I had no alternative but to act as I did. Not that my seniors thanked me. Far from it. They didn't. But at least I knew that I'd done what was right.'

'But they did promote you, sir, didn't they?' said Tench. 'That was what Brigadier Maddox told us.'

'I can only think he said it with his tongue very much in his cheek, Inspector. It was a sideways promotion. I never tried another case. It wasn't intended that I should . . . Now, enough about me. Have you got all the information that you came for?'

'I think so, sir, but there's one point I still don't fully understand.'

'Not clear in the evidence?'

'No, sir, not entirely.'

'You want to know what made Tremellen drive through the lights.'

'Yes, sir. Brigadier Maddox said he was driving straight into the setting sun. He seemed to think that he was dazzled by the glare.'

Sir Giles shook his head. 'Quite untrue, Inspector. The sun was already down. The lights were clearly visible. If it had been otherwise, Mr Drummond would surely have seized on the point. He'd have made it the cornerstone of his plea. But he never made any such suggestion. You know that. You've read the transcript.'

162

'Then why in heaven's name didn't Tremellen slow down? He must have gone through that crossing like a bat out of hell. He never even braked. It seems quite incredible.'

'It does, Inspector, doesn't it?' Sir Giles eyed him quizzically. 'But the answer's very simple.'

'Is it, sir?'

'I'm afraid so. Accidents like Tremellen's occur somewhere every day. Surely you can work it out for yourself. It doesn't require much in the way of logic.'

Tench surveyed the evidence. Nothing emerged.

'Sorry, sir,' he said. 'Perhaps I've missed something.'

Sir Giles was silent for a moment. Then he suddenly leaned forward.

'The man was drunk, Inspector. It was a very hot evening. He'd been drinking at the Club bar from six o'clock till he left at half-past eight.'

Tench stared at him. 'You knew that? At the time of the trial?'

'Everybody knew.'

'Then why wasn't it ever mentioned at the hearing?'

Sir Giles breathed a sigh. 'You've never been to India, have you, Inspector?'

'No, sir, I haven't.'

'If you had, it would be easier for me to explain . . . It was a very different world out there, very different. India's a vast country. It's oppressive, overwhelming. It crushes those who try to tame it. The British in India knew that. They were living in a land where they were outnumbered by many thousands to one; a land where disease could strike without warning and kill a man in a matter of hours; a land where British men and women and children, not so long before, had been butchered by the natives and their bodies thrown down wells. Oh, yes, Inspector, the Mutiny was always with them. It lay across their lives like the shadow of a sword. They were vulnerable. Every day they were vulnerable, and their vulnerability led them to cling together, to shut out the alien world that was around them.' He paused. 'D'you know what a laager is, Inspector?'

'I think so, sir,' said Tench. 'It's a defensive ring of ox-wagons all lashed together.'

'With a camp in the middle. Yes, that's correct. It's an Afrikaans word. The Boers laagered their wagons in self-defence. They were another beleaguered community . . . Well,

163

the British in India borrowed their idea, metaphorically at least. They created their own laagers: the cantonments, the civil lines, even the hill stations. But in all those places, the innermost laager, the tightest ring of all, was the Club. The spiritual citadel, someone once called it. Within its confines they banded together against all the hostile elements that threatened them outside . . . You understand, Inspector?'

'Mutual support and confidence?'

'Yes, exactly. That's why the whole tale was never told in court. I did, of course, have the right to call for any evidence that I felt might be needed. I could have instructed the police to make inquiries, to ascertain just how much Tremellen had drunk. But I knew such an exercise would be utterly futile. No member of the Gymkhana Club would ever testify against him, nor could any of the bearers be persuaded to give evidence. They'd have lost their jobs. And not merely that. They'd have been black-listed for any further employment . . . Oh, I debated whether or not to press for the evidence. Perhaps I should have done so. Not that the outcome would have been any different . . . But, knowing what I did, I had to take it into account when I came to pass sentence. I had to ensure the penalty matched the crime he'd committed.'

'But in the end, sir, it didn't. He got away with it,' said Tench.

'Strictly between you and me, Inspector, he got away with a great deal more than he was ever aware of. The girl's injuries proved to be far more serious than anyone had imagined. The spinal cord was damaged. In a matter of months it became apparent that she'd never walk again.'

'And the case was already closed.'

'The case was closed and the compensation paid . . . for what it was worth. But I've always had the feeling . . .'

He stopped abruptly.

'Yes, sir?' said Tench.

Sir Giles looked straight at him. 'Let me put it this way. If I were searching for someone with a grudge against Tremellen, and there weren't six thousand miles of ocean between them, it wouldn't take me long to come up with a name . . . I don't think I need to spell it out for you, Inspector.

'But then again,' he added, 'six thousand miles is a devil of a way. Unless you believe in some kind of witchcraft.'

164

# VI

## INTO THE DARK

I have heard of thee by the hearing of the ear: but now mine eye seeth thee

Job: 42.5.

# 1

Tench chose not to go straight back to Norwich. He drove a mile and a half north to Burnham Overy Staithe and parked on the hard by the edge of the creek. He needed time to think.

Leaning forward with his arms on the wheel, he watched the yachts, their sails flapping before they caught the breeze. Only pleasure craft used the narrow inlet now. A century before, there'd have been fleets of coasters, some of them more than a couple of hundred tons. They'd have tied up at the quay to load corn and shellfish, and malt for the London brewers.

And down the coast at Cley, where Lubbock had his cottage, the wharfs would have seen even greater activity. According to him, there'd been a time when the river there, now little more than a stream through the meadows, had been a wide-spreading estuary; when three-masted traders had put into the Glaven from as far away as the Mediterranean. They'd brought vegetable oil from Greece and spices from the distant ports of the Levant. Spices, Tench reflected, that might have travelled even further: all the way up the Persian Gulf from India. Six thousand miles.

He stared at the yachts.

Six thousand miles . . .

As D'eath had said, it was a devil of a way. Was it possible that murder could reach out so far?

Logic said no, and yet . . .

Logic could be wrong.

One thing was for sure. He didn't believe in witchcraft. Lubbock had brought up the same idea eighteen months before when they'd been working on the murder at Elsdon Hall, and Lawrence Bell had told him about the curse that tormented the Wilder family. 'Laddie,' he'd said, 'what's your opinion of this witchcraft business? Sticking pins in wax figures and making folk die? Laying curses on people?'

He'd told him then that, as far as he was concerned, it was all a load of nonsense. And he was still of the same opinion.

Strange things might well happen in India – that he was only too ready to admit – but he couldn't believe that someone had purposely moulded a figure of Tremellen, pierced it with a pin, and made him fall backwards down a church tower in Norfolk.

Couldn't believe and wouldn't. The idea was grotesque.

Tremellen had been pushed. He'd been pushed by a hand. The question was, whose?

Whose hand had done it?

He didn't like the answer that came into mind.

The hand of an Indian?

From six thousand miles away?

A man with a grudge?

This man Surendra Singh? Was that conceivable?

He told himself no. It seemed almost as fantastic a theory as witchcraft.

But then . . . Surendra Singh . . .

The name was somehow strangely familiar. He had a nagging impression that he'd heard it before, and recently, too. But he couldn't for the life of him remember exactly when.

He leaned back and closed his eyes . . .

It was during the past week. He was certain it was. Since Tremellen's murder.

Where had he been in that time? Norwich . . . then Salleston . . . Cambridge and Stow-cum-Quy . . . Burnham Market . . . Where had he heard it?

He went over the places, one by one, in his mind. Who had he met? Who'd mentioned the name?

It had something to do with the trips he'd made to Cambridge. He was sure that it had . . . Who had he spoken to?

Mr Parfitt . . . Sally Merivale . . . Mallender . . . Alan Summers . . .

Then, in a flash, it came back. He remembered.

He hadn't heard the name. He'd seen it.

And along with the recollection came a number of others. Links in the chain. Connections he'd never made.

He sat very still and cast his mind back, trying to work out the sequence.

Lubbock, McKenzie, Blake, Velda Reynolds, and then Alan Summers . . .

They fell into place.

'Idiot!' he said. And repeated it, 'Idiot!' This time with greater force.

He pulled a wad of paper from under the dashboard, and unscrewed his pen.

Then he scrawled a figure one, and after it wrote 'Visitors'.

Underneath he put '2' and followed it with 'Talks'.

Then, working more swiftly, he added '3' and '4'. '3' was 'Rooms'. '4' was 'Chimneys'.

Visitors, Talks, Rooms, Chimneys.

He stared for a moment at what he'd written. Then he started up the car, turned it on the hard, and drove through the village till he spotted a phone box. Wrenching open the door, he lifted the receiver, asked for a Norwich number, and then for McKenzie. His fingers drummed on the coin box till there was a click on the line and McKenzie spoke.

'CID. Can . . .'

Tench cut him short.

'Mac,' he said, 'it's Mike. I'm still out at Burnham . . . You remember that list of visitors to Salleston church? The one Lubbock gave us? Gregg checked it out, didn't he?'

McKenzie was quick to answer.

'Yes,' he said. 'That's right.'

'Is he there?'

'Standing right next to me.'

'Put him on, will you?'

He heard Gregg's voice: 'Yes, sir?'

'Andy,' he said. 'Those visitors to Salleston church. Wasn't there a local couple? Said they'd seen a man hanging round the tower?'

'Yes, sir. Husband and wife, out for the day with some friends. Came from Reepham, I think.'

'You've a note of what they said?'

'It's here somewhere, sir. Hang on. I'll find it.'

There was a pause.

'Right, sir. Got it.'

'Read it out,' said Tench.

Gregg read it.

'We dismissed it, sir,' he said, 'along with all the rest.

169

Everyone who goes to Salleston stares up at the tower. We didn't think it was important.'

'We should have looked a bit closer. What was their address?'

There was a rustle of paper.

'Norton House. It's close by the church.'

'And their names?'

'Winthrop. John and Elizabeth Winthrop. They're pensioners, sir.'

'Right.' Tench had already made up his mind. 'I'm going to Reepham, and then on to Salleston. Unless you're called out on something urgent, you and Mac stay put. I'll be with you as soon as I possibly can.'


# 2


Norton House was a small block of flats, and the Winthrops rented the ground floor front. A couple in their late sixties, recently retired from running a post office and general store in a nearby village, they were both well spoken and appeared to be healthy: a fact that Tench noted with some relief, after months of interviewing garrulous Norfolk residents who addressed him as 'bor' and insisted on recounting their multifarious ailments.

'I believe, sir,' he said, 'that you visited Salleston church. A week yesterday, 28th June. My sergeant came to see you and asked you some questions.'

Mr Winthrop, his hands spread wide on his knees, acknowledged that that was so. 'Yes, we told him what we'd seen.'

'D'you mind very much if we go over it again?'

'Why?' The man seemed apprehensive. 'Is there something wrong?'

Tench was swift to reassure him. 'No, Mr Winthrop, nothing at all. We've tried to contact everyone who visited the church on that particular day. Yours is just one among a number of statements, but we think it may prove more helpful than the rest . . . You told Sergeant Gregg that you'd seen a man hanging round the tower.'

170

'Yes, Inspector, that's right.'

'But it wasn't that day,' Mrs Winthrop said.

She was a small, slight figure, unlike her husband who was massively broad.

Tench looked at her sharply. 'Then you didn't see this man a week yesterday?'

She shook her head very firmly.

'Oh, no,' she said. 'It was when we were there earlier, wasn't it, John?'

'Earlier?'

'About a month ago,' Winthrop said.

If Tench was disappointed, he did his best not to show it. 'I understood from Sergeant Gregg it was 28th June.'

'No, Inspector, it was the first time we went. We've been twice this summer. I thought the sergeant knew that.'

'It was probably our fault, not his,' Mrs Winthrop added gently. 'We couldn't have made things clear.'

'But you did see this man?'

'Oh, yes.'

'And he caught your attention?'

Winthrop nodded. 'That's why we mentioned it when the sergeant came.'

'Can you describe him, sir?'

'Yes, he was tall. Wasn't he, Mother?'

'Very tall,' she said.

'And how tall was that?'

'How tall are you, Inspector?'

'Six foot,' Tench told her.

'Then he must have been about six foot four.'

'You said he was sun-tanned.'

'Burnt very dark,' Mrs Winthrop said. 'Looked almost foreign. But it was difficult to tell.'

'Why was that?'

'It was raining, Inspector, wasn't it? He was wearing one of those mackintosh capes, with a hood. It came down across his forehead.'

'So you didn't really get a very good look at him.'

'Well, maybe not all that good,' Winthrop said, 'but good enough to tell he'd had a lot more sun than we had. And we did see him twice, didn't we, Mother?'

Tench frowned.

'I think,' he said, 'you'd better tell me exactly what happened.'

Winthrop nudged his wife. 'You tell him, Mother. You remember it better.'

Mrs Winthrop smoothed down her skirt.

'Well,' she said, 'it was like this. We've got a granddaughter. Angie. Eighteen last month. Lives out at Lynn, and she's taken a craze for this thing called brass-rubbing. You know all about it, I suppose, Inspector. They lay sheets of paper over brass tablets and rub them with a kind of black wax or some such. It leaves a design, like it does when you pencil over a penny . . . She came to stay with us a month ago, and wanted to do some of this rubbing at Salleston church. Seems there's a brass plate in one of the side aisles. A knight in armour, life-size, with some peculiar animal lying across his feet . . .'

'Meant to be a lion,' Winthrop intervened, 'but it doesn't look like one.'

'No,' she said, 'it's more like a Siamese cat. Anyway, we took her out to Salleston. Lovely day it was. Sun was shining. But we hadn't got to Clunch before it thundered and lightened, and when we got off the bus it was spitting with rain. We hadn't taken umbrellas or macs, so we walked up the church path as fast as we could, and when we got to the porch we saw this man standing, looking up at the tower. He stared straight at us for a moment . . .'

'Like as if we hadn't any right to be there.'

'And then he moved to the far corner and stared up again. It was just as if he was looking for something. Then we'd hardly got inside when the rain came down in buckets. We'd meant to leave Angie there and take a walk down the lanes, but it really wasn't fit, so we had to wait till it cleared. It was one of those heavy summer showers that come out of nowhere. Went on for nearly a quarter of an hour, and when we came out he was still by the tower, draped in this cape thing, wasn't he, John?'

'It's a fact,' said Winthrop. 'Rain dripping off him. Looked like a drowned rat. He'd kind of wedged himself into the side of the tower. Why, goodness knows. It didn't give him any shelter.'

'What d'you mean, sir?' said Tench. 'Wedged himself in.'

'Well, he was in between one of those two projecting bits.'

172

'The buttresses?'

'Yes. They go all the way up to the top of the tower. He was leaning with his back against one of them, and I thought he was just huddling against the wall to keep out of the rain, though, with the porch so close, it seemed a daft thing to do. Then – I still can't quite understand what he was up to – he raised one of his feet and pressed it against the opposite bit of the wall. After that he kind of pushed himself up with the other foot behind him. He was clear off the ground . . . I reckoned he was one of those barmy ones. We both did . . .'

'So,' said Mrs Winthrop, 'we went back into the church to tell Angie to keep clear of him. And when we came out again, he'd just disappeared.'

Tench was more than a little interested. He was also puzzled.

'But you didn't tell Sergeant Gregg the whole of this,' he said. 'There was nothing in the statement that mentioned the buttresses.'

'Well, no,' said Mrs Winthrop. 'We didn't really have the time. When he came to see us, we were in a bit of a rush. We were just going out to catch a bus into Aylsham.

'And after all,' she added, 'we didn't think it was important. The man was just a bit mental.'

For want of a nail, thought Tench.

'Can you tell me exactly when this visit of yours was?'

'The first one?'

'Yes, when you went with your granddaughter.'

'Oh, that's easy,' she said. 'It was the day before her birthday.'

'And when's her birthday?'

'1st June.'

'So it was 31st May?'

'Yes, it would be.'

Tench flipped through his diary. 'A Monday.'

'That's right.'

'The last Monday in the month.'

She looked at him curiously.

'Of course,' she said. 'It must have been, mustn't it, Inspector?'

Leaving the flats, Tench looked at his watch. It showed a quarter to two.

Ten minutes later the Reverend Eustace Blake seated himself at his desk in the rectory, and began to write his sermon for the following Sunday. He'd chosen his text from Amos, chapter 4, verse 12: 'Prepare to meet thy God': a dictate which he felt to be eminently appropriate considering the events of the previous week. He'd composed the first sentence and was pondering the second, when there was a knock on the door.

Blake wasn't a man who took kindly to interruptions. He tossed aside his pen in some irritation and, opening the window, peered out towards the porch.

'Yes, Inspector?' he said in a voice that implied that his temper was short.

'Sorry to disturb you, sir,' – Tench read the signs – 'but would it be possible to have a few words?'

'Does it have to be now?'

'I'm afraid it does, sir, yes.'

The rector gave a sigh.

'Then you'd better come in. You'll find the door's on the latch.'

'Now,' he said, when Tench was perched on the horsehair sofa, 'you implied that this was urgent.'

'Yes, sir, that's correct.'

'Then I trust it won't take up a great deal of time.'

'I hope not, sir,' said Tench, 'but I do need the answers to a number of questions.'

'About Major Tremellen?'

'Not directly, sir, no.'

'What then, Inspector?'

'I'd like to know more about the Salleston Circle.'

'The Circle? You should really be speaking to Mrs Reynolds.'

'I intend to, sir. But before I do that, I need some information.'

'From me?' Blake's tone was almost dismissive. 'Come, come, Inspector. What can I tell you that Mrs Reynolds can't?'

'Maybe nothing at all, sir.'

'Then I have to confess that I fail to see the point.'

'There is one, sir, I can assure you of that.' Tench was soothingly diplomatic. 'Perhaps if we can just proceed with the questions . . .'

Blake pursed his lips.

'Very well,' he said, 'but please be as brief as you can. I have a sermon to prepare.'

'And I, sir,' said Tench, 'have a murder to solve.'

'Yes . . . Yes, of course.' The rector was disarmed by this sudden change of approach. For a moment he seemed flustered. 'Well then, Inspector, what is it you want to know?'

'I'd like to go back, sir, to the time we first met. You were good enough on that occasion to show me round the church, and we talked about the Circle. You said you had a wide variety of speakers, and you mentioned in particular an Indian from Cambridge. You said he'd been twice.'

'That's right . . . Dr Singh.'

Tench seemed to smile. 'That was his name, sir, was it?'

'Yes, Inspector . . . You appear to be amused.'

'I was just reflecting, sir, how easy it is to miss an obvious clue.'

'"The people that walked in darkness"? We all walk in darkness at some time, Inspector.'

'Indeed, sir, we do.' Tench said it with feeling. 'Would you happen to know the doctor's first name?'

'Ah, there I'm afraid I can't help you. I simply knew him as Dr Singh.'

'You met him, sir? You were introduced to him?'

'Naturally. Mrs Reynolds brought him over to see me before he gave his talk.'

'A tall man?'

'Yes. My own height.'

'Did you show him round the church?'

'As a matter of fact, I did. He was extremely interested. And a very good listener. He asked a number of intelligent questions.'

'Did he perhaps show an interest in the tower?'

'Yes, he wanted to know why there was no parapet. I told

him the legend, and he said he'd like very much to go up to the top.'

'And did he?'

'Oh, yes. I got George Starling to take him.'

'Was that the first time he came, sir, or the second?'

'He was introduced to me the first time. The second time he asked if he could see the church, and after that the tower. He came early that day. Spent part of the afternoon with Mrs Reynolds, arranging some photographs for display in the village hall. Connected with his talk. I invited them to tea.'

'When would that have been, exactly?'

'It was the meeting before the last one. The last Monday in May.'

'And when did he come the first time?'

The rector shook his head. 'I can't tell you precisely. It was round about a year ago. Mrs Reynolds'll have a note of it.'

'Did you attend the talks?'

'Yes, I did. I was there on both occasions.'

'Was Major Tremellen present?'

'The second time, no. The first time, I can't remember. You'd have to ask Mrs Reynolds. She keeps the minutes.'

'But didn't he make a point of attending Circle meetings?'

'Normally, yes.'

'D'you know why he wasn't there? The second time, I mean.'

'He was out of the village. I understood that he had some business in London.' The rector suddenly paused and looked at Tench keenly. 'Surely, Inspector, you're not thinking there's some connection between Dr Singh and what happened to the Major?'

'I'm not thinking anything at the moment, sir. I'm merely collecting facts.'

'Yes, I understand that. But even so . . .'

'Conclusions come later, once the facts are assembled. Till then it might be better to shun speculation . . . All speculation.'

The rector took the hint. He breathed deeper than usual. 'Of course. As you wish.'

'To come back to the talks that Dr Singh gave. What did he speak about?'

'I think I told you about the first one, Inspector. He contrasted his life in England with the one he'd known in India.'

176

'And the second? You said that was equally good, but on a very different subject.'

'Well, perhaps not so different, but he was more concerned with contrasting landscapes. He spoke about the flatlands of Norfolk and the low-lying Fens. He said they were nothing more than a speck against the spreading vastness of the great Ganges plain and its wide-flooding rivers. Then he went on to talk about mountains. Ours, he said, would be nothing more than foothills compared to what he called the Eternal Snows.'

'The Himalayas.'

'Yes.'

'Did he mention mountaineering?'

'Not, as I remember, in the course of the talk. But there were questions afterwards, and someone asked him whether he'd ever climbed there.'

'And what did he say?'

'He said yes, once or twice. He was guarded about it, but I had the impression that he'd done far more than he was willing to admit. He talked about the Garhwal Hills. How high would they be?'

'High enough, sir, I'd imagine,' Tench answered drily.


4


He'd heard Lubbock say more than once, when they'd been talking together in the cottage at Cley, that solving a murder was much like the business of cultivating roses. You needed to prune the evidence you'd gathered, discarding most of it as quite immaterial; you scratched yourself from time to time following clues that led absolutely nowhere; and then one day, after weeks or perhaps months of waiting, the case would open out like a beautiful flower.

Well, today had undoubtedly been such a day. As he walked towards the road, through the rectory garden, he looked at the Reverend Eustace Blake's roses with fresh appreciation. Sniffing the air, he scented not merely Damasks and Hybrids, but a victory snatched from the jaws of frustration. The case of Major

177

Christopher Tremellen was at last opening out, as the rector might have said, like Mandeville's miraculous roses of Bethlehem.

Or was it?

For a moment his native Lancastrian caution reasserted itself. He stopped in his tracks, staring at a full-blown standard rose by the edge of the path . . . Was it opening too swiftly? Was it doomed yet again to fade and wither, and the petals of his logic fall apart in his hands?

Mike Tench had always been a superstitious mortal, addicted to veering round ladders and throwing salt across his shoulder. As he stepped out again, up the main street, to George Starling's cottage, he remembered the advice the Chief Super had offered, and kept his fingers crossed.


George Alfred Starling lived on his own and, like many starved of company, was only too ready and willing to talk. Indeed, once wound up and running, it seemed more than likely that he'd go on for ever.

Yes, he said, he'd taken Dr Singh up the tower. Not that he'd wanted to. Climbing those bloody steps was just about the last thing he'd needed. But the Major was away, and the rector had asked him to do it as a favour. Never paid him, of course. He hadn't seen a penny piece for all the sweat and strain.

Yes, the doctor had quizzed him a lot about the tower, and that was a fact. Were there any lights, he'd asked. Where were the switches? Was the door to the belfry kept locked or not? Did the Major have a key as well as the rector?

'Spent a lot o' time, he did, pokin' his nose round th' back o' th' bells. An' he were fair taken up wi' th' trapdoor, he were. Kept openin' it an' shuttin' it, like as if he'd never seen any such thing afore. Then, when he gets up top, he walks this road an' that three or four times an' gets down on his knees an' sticks his head way out over the edge. Looks straight down th' wall right as far as th' ground. I were for grabbin' a-hold of him at one time, sir, that I were. Reckoned as he were goin' to fall an' do hisself a mischief. An' how be I goin' to explain to th' rector, an' him lyin' down there dead on th' cobbles?

'An' that weren't all. No, not by a long chalk.' Starling, it seemed, was not a man to be interrupted. 'When we gets

178

ourselves back down again to th' belfry, he tells me, sharp as a pritch, to go outside an' wait. Then he closes th' door. So I waits for him there at th' top o' th' stairs. An' waits an' waits an' bloody well waits. I'm left wi' miself, standin' there like a mawkin. So at last I says, George, ye'd best go an' see what he's a-doin' of in there. So I pushes th' door open an' can't see him nowhere. Then I thinks he's mebbe gone up top again, so I climbs up th' ladder an' out through th' trap, an' there's not a bloody soul. Naught but empty leads. Well, atween you an' me, sir, I be gettin' a mite pensy. I gives him a round o' swears an' climbs down again, and there's still neither hide nor hair of him nowhere. Then, just as I'm makin' for th' stairs a second time, what do he do but shoot hisself out, sudden-like it were, from back o' they ol' bells, an' he gurns at me like he's done a bit clever. "You're not seein' me, are you, Mr Starlin'?" he says, like as if we be playin' a game o' hide-and-find-me. Well, I looked at him, sir, an' said not a word. I were fair bloody mad. There were I chasin' up an' down ladders, an' him stowed away i' th' dark behind th' bells. I bloody nigh give him a clout, that I did.'

'I don't wonder,' said Tench. 'Did you tell the rector?'

'Not I,' said Starling. 'What were the bloody use? He'd think I gone shanny. But I be tellin' you one thing, sir, an' that be for sure. Nex' time, an' there be one, he goes up there hisself. If he reckons I'm a-goin', he'd best come on his knees wi' a fiver on one o' they silver servers. An' tied up wi' a tag o' red bloody ribbon. An' that's about as like as a calf trottin' three mile to suck at a bull.'

5

Passing the Cow and Heifer, Tench reflected that if George Starling's imagery was a trifle bizarre, his memory, thankfully, was still unimpaired.

So far, he thought, so good.

He crossed his fingers and coupled them with a prayer that he'd find Velda Reynolds at home that afternoon.

The prayer was answered. She was.

In answer to his knock, she appeared at the door swathed in a bathrobe which, once she was seated on a chintz-covered settle, revealed an enticing depth of cleavage and several inches of lustrous inner thigh. She seemed quite undisturbed by this double disclosure, though the same could hardly be said of Tench. He found it hard to keep his gaze fixed firmly on hers, and discovered a constant need to remind himself that he was searching for a string of confirmatory clues, among which Velda Reynolds' vital statistics took no pride of place.

'So Inspector,' she said, 'you and I meet again. What is it this time? More intimate questions about my married life?'

'No, not on this occasion, Mrs Reynolds,' he said. 'I need some information about the Salleston Circle, and the rector tells me you have all the details.'

'Most of them, yes.' She leaned across a coffee-table, opened a wooden box and held it out to him. The bathrobe hung a little more loosely, revealing two firm and well-rounded breasts. 'Do you smoke, Inspector?'

Tench declined politely, and made a staunch resolution to keep his mind on his work.

'Do you mind if I do?'

'Not at all, Mrs Reynolds.'

She lit a cigarette and blew out a trail of smoke.

'It depends, Inspector, on what you want to know.'

'It's mainly a matter of dates and timings,' said Tench. 'In the last twelve months you've had, I believe, two lectures given by a Dr Singh.'

'Yes, that's right.'

'The second one, I'm told was a month ago, on 31st May. Can you possibly tell me the date of the first?'

'It was sometime towards the end of last summer. If you want the precise date, then I'll have to look it up.'

'Will you do that, please, Mrs Reynolds?'

'Of course.' She swung herself up, opened a drawer in the sideboard, and took out a large leather-bound diary with a blue ribbon bookmark. Bringing it back to the settle, she flicked through the pages. Tench waited and watched and wondered when she'd tighten the sash on her bathrobe.

'It was 25th August,' she said.

'That was a Monday?'

'Yes, Inspector. We hold all our meetings on Monday.'

'Good.' Tench jotted the date down. 'Now, I understand from the rector that Major Tremellen wasn't there when Dr Singh spoke the second time. Can you confirm that?'

'Yes. He was in London.'

'And what about the first time? Was he present then?'

She leaned forward again, drew an ashtray across the table, and tapped the ash from her cigarette.

'I can't remember, offhand, whether he was or not.'

'I'd have thought,' said Tench, 'considering your close association with the Major . . .'

'At that time,' she said, 'we weren't all that close.'

'But you do keep the minutes of the Circle meetings.'

'Yes . . . Would you like me to check?'

'It's important that I know, Mrs Reynolds. Please do.'

She reached down under the coffee-table, tossed aside a clutch of women's magazines and produced a thick ring-file: a series of actions which did much to unnerve Tench and fray at least the edges of his good resolution.

She laid the file on the table, opened it, licked her finger and turned the pages swiftly. Then she stopped and examined one.

'No,' she said, 'he wasn't.'

'Have you any idea why?'

'Not the slightest, Inspector. I didn't know him well enough then to inquire.'

Tench nodded slowly.

'This Dr Singh,' he said. 'What was his full name?'

'I don't really know. When I wrote to him to make arrangements, I simply addressed the letters to Dr Singh.'

'Where at?'

'One of the Cambridge colleges.'

'Which one, Mrs Reynolds?'

'I believe it was St Margaret's.'

Tench nodded again. 'He replied to you?'

'Of course.'

'How did he sign himself?'

'I think it was S. N. Singh.'

'S.N.?'

'I think so.'

'Did you keep his letter? Is it still in the file?'

'I'm afraid not, Inspector. I simply keep the correspondence till after the lecture, and then I destroy it.'

'So you've no correspondence from him at all? Not even about the lecture he gave a month ago?'

'No, I haven't, I'm afraid.' She leaned forward again and stubbed out her cigarette.

'How did you come to hear about him in the first place, Mrs Reynolds?'

'He was mentioned at a meeting of the Circle committee when we were discussing the programme.'

'Who by?'

'I can't honestly remember who it was, Inspector. New speakers are suggested from time to time by members of the Circle. It was one of those occasions.'

'Some eighteen months ago?'

'Something like that.'

Tench seemed to be thinking. 'What time do the Circle meetings begin?'

'We get together about half-past seven to deal with the minutes and any other business. The talks usually begin round about eight o'clock. Then we have a coffee-break, and after that, questions.'

'So you finish when?'

'Roughly round half-past ten.'

'And when Dr Singh came to speak, how did he travel? Not by car, I'd imagine.'

'No, he came by train, and then by bus from Norwich.'

'So he wouldn't have been able to get back to Cambridge. The last train from Norwich leaves at ten thirty-five.'

'Yes, so he said.'

'Then where did he stay?'

'Not here, Inspector, if that's what you're thinking.'

'I'm more concerned', Tench said smoothly, 'with where he did stay, Mrs Reynolds.'

She seemed to hesitate. 'I believe it was in Aylsham. He took the last bus. I think he intended to stop the night with a friend.'

'Do you know who it was?'

'No, Inspector,' she said. 'I've better things to do than pry into people's lives. Don't you find it dull? Think of all the more fascinating ways you could be spending your time.'

Tench picked up his notebook.

'Oh, I do, Mrs Reynolds. Frequently,' he said.

# 6

He didn't bother to call at the incident room, but drove straight to Norwich at a speed which, if he hadn't been in a marked police car, would have raised a few eyebrows in Horsford and Hellesdon.

Swinging the car to a halt in the station yard, he dashed up the steps, pushed the door open with the flat of his hand, and was making for the stairs when the desk sergeant stopped him.

'Yes, Sergeant?' he said. 'What is it?'

'There's a telephone message from Mr Lubbock, sir.'

Tench suddenly realized that he'd been in Salleston for an hour and a half and hadn't given Lubbock a single thought.

'What did he have to say?'

'Said he was sorry, but he'd had to go back to Cley. Something about a windmill, sir. And would I tell you he'd give you a ring first thing in the morning.'

Kettle Hill, thought Tench. His old Chief had inherited a derelict windmill there nine months before, and had recruited a local millwright to help with its restoration. There'd probably been some unexpected hitch in the work. He shook his head in mild amusement. Show Lubbock a windmill and he'd rush to embrace it. He always maintained that there were few sights more pleasant than the sails of a mill turning slowly in the breeze against a wide Norfolk sky.

In a way he felt relieved that the old boy had gone. Perhaps it was a good thing that he hadn't been at Salleston. If he'd met him, that would have meant explanations. With Lubbock they took time, and time was at a premium.

'Thank you, Sergeant,' he said, and took the stairs at a run.

McKenzie was waiting at the door of his office.

'Well,' he said, 'what's the news? Good, still cryptic or another dead end?'

'I think', said Tench, 'we may have found our man.'

'The Indian?'

'Yes, it's more than a possibility . . . Is Gregg still here?'

'He's somewhere about.'

'Then give me five minutes and round him up. We need to do some talking.'

'The Chief Super wants to see you.'

'I want to see him,' said Tench, 'but first things come first.'

He sat down at his desk, pulled the phone towards him and dialled the exchange.

'Get me Cambridge,' he said. 'St Margaret's College. I want to speak to the porter's lodge.'

He waited impatiently. There was a click on the line, then a second and a third; and then, at last, a voice.

'St Margaret's College.'

'Is that the porter's lodge?'

'Yes, sir. It is.'

'Is Mr Mallender there?'

'I'll put him on to you, sir.'

Tench waited again.

'Mallender speaking.'

'Mallender,' he said, 'this is Mike Tench.'

'Oh, good afternoon, Mr. Tench, sir. Something we can do to help?'

'I hope so, Mallender. You remember when I came into college last week to see Dr Summers? Well, I walked round to take a look at my old rooms in Second Court.'

'P Staircase, sir.'

'That's right. There seems to be quite a varied assortment there now. A couple of Chinese students, and my own rooms are occupied by an Indian.'

'That would be Dr Singh, sir.'

'Yes, I saw his name. I take it he's a don.'

'Yes, sir. Research fellow.'

'What's he researching?'

'Oriental Languages, sir, so I understand.'

'Can you give me his full name? I was told his initials might be S.N.'

'That's correct, sir. S. N. Singh.'

'Would his name be Surendra?'

'I'm almost certain it is, sir. Wait a moment and I'll check.'

He waited yet again. Then Mallender's voice came back.

'Yes, sir, that's right. Surendra Nath Singh.'

'How long's he been with you?'

'I wasn't here when he came, sir. It was during the war. I can look it up if you like.'

'No, Mallender, don't bother. It's not really vital. It was the name that I wanted more than anything else.'

'Nothing more then, sir?'

'No.' Tench had all that he needed. 'Thanks a lot, Mallender. You've been a great help.'


'Sounds pretty conclusive,' McKenzie said. 'If it is the same chap, he certainly had the motive and he made the opportunity.'

'And he had the means,' said Gregg. 'He'd done a bit of climbing . . . Are we going to pull him in?'

'No, not yet.' Tench had made up his mind. 'We could haul him in on suspicion – we've got reasonable grounds – but we're still very much at the guessing stage, aren't we? If we have him in and grill him, guesswork's not going to get us very far.'

'It's been known to,' McKenzie said.

'Yes, Mac, it has, but far too much depends on the suspect, and somehow I don't think our friend Dr Singh's going to burst into tears and confess to a murder. Unless we can confront him with the right sort of evidence – something that links him beyond doubt to what happened at Salleston – we'll be likely to find ourselves out on a limb. He'll simply deny everything. We'll have to let him go. And I'm not one for putting a suspect on alert unless we can pin him down.'

'So where's the evidence coming from?'

'The letters,' said Tench.

'The Baradari letters?'

'Yes. Lubbock always said they were the key to this case, and he was right. They are.'

'Then where do we start to look?'

'You don't,' Tench told him. 'Sorry, Mac, but this is my job. It has to be. I'm the only one around who's got the right connections. If those letters hold the key, I think I know where to find it, but I need you and Gregg right here by the phone until I've made sure.'

'And after that, what?'

'After that, we move . . .'

*

The Chief Super listened, then he sat back and looked at Tench for quite a long time.

'This man Singh,' he said at last. 'Surely you don't think he came six thousand miles just to push Tremellen down a flight of steps?'

'No, sir, I don't. I think he was here already, and they met again by chance. The encounter between them reopened old wounds.'

'You've evidence to prove it?'

'Circumstantial evidence.'

'That isn't proof, Mike. You're going to need more than that.'

'Yes, sir, I know.'

'Then what have you got in mind?'

'I'd like your permission, sir, to go to Cambridge,' Tench said. 'Immediately, if that's possible.'

## 7

Once a student of the classics, he was only too well aware of Ovid's famous dictum that permission, once granted, takes the edge off desire; that the illicit, in other words, is always more exciting.

Driving into Cambridge down the Newmarket road, he recalled it and then dismissed it as having no relevance to Michael Bruce Tench. His one desire now was to wind up the case of Major Tremellen just as fast as he could: a desire that had suffered no sensible diminution since he'd knocked on the door of the Chief Super's office.

The light was already beginning to fade as he turned up the drive that led to the college and parked beneath the trees. Summers' car was there: an old MG Magnette that was still his pride and joy, its wire wheels gleaming in what was left of the sun; and the shadows were lengthening across the lawns of Chapel Court as he climbed the stairs to his old tutor's rooms.

*

Summers shrugged off the gown he'd been wearing to dinner and tossed it on a chair.

'Sherry, Mike?' he said. 'Or I've got an old bottle of Benedictine stowed away . . .'

Tench turned down the offer, not without some regret. 'Sorry, Alan. Not tonight. I've got to drive back to Norwich.'

'Another flying visit?'

'Has to be, I'm afraid.'

Summers eyed him thoughtfully. 'You said on the phone that you needed more help. Is this still the same case?'

'Very much the same.'

'So what are you after this time? More esoteric knowledge? How to make a traverse?'

'Not on this occasion, no.' Tench was suddenly sombre. 'This is business, Alan, an official inquiry, though I'd prefer it to be a chat between two old friends.'

Summers narrowed his eyes a fraction.

'What's the trouble, Mike?' he said.

'I'm here to see you as the Senior Tutor of St Margaret's. There's something you ought to know.' He paused. 'This is difficult.'

'Then the best thing to do is come straight to the point. So what is it? Tell me.'

'We're investigating the murder of a Major Tremellen, and we think it may involve a member of the academic staff.'

'You mean here?'

'I'm afraid so.'

Summers stared at him. 'You're joking.'

'Far from it, Alan. I wish to God I were.'

'Are you trying to tell me there's a killer on the loose somewhere in the college?'

'Well, maybe that's a little too melodramatic. I don't think our man's likely to run amok with a gun. But there's evidence that he may be connected with the murder.'

'Who is he?' Summers was clearly sceptical.

'He's one of your research fellows. Has my old rooms. An Indian called Singh.'

'Dr Surendra Singh?'

'I believe that's his name, and he has a doctorate, yes, in Oriental Languages.'

'But this is ridiculous.' Summers thumped the chair arm.

187

'He's quiet, unassuming, utterly rational. I've never seen him lose his temper. He's the last person I'd suspect of criminal violence.'

'Murderers', said Tench, 'quite often are.'

Summers shook his head.

'I'm sorry, Mike,' he said, 'but I find this quite impossible to believe. Are you sure he's the right man?'

'There's considerable evidence, though it's all circumstantial.'

'Reliable evidence?'

'From a number of different sources.'

Summers pushed himself up, crossed to the cabinet and poured himself a liberal measure of brandy. He shook his head again, as if still unconvinced. Then he sat down and looked Tench straight in the eyes. 'What d'you want me to do?'

'If I'm right, you may be able to prove the case against him.'

'Or acquit him?'

'That's possible.'

'But how do I do it?'

'Tell me about him,' said Tench. 'Start at the point when you first heard his name, and carry on from there.'

Summers set down his glass.

'All right,' he said. 'You wouldn't remember a man called Tyler-Jones, would you? The Reverend John Tyler-Jones?'

'No, the name's not familiar.'

'He was Dean of the college when I first came up in 1919. I got to know him well. He was a man of deep faith and notable charm. He left the year I took my degree, and went out to India to serve with the Circuit of Anglican Missions. They run schools out there. He was appointed chaplain of the Anglican Mission of St Mark in Lucknow. Stayed there for something like sixteen years. Then, just before the war, he retired and came back to live in Cambridge. We made him an honorary fellow. He's out at Fen Ditton.'

Summers paused to sip his brandy, and then continued.

'I think it was round about 1942. There was this vacancy for a research fellowship – Oriental Languages – and Tyler-Jones said he knew just the right man. A young student of his, a quite brilliant scholar. Had a tragic background. As a child he'd been orphaned: both his parents had died in a cholera epidemic. He'd received his education at the mission school in Lucknow, and Tyler-Jones said he was quite outstanding. Graduated from

Lucknow University, and went on from there to do research in Calcutta. We got in touch with him, the Circuit paid for his passage, and he's been here ever since.'

'And Tyler-Jones was right? He's lived up to his reputation?'

'Yes, in every way. He's now an Assistant Director of Research.'

'Is he married?'

'He had been, so we gathered from Tyler-Jones. That again was a tragedy. According to him, she was a beautiful young woman. They married while he was still a student at Lucknow, but soon after that they were both in a road smash. He got away with minor injuries, but the girl was paralysed and died some months later. Tyler-Jones said that he took it pretty badly.'

There was silence for a moment.

'Has he ever talked about his wife?' Tench asked.

'Not to my knowledge. Certainly not to me. It's not a subject that any of us would willingly broach.'

'And there's nothing further you can tell me?'

'I don't think so . . . Should there be?'

'I was hoping perhaps there might be.'

'Then all I can do,' said Summers, 'is confess that I've no idea what it is.'

'You're sure about that?'

'Yes, I've told you everything, as far as I know.'

'Not quite everything,' said Tench. 'You haven't mentioned The Night Climbers.'

'Advisedly, Mike.' Summers took another drink. 'This is an official inquiry. You said so yourself. Officially they don't exist.'

'But unofficially they do.'

'So I've heard from time to time.'

'Then unofficially, off the record, between you and me, our friend Dr Singh is one of them, isn't he? He goes around climbing buildings at night.'

'Do I have to answer that?'

'I'm afraid so, Alan.'

'Then the answer, reluctantly, has to be yes.'

'How good is he?'

'Very good.'

'Good enough to chimney up Salleston church?'

'I don't think he'd find it a serious problem.'

'Has he ever climbed King's?'

189

'Yes, I believe so.'

'Did he tell you about it?'

'No.'

'Someone else told you?'

'Not that I recall. Such things aren't discussed.'

'Then there's only one way you could possibly know,' said Tench. 'He made an entry in the log-book, didn't he, Alan?'

'That's always been the custom.'

There was silence again.

'You realize, don't you, that I'm going to have to see it?'

'Is that absolutely necessary?'

'It's a murder case, Alan. The evidence may be vital.'

Summers drew a deep breath. He got up from the chair, took a key from his waistcoat pocket and unlocked his desk. Pulling open a drawer, he produced a heavy day-book, bound in leather, and handed it to Tench.

Tench didn't take it. 'The entries aren't signed?'

'You know they aren't, Mike. No one ever signs his name.'

'Then do me a favour. Find me the entry that Dr Singh made.'

Summers turned the leaves. Then he held out the book.

'That's one of his,' he said.

Tench glanced at what was written: 'We reached the chapel shortly after midnight, and made our way to the chimney on the north-east turret, at the end of the north wall . . .'

He didn't need to read further.

The writing was in copper-plate. It streamed across the page.

8

'I'll have to take this away with me, Alan,' he said.

Summers shrugged. He seemed resigned. 'If you must, then you must . . . What are you going to do with it?'

'Send it to a handwriting expert,' said Tench. 'Then, if it shows what I think it does, we'll have the relevant passages photographed and the prints of them filed. Once that's done, we'll return the book to you.'

'The relevant passages. Which would they be?'

'Those proving that certain letters were written by Dr Singh, and others that show he was skilled at climbing buildings, particularly chimneys.'

'And if they confirm your suspicions, I presume they'll be produced as evidence in court.'

'Yes, they'll have to be, but they'll simply be recorded as samples of handwriting. There's no reason why you should be involved in any way.'

'But I am involved, aren't I?' Summers tossed down the last of his brandy. 'You made that clear right at the start. I'm the Senior Tutor. I'm responsible to the Master. He'll have to be told, Mike.'

Tench agreed. 'Yes, he will.'

'So I'll need to know the strength of the case against Singh. How much can you tell me?'

'Enough to prove we've sufficient grounds to take him in for questioning . . . Is he here, by the way?'

'He's in residence, yes, but at the moment he's not in college.'

'Then where is he?'

'Out at Hilderfield. Conducting a course at the Village College. Went yesterday morning. He's staying at the Hall.'

'And when's he due back?'

'Not till Thursday evening.'

'Then that gives us time. Forty-eight hours. It should be more than enough . . . You'll have to inform the Master, I realize that. But no one else must know. I don't want Singh alerted.'

'Don't worry. Nothing's going to go beyond the walls of the Lodge. The Master won't want rumours flying around.'

Tench nodded. 'Fair enough. Then, if all goes well, we can pick him up at Hilderfield. There won't be any need to disrupt the college.'

Summers sighed. 'But there's bound to be a scandal, Mike. You know that.'

'I'm afraid it's unavoidable. Once the papers get hold of the tale, there'll be a spate of banner headlines . . . COLLEGE DON ARRESTED ON MURDER CHARGE . . . ST MARGARET'S MAN HELD FOR SALLESTON KILLING . . . The only thing you can do is ride out the storm.'

'Isn't there any way we can keep it under wraps?'

'Can you think of one? I can't.'

'*Fiat justitia*, though the heavens crack open above St Margaret's?'

'That,' said Tench, 'and the other old adage . . . Justice needs to be seen to be done.'

Half an hour later, carrying the log-book, he made his way thoughtfully out to the car. He dropped the book on the rear seat, slammed the door shut and stood for a moment staring up at the long east range of Chapel Court. Then, on what was almost an idle whim, he turned on his heel and strolled back through the gatehouse.

What drew him towards his old rooms that evening he never really knew. Some strange nostalgic urge? Summer evenings remembered, when he and his friends, bewitched still by innocence, had lounged on the grass and tried to persuade themselves war was just a myth? Whispering voices that he'd never hear again, stilled for ever in the desert, on the Normandy beaches, in the forests of Burma? Any one of them, perhaps, could have called him back. Or the voice of his own youth, lost and locked in the stones?

Whatever the call was, it directed his steps, round the lawns, through the archway and into Second Court.

It was dark. The college windows were studded with light. At the foot of his own staircase, a single bulb threw a dim yellow gleam on the ancient flags and the pitted stone walls. He stood there, looking up at the six leaded panes behind which he'd spent a whole year of his life. The rooms were in shadow, and he knew very well that the heavy oak door at the head of the stairs would be closed and locked; but he suddenly felt an impulse to do what he'd done so many times before: to climb the steps and stand outside the door; reliving the past, regressing ten years to the day when, an apprehensive young freshman, he'd stood there, key in hand, and wondered what lay behind those stout oaken panels.

Nowadays he knew. There was a claustrophobic lobby, and, opening off it, four separate doors: to the left a study; next to it a water-closet with a rusted chain, then the bedroom with its bleak bedstead, and last of all the cubby-hole that held a set of fitted cupboards, a sink and a gas-ring.

Stark as they were, he'd left a part of his younger self behind in those rooms . . .

192

He saw the name, Dr Singh, white-lettered inside the flat-tened arch of the entrance.

Could walls absorb speech, perhaps even thoughts? How many of his own were still trapped inside them?

How many now of Singh's?

He set his foot on the bare wooden tread at the bottom and started to climb, his footfalls sounding up the well of the stair. Then, half-way up, he stopped, his gaze fixed on the landing.

When rooms were left vacant, the outer door, the oak, was invariably shut. But Singh's was wide open, flung back against the wall . . .

Yet the man was out at Hilderfield, twenty miles away. And the windows had been dark.

Caution told him to stop, to turn round and go down; but he didn't, he went on . . .

Reaching the landing, he peered into the lobby. The inner doors were shut, and there was no streak of light.

Curiosity gripped him: a potent curiosity that demanded satisfaction. He put his hand to the knob of the study door and turned it, expecting to find it locked. But it wasn't. The door yielded. It opened with the same old creak that he remembered from his undergraduate days.

He hesitated a second, wondering. Then he stepped inside.

As he did so, the room exploded into light. A lamp was switched on, and a tall, lean figure uncoiled itself from a deep armchair. The voice that spoke was soft, with a rhythmic inflection.

'Inspector Tench?' it said. 'Do please to come in and find yourself a seat. I was expecting you to call . . .'

## 9

That was when Tench knew that things were going wrong.

He tried to keep calm.

'Dr Singh?' he said.

'So people call me.' Tench saw the high forehead, the bur-nished cheekbones, the aquiline nose.

'Then I'm sorry to intrude. I was led to believe you were away on a course.'

'You were not misled, Inspector.'

'I saw the door open . . .'

'And you were naturally curious. That is understandable.' The doctor was the very quintessence of reason. 'Please to sit down. What would you care to drink? A sherry? A small liqueur? I have a very fine Armagnac. Perhaps you might prefer that. It has an air of strangeness, an unusual warmth.'

Tench raised a hand. 'Not for me, Doctor.'

'But you must. I insist. We have a lot to discuss, and the night, as they say, is still very young.' He took a bottle and two small glasses from a handsome mahogany cabinet, poured two full measures and handed one to Tench.

'I really do think it would be better if you sat down, Inspector,' he said. 'Relax and let us enjoy our time together. You are clearly very interested in me, and I also in you. Our meeting holds the promise of a worthwhile encounter. Would you not say so?'

Tench took the glass, and lowered himself on to the edge of a chair.

He didn't drink. Singh did.

'Jai Hind,' he said. 'And now, perhaps, you would like to ask the first question.'

Go along with him, Tench thought. Let the man talk. It was the only thing to do.

He ran his tongue across his lips.

'Why are you here, Doctor,' he said, 'and not at Hilderfield?'

'Let us say that I was called back on urgent business. That should, I think, be an adequate explanation.'

'Perhaps,' said Tench. He was slowly but surely recovering his poise. 'But it fails to cover all the eventualities.'

'It does?' Singh raised his eyebrows. 'Now how can that be?'

'I think you know very well. You said you were expecting me. Why was that?'

'I came from the station by taxi, Inspector. Your car was parked by the Chapel Court gate. Police cars are easy to identify. No?'

'And you assumed that I'd come to pay you a visit?'

'Of course.'

'But we've never met before, Dr Singh. So why on earth should I want to see you?'

'I can only reply, Inspector, with much the same question. Why did you climb the stairs and open my door?'

'You find that perplexing?'

'Not entirely. You must have had some very good reason. Shall we say that, like you, I have a natural curiosity?'

'The answer's simple enough, Doctor.'

'It is?'

'Yes, I merely wanted to see this room.'

The doctor sat back and took a sip from his glass, but his gaze never wavered.

'Do forgive me,' he said, 'but I find that hard to credit. You wished to see my room? But why should it exercise such a fascination?'

'I think you'll find the explanation credible enough.'

'Then perhaps I could hear it.'

'Willingly,' said Tench. He felt himself once again on safe ground. 'This may be your room, but when I was a student here it was mine.'

If Singh was surprised he gave no indication. 'You wished to see it again?'

'I spent some happy times here.'

'That I can imagine.' The doctor raised his glass. 'Then let us both drink to happiness, Inspector. Come. Grant a dead man at least one small favour.'

'A dead man?'

'Quite dead . . . Please drink . . . To happiness.'

Tench lifted his glass and drank.

'To happiness,' he said.

'Thank you.' Singh studied him. 'It was perhaps not so difficult? To drink to happiness?'

Tench was wary. 'Not so difficult, no.'

'Have you ever considered the fleeting nature of happiness, Inspector? It is with us one moment and dissolves away the next. Someone once called it a dream of perfect bliss, too beautiful to last. But I much prefer the line in Byron's *Don Juan*. "Happiness is born a twin". It needs to be shared. Without sharing, it dies.'

Tench made no comment. He felt there was none he could profitably make.

195

'You say you were happy here,' the doctor continued. 'Who did you share your happiness with?'

'Three very good friends.'

'And where are they now?'

'Two of them are dead. They were killed in the war.'

'And the third? Where is he?'

Tench suddenly saw himself sitting with a man he had every intention of arresting for murder. Engaged in a philosophical discussion. It was farcical. He had to end it. He had to get away. Give himself time to think.

'I can't see that it matters, Doctor,' he said. He emptied his glass and stood up. 'Thank you for the drink. And now, if you'll excuse me, I've an appointment to keep.'

Singh remained seated. 'You disappoint me, Inspector.'

'I'm sorry about that, but I have to get back to Norwich.'

'Without an answer to your question?'

'What question was that?'

'You wanted to know why, since we were strangers to one another, I was expecting you to call.'

'I can guess.'

'I hardly think so.' Singh uncoiled himself again from the chair. He walked across to the window and closed the curtains. Then he moved towards a bureau set against the wall. 'I asked you to grant a dead man a small favour. To drink to happiness. You remember, Inspector?'

'I could scarcely have forgotten in such a short time.'

'Did it never cross your mind that the phrase, a dead man, was a little bizarre?'

'I assumed you meant yourself.'

'But that would be completely illogical, Inspector. I am here, in front of you, very much alive. You can reach out and touch me. Why should I speak of myself as dead?'

Tench felt that reality was slipping away. He was caught in a debate that had just as little meaning as his own quite irrational presence in the room.

'I have to go,' he said.

'Your appointment?'

'Yes.'

'It is vital you should keep it?'

'Imperative,' said Tench.

'Then of course it would be grossly discourteous of me to attempt to detain you. But permit me my regrets. I was hoping we might talk at much greater length . . . However, before you leave, I would ask you, Inspector, to grant me another favour. I have something to show you. Please to come and see.'

Tench hesitated, then he moved reluctantly closer.

Singh took a photograph in a heavy metal frame from the top of the bureau, and held it out between his hands.

'Her name', he said, 'was Kamala. She was beautiful, Inspector. Would you not agree?'

Tench looked. The young woman in the picture was undeniably lovely. She was seated on a couch, her elbow on the armrest, one hand beneath her chin and the other in her lap. She was dressed in a sari, the fringe of it draped across her smooth black hair, and she looked straight at the camera, pensive and yet, at the same time, adoring.

'Yes,' said Tench, 'I would.'

The Doctor traced the outline of her face with a fingertip, tenderly, almost lovingly.

'She was, as one might say, the indispensable twin to my happiness, Inspector. We shared it together . . . and then . . .'

'Then?' said Tench, in spite of himself.

'She was murdered.' The doctor's tone, for the first time, was harsh. 'Killed by a madman. A man who cared nothing at all for happiness. Whose only concern was self-gratification . . . Have you ever, Inspector, watched someone die? Someone you loved with a love that couldn't die? Have you ever seen them slowly drifting away from you month after month?' He looked up, and Tench saw the pain in his eyes. 'No, I think not. Nor would I wish you to know such anguish . . . But all through those months I remembered one thing. I remembered her lying there, broken on the road, her arms flung wide like those representations of the crucified Christ on the walls of the mission; and I carried always in my mind two verses from the Bible that were read to us as children. The first was from Luke 6.29, the words of Jesus himself: "To him that smiteth thee on the one cheek offer also the other." The second was from Deuteronomy 19.21, the words of Moses: "And thine eye shall not pity; but life shall go for life, eye for eye, tooth for tooth, hand for hand, foot for foot . . ." I sought the chaplain in my misery and asked which I should follow. He told me that deep in my heart I must know. "Put your trust in justice, Surendra Nath," he said.'

The doctor stared at the picture.

'Put your trust in justice.' There was bitterness in his voice. 'But Justice is blind. Did you know that, Inspector? She stands above your Central Criminal Court, but she cannot see the scales that she holds between her fingers. She cannot see the hand that secretly tilts them. If she knew it was there, she would strike it off blindly with the edge of her sword . . .'

He suddenly raised his eyes.

'I sometimes think,' he said, 'that in that moment when he struck her down on the crossing, he and I, like the rulers of Jerusalem, made a covenant with death. When I held her in my arms and knew at last that she was gone, I spoke to him again across her dead body. I told him that because I had no wish to die alone, he must die with me. That, Inspector, was always my design. But then she intervened. No, my love, she said, life is worth living. Take his life, yes, but let me live on with you. Let me share with you what remains of happiness.'

He looked again at the picture.

'For a while I was deceived. I thought it might be possible. But one cannot renege on a covenant with death. All one can do is extend its compass. There is another line from Byron that I remember, Inspector, and find strangely appropriate. Perhaps you may also keep it in memory. "Hope withering fled and Mercy sighed farewell." It has a ring of truth that is not unacceptable.'

He replaced the picture, almost with reverence.

'I, too, have an appointment to keep,' he said.


What happened after that, Tench, for long, found difficult to believe.

The man simply walked passed him into the lobby, and, even as he turned, he heard the outer door close.

A key rattled in the lock, and then footsteps clattered away down the stairs.

# VII

## BETWEEN THE WALLS

We have made a covenant with death

Isaiah: 28.15.

# 1

The outer doors were thick; so were the college walls; and when he flung back the curtains and opened the window, the court stretched away from him dark and deserted.

It took him all but five minutes of hammering and shouting before he managed to alert the Chinese student who had the rooms below, and it was another five minutes before Mallender arrived with a bunch of master keys and unlocked the door.

Ten frustrating minutes while he railed at himself for downright negligence. Why on earth had he been so bloody irresponsible? He should have been on his guard. What the devil had made him forget all his training? Once you have a suspect within your sights, Lubbock had warned him, take extra care. Never, never let your attention wander. The old man had told him that time and time again. And what had he done? He'd allowed this suspect to bemuse him with words. He'd been listening, not watching. And what was the result? Singh had locked him up and walked away with the key. And he'd helped him to do it.

As he waited for Mallender to open the door, he swore to himself as he never remembered swearing since a booby-trapped bomb had blown out the wall of his office in Naples.

Mallender was quite understandably bewildered. Questions formed on his lips, but Tench already had his feet on the stairs.

'Don't ask me what happened, Mallender,' he said. 'Have you seen Dr Singh?'

'Not since yesterday, sir.'

'He hasn't gone out tonight? In the last ten minutes?'

'Not by the Chimney, sir.'

'Right. Thanks a lot.'

If Mallender was confused, that was just too bad. He hadn't time to explain.

He dashed down the stairs and sprinted across to the Chapel Court gatehouse. The huge double doors were closed and the wicket was bolted. He looked at his watch. They would be, of course. The porters locked up at ten.

He didn't wait for the man to come out of the lodge. He pulled back the bolt himself and stepped outside. His car was still parked next to Summers' MG, but the paths that led away to the outer gates showed no sign of life.

He turned back inside. The porter was there.

'Are you going out, sir?' he asked.

Tench ignored the question. 'Have you let anyone out in the last few minutes?'

'No, sir, not since the gates were closed.'

He left the porter standing by the open wicket, raced across the lawns and up the staircase to Summers' rooms.

If Singh hadn't left by either of the gates, he'd gone over the wall.

He thumped on the door and went on thumping till Summers appeared. He was wearing a dressing-gown and pyjamas.

'Good God, Mike,' he said. 'I thought you'd be half-way back to Norwich by this time.'

'Has Singh got a car?'

Summers stared. 'Why, what's wrong?'

'Has he got a car?'

'I believe so, yes.'

'What make?'

'I don't know.'

'Colour? Registration number?'

'I haven't the faintest idea. Why d'you want to know?'

'Can't you tell me anything about it at all?'

'Nothing, I'm afraid.' Summers was almost as bewildered as Mallender. 'He had an old Morris, but he changed it last week. I don't know what he's got now. He doesn't normally bring his car into college.'

'Where does he keep it?'

'Has a lock-up, I think.'

'Where?'

'Somewhere on Park Street.'

'But you don't know exactly where.'

'No, I don't.'

'Does he get any extra petrol? A supplementary ration?'

'Not that I know of.'

'Park Street. That's what? Five minutes' walk?'

'Three, at a run.'

'Right . . . Listen, Alan . . . No, don't ask me any questions . . . I want a description of his car, and I need to know if it's still in that lock-up. I'm off back to Norwich. If you can find out anything, ring my office there and ask for Sergeant McKenzie or Sergeant Gregg. If you can't reach either of them, leave a message with the desk.'

'You mean tonight?' Summers was clearly on the verge of disbelief.

'Yes, if possible. Pull out all the stops.'

'But what in heaven's name's happened?'

He didn't get an answer.

By that time Tench was half-way down the stairs.


He sat in the car.

Told himself to slow down. Slow down and think.

What had Singh said?

'I, too, have an appointment to keep.'

But where? And who with?

He'd said no one could renege on a covenant with death. What had he meant?

Suicide? Was that what he had in mind?

It was logical, yes. He'd as good as admitted to killing Tremellen. Why would he do that if he wanted to live?

But he didn't want to live. He'd made that plain enough.

'Happiness is born a twin.' That was what he'd said. He'd quoted Byron. 'It needs to be shared. Without sharing, it dies.'

And what was left without happiness? Nothing but self-deception.

Suicide? Yes, it all pointed that way . . .

And yet he wasn't sure.

Other phrases of Singh's came back into mind. Words that didn't fit.

Something about protracting the covenant with death. Extending its compass.

What the hell had he meant by that?

He admitted to himself that he didn't really know.

But just what did he know?

Nothing for certain. Nothing he could prove. Singh had treated him to a philosophical monologue, and what did it contain when all was said and done? Nothing that could possibly be classed as evidence. Nothing but a half-confession of guilt, unsubstantiated, unrecorded . . .

There was still no valid evidence to link the man with murder. The only chance of that lay in matching the letters with what he'd written in the log-book.

The log-book! He'd forgotten all about it!

He swung round in his seat and breathed a sigh of relief.

It was still there, safe.

He pushed it out of sight, underneath his coat . . .

What was he to do?

For a moment he debated whether to put out a call and have Singh picked up, but it went against the grain, against all his inclinations.

This was his case. To turn it over to someone else would be too much like an admission of failure. And he wasn't prepared to admit that he'd failed.

If he'd made a mistake, it was his responsibility. It was up to him to retrieve it.

But how?

He hammered with his fist on the steering column. How, he said, how?

What would Lubbock have done?

He'd never have let the man get away in the first place, but suppose that he had . . .

He found himself echoing Lubbock's own words. Think, laddie, think.

He had a strange conviction that there was something he'd missed. Something that was a clue to the man's intentions.

He closed his eyes and tried to bring back to mind exactly what Singh had said.

He'd stood there, holding the picture in his hands, and talked about hearing his dead wife's voice. She'd pleaded with him not to take his own life.

What were the words she'd used?

'Let me . . .'

Let me what? He had to get it right.

204

'Let me live on with you.'

He repeated the words.

'Let me . . . live on with you.'

For a moment he sat rigid, absolutely still. Then he gripped the wheel tightly and told himself what a blind fool he'd been.

Why hadn't he guessed before? Why hadn't he made the obvious connection?

He leaned forward, started up the car, drove out through the gates and turned right and then left on to the Newmarket road.

At Bottisham, six miles out, he stopped at a phone box and rang through to Norwich.

Then he rammed his foot down.

Running into Newmarket, he hit the alarm bell.

No-one was going to stop a police car on call.

And he was answering a call.

What he'd told Singh was no more than the truth.

He did have an appointment.

And one that now, more than ever, it was imperative to keep.

# 2

Salleston had never been a place where people went to bed late, and on that Tuesday night its inhabitants saw no reason to vary the pattern. By quarter past eleven there were few lights still burning, and one by one they winked out into darkness. Henry Bebbington had already been in bed a full hour, and old George Starling at least half that time. At twenty past eleven, when Velda Reynolds turned off her bedside lamp and slipped between the sheets in her satin pyjamas, only one lighted window remained in the village. That was in the rector's study, where the Reverend Eustace Blake was still wrestling to find a fitting peroration to his sermon on the strangely erratic nature of death. Then he, too, shuffled his papers together, laid them neatly in a drawer and locked up his desk.

Constable Grenville, standing in the shadows by the incident room, watched the lights in the rectory go off one by one: first the study, then the landing, and after an interval the one in the bedroom.

The village lay dark and silent. He peered at the luminous face of his watch.

It showed 11.28.

He waited and watched. That was what he'd been told to do.

At half-past eleven two cars coasted to a halt in a narrow lane at the back of the church.

Five figures emerged: Sergeants Gregg and McKenzie, and the three detective constables, Rayner, Lock and Spurgeon.

Grenville saw them approaching.

'You've opened up?' McKenzie asked him, almost in a whisper.

'Yes, Sarge.'

'Give the key to DC Lock.'

Lock took the key, dropped it in his pocket and made his way into the incident room. Leaving the place in darkness, he sat down at a table and pulled the phone towards him.

McKenzie turned back to Grenville. 'She's in?'

'Yes, Sarge. Just gone to bed.'

'Is she on her own?'

'I wouldn't know for sure.' Grenville stared across at the unlit windows. 'There hasn't been anybody else around. Not for the last half-hour.'

'Right.' McKenzie tapped Gregg on the shoulder. 'Andy, you and the others stay with Lock for the moment . . . Let's go,' he said to Grenville.

They walked down the path and straight across the road. McKenzie pressed the bell. He waited, then pressed it again, a second time. They heard it ring inside the house. Then a light went on upstairs and a window was opened.

'Who's there?'

A woman's voice.

'It's the police, Mrs Reynolds,' McKenzie said. 'Please come down.'

The window closed. There were footsteps on the stairs, a key turned in the lock and the door was pulled back. Velda Reynolds stood there. Red satin pyjamas. Red satin night-robe. She tightened the sash.

'Yes?' she said. 'What is it?'

McKenzie produced his card. 'I'm Detective Sergeant McKenzie,' he said, 'and this, as you know, is Constable Grenville. Can we come in?'

206

She gave a little shrug.

'I suppose so,' she said.

She stood aside to let them pass, closed the door behind them, led them along the hall and switched on a light.

'You'd better come in here.'

McKenzie stepped past her. Grenville followed.

She reached down, took a cigarette from a wooden box on a coffee-table, lit it with a gold-plated lighter and calmly blew out a long trail of smoke.

'Now, Sergeant,' she said, 'what is it you want?'

'Are you alone, Mrs Reynolds?'

She eyed him with some amusement. 'Did you think I wasn't?'

McKenzie ignored the question. 'Your husband?'

'He's at work.'

'And you have no other visitors?'

She raised her eyebrows.

'Really, Sergeant,' she said, 'you should know better than to ask a lady such a question. After all, I was in bed.' She was suddenly serious. 'Now what have you come for?'

McKenzie wasted no time. There was little enough left.

'We've received some information, Mrs Reynolds,' he said. 'It leads us to believe that you may be in some danger.'

She frowned. 'Danger? Who from?'

'I'm afraid I'm not at liberty to disclose that, Mrs Reynolds. My instructions are simply to take you to a place where we know you'll be safe.'

She sat down and crossed her legs. 'Are you telling me that you want me to leave my house?'

'We think it would be best.'

'And what if I refuse?'

'That wouldn't be very wise, Mrs Reynolds.'

'Why not?'

'We'd have to take you into custody. Protective custody. We don't want to have to do that.'

'You mean you'd arrest me?'

'If necessary, yes. We have to ensure your safety.'

She stood up.

'You expect me to believe all this nonsense?' she said. 'I think you'd better leave and let me go back to bed.'

She stubbed out her cigarette and moved towards the door.

207

Grenville stepped in her way.

'It really would be best, Mrs Reynolds,' he said, 'if you came with us now. You are in some danger. If you weren't, we'd not be here.'

She looked at both of them in turn, searching their faces. All at once she seemed weary.

'And just where do you propose to take me, Sergeant?' she asked.

McKenzie was still determined to play it by the book.

'Our orders', he said, 'are to take you to the police house. You'll be safe enough there . . . And now perhaps you'd care to get dressed. As quickly as possible, please, Mrs Reynolds. We've other things to do.'


3


Tench drove faster that night than he'd ever done before. He swept through Mildenhall and Thetford, his alarm bell ringing, his headlights cutting a swath through the darkness as he swung on to the long straight stretch that led to Wymondham. The roads lay empty under a night-clouded sky. With petrol for private motorists still restricted to a miserly ninety miles a month, few people were going to waste it by driving in the dark. He was thankful for that. His one concern was to lessen the lonely miles that lay between him and Salleston.

He knew that he was working partly on intuition – something that Lubbock professed to despise – but it was intuition sprung from at least a grain of logic: a deep-rooted conviction that if Singh was determined to keep an appointment, it had to be in Salleston.

He wasn't trying to find him. He didn't expect to overtake him on the way. No man in Singh's predicament would have chosen this route. Not the main roads. For all he could know, police all over Norfolk might be on the alert. He'd have turned off somewhere, probably at Thetford, threading the lanes that wound through the Breckland and then around Dereham.

That was bound to slow him up.

Tench didn't want to catch him before he reached Salleston, but he had to get there before him.

He rammed his foot to the floorboards, oblivious to everything but the beat of the engine, the headlights dancing up and down on the road, and the sound of the bell ringing wildly across the flat Norfolk fields.

Buildings flashed by, held for an instant white in the lights, then vanishing behind him.

Farmhouses, barns, long rows of cottages, the desolate stub of one of Lubbock's dead windmills . . .

Attleborough, Besthorpe, Wymondham, Hethersett . . .

Then he was twisting and turning through Norwich, and out on the road to Holt.

He switched off the bell.

It was twenty to one by the dashboard clock when, rising through the gloom, he saw the tower of Salleston church.

He drew to a halt behind the two parked police cars.

The village seemed dead to the rest of the world.

Cutting down a passageway between the clustered cottages, he made for the village hall. As he reached it, McKenzie's bulky figure emerged from the shadows.

Tench nudged him inside the incident room.

'All set?' he whispered.

'Yes, everything's fixed.'

'Velda Reynolds?'

'She's with Grenville. Been there an hour.'

'And the cottage?'

'All secure.'

'Where are the others?'

'Lock's here on the phone. Gregg and Spurgeon are round the back, and Rayner's out at the front with me.'

'No sign of him yet?'

'No, not a flicker.'

'Right.' Tench relaxed. 'Anything from Norwich?'

'Yes. Message from a Dr Summers in Cambridge. The car. It's a pre-war Hillman Minx saloon, colour dark green. And it's not in the lock-up.'

'Any number?'

'No, just the make and colour. Still, that's enough . . . What time did he leave?'

209

'Must have been just after half-past ten.'

'And you've seen nothing of him?'

'Nothing at all. He must have opted for the side roads . . . How long would it take him?'

'In a pre-war Minx?' McKenzie gave a shrug. 'Two and a half hours. At least that long . . . But he must be getting close.'

'If he's got enough juice to get him this far. It's all conjecture, Mac.'

'But he's making for here.'

'I've nothing to prove it, but yes, I'm pretty sure. And if I'm right, and I'm reading what's in his mind, he won't want to rouse the village. It's my guess he'll leave the car somewhere outside and come in on foot.'

'So we wait.'

'We wait,' said Tench, 'and watch, and hope he turns up. It's all we can do.'

# 4

It wasn't the darkness that defeated his plans, though it did play a part.

The two sides of the main street that ran through the village differed greatly in character. On the side where the church, the rectory and the village hall stood, the frontage was broken, the roof-line irregular. The buildings were spaced out with gaps in between: semi-detached Victorian houses, small groupings of shops and, at the opposite end to the church, a farm with its scattered adjuncts: stables, cowsheds and a brick-and-flint barn.

On the other side, the side where Velda Reynolds lived, there were simply three long rows of identical cottages, pierced by two passages giving access to a series of small back gardens; while beyond the gardens lay a narrow lane that ran the length of the rows. Velda Reynolds' cottage was in the middle row, and five doors away was the one that Constable Grenville used as a base.

The village was dimly lit. There were only three street lamps, one in the centre of each of the rows, attached to brackets that projected like gallows from the walls of the cottages. Behind the rows there were no lights at all, and those on the main street served merely to throw the backs into deeper shadow.

There was no moon that night, and Gregg and Spurgeon, watching at the rear of Velda Reynolds' cottage, found it difficult to see any distance through the gloom. From half-way down the garden where they'd first taken cover, it wasn't possible to pick out the door or the windows, and they were forced to creep closer.

As time wore on, they had to make a second move, and after that a third, till the roof-line was hidden by the guttering above them.

That was why they never saw Singh when he came.

It was the mist that drew them in: the mist that made effective surveillance impossible.

It gathered above the fields, as it often did at that time of year in Norfolk, and then swiftly and stealthily invaded the village.

Half an hour after Tench arrived, it was cloaking the gardens, rising inch by inch like a soft grey sea, hiding the cottage walls, enveloping the windows, curling like smoke around the roof-tiles and chimneys.

And as it thickened, so Gregg and Spurgeon had to move.

Out at the front, McKenzie and Rayner huddled behind a wall and peered across the road at cottage doors and windows dissolving into blurs.

And Tench, crouching down, swore at the Norfolk weather, as he dodged this way and that amid the brick and flint of Salleston, listening for the sound of footsteps in the night.

But just as Gregg and Spurgeon never saw Singh, so Tench never heard him.

Gregg, at one point, thought that he did.

It was just after two o'clock when he caught what could have been the creak of a hinge as a door or a window was quietly opened.

He gripped Spurgeon's arm and they both listened tensely.

There was silence. Then a dog barked somewhere in the distance.

211

They crept forward, edging along the wall of the cottage, testing the door and the ground-floor windows.

All were firmly shut.

Gregg shook his head and they backed away, still alert for any sound, any sign of movement.

They listened and watched.

Nothing.

Then, out of the darkness, from high in the house, came the noise of running feet, a crash and a terrible splintering of glass.


At the front, McKenzie heard.

Swearing, telling Rayner to stay where he was, he raced across the road, unlocked the front door and switched on a light.

The hallway was empty. The cottage was quiet.

He stood for a moment, still, trying to guess where the noise had come from. Then he heard someone moving, way above his head.

He pounded up the stairs to the landing, throwing back doors and switching on lights.

First a bathroom, empty.

Then a bedroom, empty too.

He flung open the third door, Velda Reynolds' room, and flicked on the light.

'Bloody hell,' he said.

The room was a shambles.

The dressing-table lay on its side. Brushes and combs, bottles of perfume and boxes of powder were strewn across the floor. A silver trinket box had been smashed against a wall, spilling brooches, ear-rings and strings of pearls. The wardrobe stood open, its twin mirrors shattered, and the clothes it had held were flung around haphazardly: dresses and skirts, coats and blouses, slashed from top to bottom.

But what riveted his gaze was Velda Reynolds' bed. The covers had been savagely tossed aside, and protruding from the mattress below one of the pillows was the hilt of a knife.

He stared at it, for an instant utterly bemused.

Then, out of the silence, he heard the sound of feet.

Tap-tapping across the roof.

Gregg and Spurgeon saw the lights, and heard McKenzie shouting from the window above. Stepping back from the wall, they were just in time to glimpse the figure of a man, crouched low on the tiles, feeling his way across the chain of connected roofs. Then they lost him in the mist.

Rayner, running down the street, picked him up as he crossed the roof-ridge at the end of the row and came down a drainpipe. Yelling to the others, he set off in pursuit.

Tench heard the commotion as he moved down the lane at the back of the church. Taking the nearest path through the grounds of the rectory, he saw him vault the churchyard wall before he, too, lost him as he twisted between the gravestones.

Rayner was the closest. Breathing hard, he sprinted up the path to the church, but even he was too late. By the time he reached the foot of the tower, a black shape, folded double against the stones, was rising foot by foot between the two buttress walls. As he watched, it vanished from sight in the mist.

Then Tench was beside him, staring up at the tower.

'Couldn't catch him, sir,' said Rayner. 'Went up there like a monkey.'

Gregg and Spurgeon appeared, then the breathless, thick-set figure of McKenzie.

Lights were springing out all over the village.

Tench turned on his heel.

'Andy,' he said, 'tell the folk to stay inside. I don't want a crowd.'

He rounded on Spurgeon. 'We need the key to the tower. It's in the filing cabinet in the incident room. Get Lock to open up.'

McKenzie was peering up at the sheer stone wall.

'What the hell do we do now?' he said.

Tench remembered. McKenzie was better on the ground.

'You stay here, Mac,' he told him. 'When Spurgeon comes

back, I want him round the other side. Once we get the key, I'll go up with Rayner.'

He turned the key in the heavy door at the bottom, and they dashed up the winding stairs two at a time.

'How much further?' panted Rayner, when they got half-way up.

'As far again,' said Tench. 'Just keep going.'

'The man must be off his rocker. Why the hell go up there?'

'Save your breath.' Tench was grim. 'We've got to get to him, fast.'

They reached the landing. The belfry door.

Tench gripped the iron ring, turned it and pushed. The door didn't move.

He charged it with his shoulder. It still didn't move.

He took three steps back and rammed his foot against it. It shook, but that was all.

They attacked it together. It shook a second time and sprang back into place.

Tench was sweating. 'Hell and damnation.'

'Must be locked, sir,' Rayner said.

'It's never locked,' Tench told him. 'He's wedged it with something.'

Rayner looked around helplessly. 'We need a sledge-hammer.'

'No time,' said Tench. 'You stay here. Keep on trying.'

He raced back down the stairs.

McKenzie was still staring up at the tower.

Tench pushed him aside.

'He's wedged the bloody door. Go up and join Rayner. Use that weight of yours. See if you can shift it.'

'What are *you* going to do?'

'At the moment, God knows. Just get up there fast.'

He watched McKenzie disappear into the porch, then he stepped back and looked up at the wall of the tower. The double buttresses stretched away into the mist.

He told himself he was mad. He was crazy to think of attempting such a thing.

214

And yet . . .

What had Summers said?

'If you want to climb a building, look for a chimney . . . Climbing up a chimney's just a rhythmic action . . . Nine out of ten young people can do it.'

Well, maybe so.

Maybe he was the tenth.

And how did they train, these nine young people?

By chasing up and down a hundred and forty steps?

He looked up again. Singh was up there. He'd already let him slip through his fingers once. If he wasn't stopped this time . . .

What?

He knew only too well, and knew he had to go up.

He stripped off his jacket, took a deep breath, stepped inside the chimney and stood between the walls. Then, closing his eyes, he tried to recall exactly what Summers had said.

'Rest your back on one wall.'

He took another deep breath and leaned back. Felt the stones against his spine.

'Stretch your right leg out, and press your foot against the opposite wall.'

He raised his leg and pressed.

What the devil came next?

'Double your left leg underneath you. Place the sole of your foot on the wall behind.'

He doubled it. Pressed hard with both feet.

He was clear of the ground.

'Straighten your left leg.'

He straightened it and felt himself rise up the wall. The stones brushed his back.

'Change feet. Press again.'

He rose again slowly. Felt the strain on his ankles.

Don't look down, he told himself. Never look down.

Don't even look up.

Look straight at the wall ahead. If you don't, you'll never make it.

'How do you climb a chimney?'

'In essence, you walk up it.'

'You make it sound easy.'

'It is, if you're a climber.'

215

But he wasn't a climber. Never had been a climber.
He gritted his teeth and changed his feet a second time.
Straightened his leg.
Pressed himself up.
Began to walk up the wall.

# 6

He knew it was one of those madcap endeavours that, once survived, he'd never in the whole of his life attempt again.

But he kept on walking, dragging himself up step after step.

He was half-way up – at least half-way – when his feet began to slip. He was sliding away suddenly, down between the walls.

He'd thought, till that moment, that he knew what fear was; but terror, he discovered, had no dimensions.

He thrust out hard with his foot, jammed his back against the stones and somehow managed to stop himself falling. His pulse was thumping wildly, the sweat standing out wet and cold on his brow. His legs, though rigid, felt irrationally weak.

He knew then, all at once, that he was never going to make it to the top of the tower. How high had Blake said it was? A hundred and twenty feet? If he was half-way up, that meant he still had sixty feet to go. Sixty steps up the wall. Too far. He couldn't do it. He'd have to go down.

He felt another snatch of panic. How the devil was he to get down? How could he reverse every step that he'd taken? He'd have to relax his grip. He'd start to slide again. Down he'd go, flailing out from the tower, clutching at nothing but handfuls of mist.

He shivered.

No, he told himself almost too firmly, he had to go on. To do that was safer than trying to go down.

Rest, he said. Rest. Wait till you feel you can take another step . . .

Then something flashed back. Something Summers had said.

'You can use your hands to press on the wall behind.'

He waited, then he changed his feet yet again, straightened his leg and pressed back with his hands. He moved up the wall.

Moved up slowly . . . one step, then two . . .

After five he stopped and rested, then changed his feet for what seemed the thousandth time, pressed down with his hands, tried to keep the rhythm going . . .

Then his feet slipped again.

He rammed himself instinctively rigid, and stopped. Braced himself, every nerve in his body a-twitch.

It was the soles of his shoes. He hadn't got rubber soles.

'Of course, there are some men who climb in bare feet. It isn't painful, and sometimes it gives a better grip.'

That was the last thing Summers had said. An afterthought. An epilogue, thrown out at random . . .

He braced himself again with his back to the wall and, reaching down, jerked off his left shoe and dropped it. He heard it hit the ground. Then he stripped off his sock and let that fall, too.

He felt the stone, icy cold against the sole of his foot; then both feet were firm against the opposite wall. Carefully, holding his left leg tense, he drew back his right, slid off the shoe and let it slip from his hand.

After that, the sock.

Planting his foot on the wall behind him, he pressed with his hands, and felt his back slowly slide up the wall. He changed his feet, pressed a second time . . . three steps, then four . . . staring straight ahead at nothing but stone: cold, black, merciless, adamantine stone that never seemed to end . . .


He climbed more cautiously now.

Stopping, resting, then pushing on again.

At last, after what seemed an agonizing age, he dared to look up.

Peering through narrowed eyes, he thought he could just see the top of the tower, the rim of it standing out, darker than the mist.

He forced himself another two steps up the wall, held his breath and looked again.

He was right. He could see the rim, and below it the grotesque projecting shape of a gargoyle.

How far? Fifteen feet? Three more rhythmic stages, another fifteen steps, and he'd have the ledge between his fingers.

He closed his eyes and breathed deeply.

Set himself to move on . . .


That was a moment he never cared to remember.

All at once he heard a scuffling sound up above.

He jerked back sharply and glimpsed a black figure right above his head, rising out of the mist on the edge of the tower.

Then it began to fall.

Sheer instinct clamped him tight between the walls, but in that same second he knew that he was lost. He tried to cry out a warning, but all he heard was the catch of his indrawn breath. Darkness was coming down on him, sweeping him away . . .

He thrust his arms up towards it, trying to ward it off . . .


The next instant lasted longer than any he'd known.

Then he knew he wasn't falling.

His leg was still stretched out taut against the wall, the stone against his back.

For a moment he found the simple fact of his existence hard to believe.

Nothing had happened.

He was still alive, suspended between heaven and the hell that lay beneath.

He moved his head warily, bending back, looking up between the walls.

Then he saw them.

They swung like a pendulum that someone had carelessly tilted out of true.

Two rubber-soled shoes twisting and turning a yard above his head.

## 7

McKenzie and Rayner had been battling to force back the door of the belfry.

It yielded no more than stubbornly, inch by inch; but, sweating and straining, they at last made a gap for Rayner to slip through, and once he was inside, McKenzie charged it with his shoulder in a final ferocious bid to smash it wide open. It gave another inch and he squeezed himself through.

Rayner had already pushed up the trap and reached the top of the tower. Apart from the clinging mist it seemed utterly deserted. He ran towards the far side, tripped over something he never even saw, and stumbled forward on the tiles. Swearing viciously in the half-light, he looked back beyond his feet. There was a rope. It was knotted round the base of the flagstaff and stretched out taut across the roof of the tower. He traced it as far as the edge and stared down. Then he heard Tench shouting from somewhere below.

'Anybody up there?'

'Yes, sir. Rayner.'

'Where the devil's McKenzie?'

McKenzie was heaving himself through the trap.

'He's coming, sir, now.'

'Then haul the man up for God's sake' – Tench sounded desperate – 'and throw me the rope.'


It was another ten minutes before they lowered the dead weight to the floor of the belfry. Spurgeon was already on his way to fetch a doctor, and Tench had sent Rayner to the incident room with instructions to ring through to Aylsham for an ambulance.

He and McKenzie stared down at the body.

'We needn't have bothered,' McKenzie said. 'The Salleston Circle won't be seeing him again.'

Tench squatted down. In the dim light thrown by the low-wattage bulb high above the bells, he studied Singh's face.

'What a waste,' he said. 'What a bloody awful waste.'

'Good riddance.' McKenzie was unsympathetic. 'He killed Tremellen and he could have killed you. If you'd been a couple of yards further up that tower, you wouldn't have stood a chance.'

Tench knew he was right. He was suddenly shaking. He pulled himself up and leaned over the bell-frame. Then he vomited on the bells.

'Mac,' he said faintly, 'why do people climb mountains?'

'God knows,' McKenzie said. 'They must have a death-wish.'

'You should be the one throwing up, and not me.' Tench was almost indignant. 'You're the one with vertigo.'

'Couldn't see the ground for the mist,' McKenzie said. 'If I can't see the ground, then that's it. There's no problem.'

Tench slid down the frame and bent his head between his knees.

'He told me it was simple.'

'Who did?'

'Summers.'

'Told you what was simple?'

'Walking up a wall.'

'It is for spiders' – McKenzie was quite laconic – 'but they have got eight legs . . . Feeling any better?'

Tench dragged himself up. 'Can't afford not to be. We've still got things to do.'

McKenzie eyed his bare feet. 'What happened to the shoes?'

Tench glanced down wearily.

'Lost them on the way,' he said. 'What does it matter? Spiders don't need shoes.'


The Reverend Eustace Blake did, though apart from them and his black ceremonial hose, he was wearing nothing else but a dressing-gown and a pair of pyjamas.

As he toiled up the hundred and forty steps, he consoled himself with the knowledge that Christian duty demanded his presence at the top of the tower. He was, after all, the rector of Salleston.

Reaching the belfry landing, he rested for a moment, leaning on the wall and gathering his breath. Then he pushed at the door.

It resisted. He pushed again, and then, with some discomfort, edged through the gap.

He saw Tench and McKenzie, then the body on the floor.

'Good heavens.' He stood there utterly bemused. 'What's been happening up here?'

'I'm afraid, sir . . .' said Tench.

The rector stepped forward, peering down. 'Is that . . .?'

'Yes, sir. It's Dr Singh.'

'Is he . . . dead?'

McKenzie had never taken too kindly to the cloth, and he wasn't in any mood for diplomatic niceties.

'Hanged himself,' he said bluntly.

'Here? In the church?' The rector seemed affronted. His tone of voice implied that there were plenty of trees.

Tench felt a spurt of anger. He looked at Blake with some distaste. Then he picked up the rope.

'D'you happen to know anything about this, sir?' he said.

The rector examined it. 'Yes, it's a bell-rope.'

'Was it left up here?'

'Yes, Inspector, it was.' He spoke as if patience was something of an effort. 'We always keep a spare one stowed behind the bells. In case one should break.'

Tench tossed it aside and jerked his head towards the door. 'Sergeant,' he said, 'you're wearing shoes. Kick those wedges away.'

McKenzie wrenched the door shut and kicked the wedges free. Tench held one out.

'And these?' he said sharply. 'Were they kept here, too?'

Blake turned the wooden wedge between his hands.

'They must have been left here. The workmen used them, I believe, when the bells were rehung.'

Tench looked down at Singh's body. Then all of a sudden he turned on the rector.

'Made it easy for him, didn't we, sir?' he said bitterly. 'Everything he needed, ready to hand. It's a pity Mr Bebbington isn't around. No doubt he'd find a stake hidden somewhere behind the bells. And he'd need one, wouldn't he? Suicides have to have a stake through their hearts.'

He knew that what he'd said wasn't fair – it wasn't logical – but he, like McKenzie, was in no frame of mind for dispassionate deduction.

He had to vent his frustrated anger on someone, and the Reverend Mr Blake, like the rope and the wedges, happened to be close at hand.

At that precise moment Mr Zaccheus Case was trudging down the side of a turnip field between Salleston and Clunch.

Old Zack was a tramp or, as he preferred to be known, a gentleman of the road. He wore a battered felt hat that was lacking a crown, a frayed woollen jersey riddled with holes, a pair of baggy trousers tied up with string, and boots that were splitting apart at the toes.

Reaching the road, he paused.

There was a car. It was empty.

He looked one way, then the other. All he could see was mist.

He tested the rear door. It swung open with a click.

On the back seat inside he could see a pair of boots.

Snatching them up, he shuffled back across the road and into the field.

He sat down and tried them on.

They weren't quite his size, but they were good, sturdy boots with nails in the soles.

They were just what he needed. They'd last him for years.

He tossed his own into the turnips, and set out towards Clunch.

## 8

Tench surveyed the wreckage of Velda Reynolds' room.

'Why this?' said McKenzie.

'Because she wasn't here. And from the look of that knife, it's a good job she wasn't.'

'Then you think he meant to kill her?'

'We'll never know,' said Tench, 'for sure, but we couldn't afford to take any chances. We had to move her out, and it was lucky we did. If we hadn't, God knows what we'd have found in the morning.'

'What was it, d'you think? Jealousy?'

'She's the one to tell us . . . The immediate question is how did he get in? The house was locked, the windows were checked, and yet no one heard a sound until he was inside. So how did he do it?'

'You want me to show you?' McKenzie said grimly.

He beckoned Tench towards the door and pointed to a stair that led up from the landing.

'See that? At the top there's an attic . . . Now, the first thing to do is switch off all the lights.'

He plunged the landing and Velda Reynolds' room into darkness.

'Follow me up,' he said, 'and be careful. Watch your step.'

Tench followed him. At the head of the stair was a door. McKenzie pushed it open.

'Now, Mike,' he said, 'what can you see?'

Tench couldn't see much at all. Slowly, as his eyes adapted to the dark, he made out vague shapes.

'Looks like a lumber room.'

'Right. That's what it is . . . Now take a step to the left.'

Tench stepped to one side.

'See anything else?'

'I think there's a window.'

'There is. It's a dormer.'

'Did you check it?'

'Yes, it's fastened.'

'So where did he get in?'

McKenzie gave a hollow laugh. 'Once she'd left with Grenville, I turned off all the lights. Couldn't afford not to. I didn't know how much of a start on you Singh had got. As far as I knew, he could have turned up any minute, and he had to find the cottage as we'd found it, in darkness . . . I locked the front door. Then I went through and locked and bolted the back, and started checking the windows. I made sure all those on the ground floor were fastened. After that I came upstairs. I checked the windows in all three rooms, then I climbed up here.'

'And this was all you could see.'

'Even less. It was darker . . . Now switch on the light.'

Tench flicked the switch. He saw a couple of tea-chests, a dilapidated bicycle reared up against them, and an old chest of drawers that was thick with dust. The rest of the lumber was shrouded in sheets that had once been white, but were now a dirty grey.

'Now look up,' said McKenzie.

He looked and saw the skylight.

'Never even bloody well knew it was there. If you climb up on top of that chest of drawers, you can push it wide open. It did have a latch, but it's rusted away . . . There are footprints in the dust . . . My fault. No one else's. I'm the one to blame.'

'Forget it,' said Tench. 'No one's blaming anyone. Who's going to search the roof of a pitch-dark room? If I'd been checking windows, I'd have missed it myself.' He paused. 'But Singh must have known about it, mustn't he, Mac?'

They made their way down and into the street.

McKenzie locked the front door.

'Keys?' he said.

'I'll take them.' Tench dropped them in his pocket. 'I want the whole team out here at first light: photographers, fingerprints, forensics, the lot. They're to scour those two rooms. Till then it stays locked.'

'Reynolds must have a key.'

'Yes, but he won't be using it. Rayner should be over at the post office now. Our friend Leslie Reynolds can spend the rest of the night with his widow in Marsham.'

'And Velda?'

'Bring her over to the incident room,' said Tench. 'I'll do the talking.'

McKenzie showed her in.

Without make-up, she looked older and desperately tired.

Tench let her stand.

'Velda Reynolds,' he said, 'I'm arresting you for the murder of Christopher Tremellen. It's my duty to warn you that you're not obliged to say anything unless you wish to do so . . .'

That was as far as he got.

McKenzie caught her as she fell.

# EPILOGUE

## RUN TO EARTH

For there is nothing hid, which shall not be manifested

Mark: 4.22.

# 1

They were sitting in the parlour of the cottage at Cley.

On a table between them were a pot of coffee and a second that was steaming with strong Darjeeling tea.

'Tell me, laddie,' said Lubbock. 'What was it that put you on to Velda Reynolds?'

'Oh, a number of things,' said Tench. 'The first time I questioned her I found it hard to work her out. She admitted she'd been having an affair with Tremellen, and it was still going on the night before he died. But she seemed to accept his death as a matter of course. There were no signs of grief. She didn't shed any tears. Mac simply dismissed her as a cold-blooded bitch, but I wasn't so sure. I thought even then that she was acting a part. Well, she was, but I read the signs wrong. Mac was nearer the mark. She couldn't have cared less about Major Tremellen.'

Lubbock stoked up his pipe, and dropped the spent match into a battered tin ashtray he'd won years before at a fairground in Yarmouth. 'You can hardly blame yourself for that. We all missed the signs.'

'Yes, I know, but when I spoke to her last Tuesday, I still wasn't very much closer to the truth.'

'Then what made you suspect she was involved?'

'To begin with,' said Tench, 'it was Singh himself. I wasn't expecting to see him that evening in Cambridge. He was supposed to be staying at Hilderfield Hall, conducting a course. But he wasn't. He was waiting for me, there in his rooms, and when I asked him what it was that had brought him back, he said he'd been called back on urgent business.'

'Did he say what the business was?'

'No, but I knew it couldn't be connected with the college,

227

because Summers knew nothing. If it had been, he'd have known. He's the Senior Tutor.'

'Did he tell you who'd called him?'

'No. I didn't ask. I think I was too bewildered at finding him there.'

'But he was waiting for you. Expecting you to call.'

'That was what he said. And he knew my name.'

'A lot of people know our names. Folk we've never even met. He could have read it in the press . . . But why was he expecting you?'

'I did ask him that. He said he'd come from the station by taxi and seen my car. I'd parked it in the grounds. Police cars, he said, were easy to recognize.'

'Well, that's true enough.' Lubbock emptied his cup and poured himself another. 'But it's hardly the most convincing explanation.'

'No, it isn't,' said Tench. 'There could be only one convincing explanation. Someone had tipped him off. Told him I was getting too close for comfort.'

'Velda Reynolds?'

'It had to be. I'd seen her that afternoon, and asked her some pointed questions about Singh. She must have had his telephone number at Hilderfield.'

'And that implied they knew one another pretty well.'

'Better than she was prepared to admit. He was probably telling the truth when he said he saw the car. He'd draw his own conclusions. From what he'd been told, he'd know we were on his track. So why would a policeman, all the way from Norfolk, be visiting the college, if not to see him?'

Lubbock blew out a rippling cloud of smoke. 'But that wasn't enough to make you go haring back to Salleston. There must have been something else.'

'Yes, there was.' Tench stirred his coffee. 'It was something he said. He was talking about the accident on the Baradari Crossing. When his wife died, he said, he made a vow that he and Tremellen should die together. A covenant with death: that was what he called it. He'd kill Tremellen and then kill himself. But then he went on to say something very strange . . . I'm trying to quote his words as best I can remember . . . "That, Inspector," he said, "was always what I intended. But then she intervened. No, my love, she said, life is worth living. Take his life if you must, but let me live on with you. Let me share with you what remains of happiness."'

He paused and shook his head as if the words were still a riddle that he needed to solve.

'Well, up to that point he'd been talking about his wife, and I thought he still was. He seemed to be telling me that, although she was dead, her voice was urging him not to kill himself . . . It wasn't till I got inside in the car that I realized what it was that he'd actually been saying.'

'Go on,' said Lubbock.

'It was those four words: "But then she intervened." You can say them in two entirely different ways, and the meaning changes. You can say them in a normal, straightforward way: "But then she intervened." Or you can emphasize the "she": "But then *she* intervened." That implies that "she" is a different person . . . He hadn't laid a heavy emphasis on "she", but just enough, once I began to think back, to make me think again. "That was what I intended, but then *she* intervened." He wasn't talking about his wife, he was talking about Velda Reynolds. "Take his life," she said, "but let me live on with you." That could only mean one thing: she knew that he intended to kill Tremellen; they were in it together. And that gave an altogether different twist to the rest of his words. He said something about thinking for a while that it might be possible, but the hope had proved false. "I was deceived," he said. Then he talked about extending the covenant with death, and quoted a line from Byron: "Mercy sighed farewell" . . . "I've an appointment to keep." That was the last thing he said to me . . . It all pointed to the fact that he'd made up his mind to kill Velda Reynolds.'

'And you still think he had?'

Tench gave a shrug. 'We'll never know, will we? But what clinched her involvement, as far as I was concerned, was that knife in the bed and the skylight up above. He must have known about that skylight. He made straight for it across the roof. That meant that he'd used it at some time before.'

Lubbock sipped his tea. 'It was still all circumstantial. You were taking a risk, arresting her for murder.'

'I was,' Tench admitted, 'but I was pretty sure she'd crack once we put her under pressure.'

'You were lucky. She did.'

'It took a hell of a lot longer than I ever thought it would.

229

There was a time when I looked at Mac and we almost gave up. But it wasn't exactly luck that did the trick. It was a bit of bluff on our part. A grain of deception. Oh, I suppose, in a sense, it *was* a last desperate throw of the dice . . .'

'But the numbers came up.'

'Double six,' said Tench.

## 2

It was half-past seven in the morning.

They'd been questioning her, he and McKenzie, for an hour and a half.

Tired and drawn, she was still defiant.

'Tell me again,' said Tench. 'When did you first meet Dr Singh?'

She looked up at him. 'How many more times?'

'As many as it takes for you to tell me the truth.'

'I've told you the truth.'

'I don't think so, Mrs Reynolds. When did you first meet him?'

She took a deep breath. 'As I said before, Inspector. It was the first time he came to give a talk at the Circle.'

'That was August last year.'

'You know it was. You asked me. I checked the date for you.'

'And when did he first mention Major Tremellen?'

'He never did, to me.'

'Never?'

'I've said so.'

'Are you telling me that in your long association with Dr Singh, he never once mentioned the Major's name?'

'There was no association with Dr Singh, Inspector. The only times I met him were when he came to Salleston and gave his talks.'

'You expect me to believe that you only met him twice? At the Circle meetings? There was nothing else between you?'

'Believe what you like, Inspector,' she said. 'I can only tell you what I know.'

'Then why did you ring him up at Hilderfield yesterday?'

'I didn't.'

'You're sure about that?'

'I've told you, I didn't even know he was there. I've never heard of Hilderfield.'

McKenzie leaned forward. He was less diplomatic. 'You're a liar, Mrs Reynolds. You rang him up and told him that Inspector Tench had been to see you.'

She turned towards him, still the essence of reason. 'Why should I do that? Why should I ring up a man that I'd only met on a couple of occasions?'

'You know the answer to that,' McKenzie said. 'You'd met him more than just twice. You'd slept with him, hadn't you? How many times had you slept with him, Mrs Reynolds?'

'You're imagining things, Sergeant.'

'How many times, Mrs Reynolds? Five? Fifteen? Twenty? Twenty-five, was it?'

'I never slept with Dr Singh.'

'You found him attractive, didn't you? A tall, handsome Indian? You'd never had a coloured man before, had you? Plenty of white men, too many to count, but he was something different, wasn't he, Mrs Reynolds? You were tired of Tremellen. You were ready for a change. You conspired with Singh to get rid of him, didn't you? Admit it.'

She looked him straight in the eyes. 'How many times do I have to repeat it? I didn't kill Chris Tremellen.'

Tench opened a drawer and took out a file. He slid it across the table towards McKenzie.

'Mrs Reynolds,' he said, 'perhaps we aren't making ourselves very clear. There are many different ways to murder a man. You can shoot him, poison him, beat him to death. You can push him down a flight of steps. You can even kill him by a few whispered words on a phone. Or perhaps in a bed. You can incite other people to do the killing for you. You can pay them. Or aid and abet them to do it. Whichever way you choose, you may well find yourself facing a charge of murder. You may not have fired the fatal shot yourself, but if you've conspired with someone to do it, paid him to do it or helped him to do it, then justice decrees that you be so charged. When several persons together commit a felony, the law regards the act of any one as

231

the act of all, and the punishment is the same . . . Now we know it was Dr Singh who pushed Tremellen down the steps of the tower, but we also know that you helped him to do it.'

McKenzie lolled back in his chair. 'She didn't merely help him. She paid him to do it. Didn't you, Mrs Reynolds?'

'How could I possibly have paid him?' There was scorn in her voice. 'I haven't that sort of money.'

'I hardly think, Mrs Reynolds,' Tench said quietly, 'that Sergeant McKenzie was talking of money.'

She was still, so it seemed, determined not to yield.

'I didn't pay him. I didn't help him. Why should I do either? I only met him twice.'

'But we know that isn't true.' Tench was quite deliberate. 'You see, Mrs Reynolds, before Dr Singh killed himself, he made a statement to the police in Cambridge. It implicated you . . . Perhaps, Sergeant, you'd like to read out what he said.'

McKenzie opened the file.

'The statement was made to a detective inspector, and witnessed by him. These were Dr Singh's words. "I made a covenant with death. Tremellen must die with me. I would kill him first and then kill myself. That, Inspector, was what I always intended. But then she intervened. No, my love, she said, life is worth living. Take his life, yes, but let me live on with you. Let me share with you what remains of happiness . . ."'

'And you still maintain' – it was Tench's turn to be scathing – 'that you met him only twice?'

There was silence for a moment.

'I think, Mrs Reynolds,' he said, 'we'd better start again. Right from the beginning . . . You say you first met Dr Singh at the Circle meeting in August last year. Now tell me, and this time tell me the truth. When was the first time that he spoke to you about Major Tremellen?'

All at once she seemed unutterably weary.

She was hollow-eyed, haggard.

The silence dragged on.

At last, when she spoke, her voice was a whisper.

'It was . . .'

'Yes, Mrs Reynolds?'

She was fighting with herself.

'Yes, Mrs Reynolds?'

'. . . when he came the second time.'

'A month ago?'

She nodded.

Tench waited, said nothing.

'There was a notice on a board inside the village hall. It asked for volunteers to clear the grass in the churchyard . . .'

She closed her eyes, tossed her head, as if something within her still struggled to deny the very words she was speaking.

'And?' prompted Tench.

'It said that if anyone was willing to help, they should contact Chris Tremellen. It gave his address . . .'

She sighed.

There was another long silence before she spoke again.

'Dr Singh saw it. He said that he'd once known a man called Tremellen. He asked me . . .'

'What, Mrs Reynolds?'

'He asked me wasn't it a very unusual name.'

# 3

Lubbock wreathed himself in smoke.

'So that was when it started?'

'According to her, yes. The following week he invited her out to lunch.'

'At the Blue Boar?'

'Where else?'

'And they discovered they had a community of interest.'

'I think to begin with they were both a bit wary. They must have picked their way through a minefield of speculation, but they pretty soon realized they both wanted the same thing: to be rid of Tremellen. Velda Reynolds, of course, is a pathological case. She's clearly a nymphomaniac. I couldn't understand, that first time I met her, why she treated Tremellen's death in such a casual manner. But when Mac and I told her that Singh had hanged himself, she was just as unresponsive. She simply shrugged her shoulders, as if to say, so what? I don't think there was any real affection between them. Nymphomaniacs don't know the meaning of love. They just drift from man to man for sexual satisfaction. Six months and she'd had her fill of Tremellen. He was becoming a nuisance. Wouldn't take no for an answer. And what made it worse was his living so close. She'd finished with him, wanted him out of the way.'

'And we know Singh's motive.'

'Partly. Beyond that, it's all a matter of guesswork. He must have realized he could use her. She was the one who could ease his path to Tremellen; and she is, after all, a very attractive woman. There may have been an element of conquest about it, a part of his twisted pattern of revenge. She was white, and that may have counted for a lot. Back in India, she'd have been way beyond his reach.'

'Did she ever admit that they'd slept together?'

'Not in so many words, but we played another hunch. Sent Gregg to the Blue Boar to check on the register. Singh had stayed overnight half a dozen times between the beginning and end of June. Each time there was another name in the register: a woman who'd signed herself in as Margaret Paterson. They'd had adjoining rooms . . . We had a few words with Leslie Reynolds. That was her maiden name. Velda Margaret Paterson.'

'Made the most of it, didn't she? While the cat was away at Marsham, the mice were having a nice little game in Cambridge.'

'If Reynolds had known, he wouldn't have bothered. I fancy she'd had a string of men since they were married. He'd come to expect it. He told me that, as far as he was concerned, she could do as she liked.'

Lubbock frowned. 'Then you don't think Singh realized Tremellen was around until he saw that notice.'

'No, I don't think he did. According to Velda Reynolds, when he first came to England, he had no idea where Tremellen was or whether he was still alive, and she didn't think he had any idea of trying to trace him. She could be right there. After all, his bitterness against Tremellen had had six years to burn itself out. He'd made a new life and a reputation for himself in academic circles. He certainly gave no sign that he was brooding on the past. Summers said that he never mentioned his wife.'

'Then seeing that notice opened up the wounds.'

'Must have done, yes.'

'Then what about the evening when Tremellen took that young girl out to dinner?'

'Miss Merivale?'

'Yes. We assumed that they'd seen one another that evening. Were we wrong?'

'Maybe not altogether wrong,' said Tench. 'Certainly Singh never mentioned the meeting to Mrs Reynolds, and he had plenty of opportunities. The trouble is we can't ask either of them about it, so we just have to work on conjecture. I think he may have seen Tremellen, but if he did, he didn't recognize him. That's logical enough. If he saw him at all, it could only have been for a couple of seconds before he took off. And don't forget, Singh would have been seeing a different face. Since the last time he'd seen him, Tremellen had lost part of his jaw. As Miss Merivale said, it made him look lop-sided.'

'But you still believe Tremellen recognized him.'

'He must have done. That was why he walked out and left her. That was why the next morning he rang up Parfitt and told him to put the cottage at Stow up for sale.'

Lubbock shifted restlessly. He pulled up a stool and stretched out his legs.

'There's one thing about this business still puzzles me,' he said. 'Singh told you that Velda Reynolds had deceived him. What did he mean by that?'

Tench drained off his coffee. 'That was where we made another wrong assumption.'

'What about?'

'What happened last Tuesday . . . We assumed that, after I'd been to see her, she made a dash for the phone and rang up Singh at Hilderfield Hall. When she told us she hadn't, we took it for granted that was just another lie. To save her own skin, she had to deny everything. But now she says – and I'm ready to admit it makes sense to believe her – that it was he who phoned her. She was expecting the call. Seems they'd made arrangements to spend another night in Cambridge once his course was finished, and he'd promised to ring her up to confirm that he'd been able to book the same rooms. But when at last he rang, she'd had time enough to think, and by then she was scared. All those pointed questions I'd asked about Singh had put the wind up her good and proper. Things were getting too hot. According to her, she told him he'd better get out of Cambridge fast before we arrested him, and that was when they found themselves completely at odds. He felt that if things were as bad as she made out, they must get away together. I reckon he didn't trust her not to spill the beans. She knew her only chance was to stay where she was and deny she'd had any connection with him. It'd be madness, she told him, for both of them to vanish. The police would put two and two together right away. I think she made it pretty plain that we might be on to him, but we weren't on to her, and if he thought she was going to put her neck in a noose just on his behalf, then he'd better think again. Stay away from me, she told him. Don't come anywhere near Salleston. She said he kept on insisting she had to go with him; it wasn't part of his plan to leave her there on her own. She went on telling him no; she was staying where she was; and at last he lost his temper, and words began to fly. At that, she rang off, and when the phone went again, she simply ignored it.'

'So he made off back to Cambridge, and when he got there he saw the police car.'

'Yes. We can't possibly know just what his thoughts were, but I think when he saw it he knew the game was up, and he made up his mind to finish it all. He probably sat there in the darkness of his room, brooding about it. He daren't switch on the light. He didn't want anyone to know he was back. But he made one mistake. In his turmoil of mind, he forgot to close the outer door to his rooms. Then I turned up, and sometime during our talk – I'm only guessing, of course – his thoughts began to turn again to Velda Reynolds. Why should she get away with it? She was as guilty as he was. Perhaps that was when he took the decision to kill her. If he had to die, then, like Tremellen, she was going to die with him.'

Lubbock knocked out his pipe and scoured it with a penknife. 'Looks like he was right. They've topped women before. She wouldn't be the first and she won't be the last.'

'I suppose not,' said Tench. He didn't sound happy. 'I've never thought hanging was the answer. What good does it do?'

'In her case, a lot. It makes sure she can't give her sweet kiss of death to anyone else . . . Surely they must have planned it all between them, she and Singh.'

236

'Oh, they did. We know that. The last time they met in Cambridge, she brought his climbing boots back to the cottage and hid them in the attic. Then, while she was entertaining Tremellen that night, he came in across the roof in his rubber-soled shoes, picked up the boots, slung them round his neck and slid down a drainpipe at the back.'

'And at four o'clock in the morning, she kissed Tremellen goodbye and sent him off to his death.'

'That's about it. The irony is that Tremellen himself unlocked the church doors, and they were Singh's escape route. Out and across the fields.'

'Then if that's what she did, she deserves to die.'

'As the law stands, she may.'

'But you don't like the law.'

'Not much,' said Tench.

Lubbock stared at the teapot. 'Well, you may be right, but it's a dangerous step to do away with the rope. It's the ultimate deterrent . . .'

His voice trailed away. For the first time that evening, the cottage was quiet.

'Strange, isn't it,' said Tench, 'that all this should have started with a minor shunt on a crossroads six thousand miles away?'

Lubbock shook his head. 'It was more than that, laddie. When those two cars smashed into one another on the Baradari Crossing, two cultures collided. East and West. Black and white. Ruler and ruled. An explosive mixture. It blew up like a bomb. An atomic bomb.'

'And the fall-out was murder.'

'Death, grief, injustice, resentment and murder. A whole catalogue of ills.'

'And it's not finished yet.'

'No, it isn't,' said Lubbock. 'But make no mistake. However far away it started, once Tremellen was found at the foot of those steps, it came home to Norfolk. It was here on your patch, and it was your job to track down the man who'd done it. That was what you did.'

'With a good deal of help.'

'I've told you before, laddie, all of us need help. Solving a murder's a matter of teamwork. Never mind the method. You sifted out the truth. And how long did it take? Seven days?

Eight? That's quite an achievement. It's better than Maitland could ever have done. So forget all the doubts. It's time for celebration. Shall I tell you a joke?'

Tench stared at him. 'A joke?'

'Don't sound so surprised. I do know one or two.'

'Go on, then. Tell me.'

'Well,' Lubbock said, 'last Tuesday afternoon when I tried to reach you on the phone, it wasn't just to explain why I'd come back here.'

'It wasn't?'

'No, it wasn't. I intended to give you a very hot tip. Something Reg Denstone mentioned before I left. Just a casual remark about an Indian giving a talk to the Salleston Circle. I thought I'd better tell you. I had the strange feeling it might possibly have some connection with the case.'

'Well, it had. You were right.'

'I was right, but too late.' Lubbock poured himself a third cup of tea. 'Far too late. I must be getting old. I'm losing my grip. So I've reached a conclusion.'

'You have?'

'Yes.'

'What is it?'

'I've come to the conclusion I was right to retire.'

There was a flicker of a smile from Tench. Then it changed to a frown.

'I remember,' he said. 'You did tell me once you were thinking about it, but I had the impression you'd never made up your mind. Now what could have given me that idea?'

Lubbock raised his bushy eyebrows.

He looked at Tench. Then he laughed.

'How about another pot of coffee?' he said.

# AUTHOR'S NOTE

The source of this tale was an incident that occurred in Rangoon more than sixty years ago, recorded by Maurice Collis in the autobiographical account of his career as District Magistrate. I have modified the facts, changed the location and created my own characters. Much has been omitted, much more altered, even more invented; and the story as it stands is no accurate reflection of the truth which inspired it. Those who prefer fact to fiction should refer to Collis's account in his *Trials in Burma*, and especially the section which deals with the man he diplomatically calls 'The Lieutenant of the Camerons'.

I must also acknowledge my debt to 'Whipplesnaith', the anonymous author of *The Night Climbers of Cambridge*, from which I derived much useful knowledge about this clandestine group and its climbing techniques.

Finally, my thanks are due in no small measure to Frank in Newmarket for a piece of swift detection which no character in this story could possibly have bettered.